Angel in Shadow

by

Annette Miller

Angel Haven, Book 4

Angel in Shadow

Cover Art by *Kristian Norris*

The Wild Rose Press, Inc.
PO Box 708
Adams Basin, NY 14410-0708
Visit us at www.thewildrosepress.com

Publishing History
First Fantasy Rose Edition, 2019
Print ISBN 978-1-5092-2861-4
Digital ISBN 978-1-5092-2862-1

Angel Haven, Book 4
Published in the United States of America

As much as Grayson didn't want to admit it, Jericho made a good point. He needed to come clean. If she found out on her own, all hope of being with her would be gone. Gone and wouldn't ever come back.

Several minutes later, Kristin came out and sat beside him. "Vertigo attacked Cole. I got her to back off, but it's reasonable to expect she won't keep her word. She admitted to me she plans to kill Jack and Adam. She wanted to have Cole with her now, too. I'm not sure how much time they have left."

He turned to look at her. "Where's Jericho? Did you tell him?"

"Yes. He's with Cole. I think it would be best if I stayed with him until he's better."

"Why are you out here?"

"I thought you'd like to know what I found out." Kristin turned to go back inside. "I know you have secrets. Remember, everyone in our line of work has secrets. Even me."

He turned and stared at her. "And what's your big secret? It can't be worse than mine."

"Are you sure? Well, here it is." She stood. "I'm not a real human."

As she walked back into the house, her cryptic statement rooted him to the spot. He knew his magical origin, but Kristin? He stared at the door. She had to be human. What else could she be?

Dedication

Dedicated to my husband, Brian,
and my sons Scot and Alex.
You guys made me believe
I could achieve my dreams.

Prologue

Kristin Mentor slid her lecture notes into the side pocket of her messenger bag. In two days she was addressing bio-engineering students at Temple University in Philadelphia. This was the job she liked the best. As one of the country's leading bio-geneticists, Kristin always had a full lecture schedule.

She leaned back in her chair and stared out the window. There were times it was hard balancing everything she did in her life. She had her research, her speaking engagements, and then there was her other life. The one no one outside of her friends knew about. Kristin led the superhero team, the Angels, in her hero identity as Proto.

She didn't think when she and her friends started using their powers they'd become one of the more well-known teams in New York City. The other established teams were popular, had a little more experience, and were stronger. In the overall scheme of things, the Angels were still a "new" superhero team. People identified more with them than the teams with a higher number of male members. Kristin's theory was that her team was more approachable than the others. The Angels weren't too imposing. They appeared more, for the lack of a better word, human.

She thought about the term "superhero." It was such an iconic word and, at the same time, completely archaic. It brought to mind pompous monologues and larger than life men and women. By the same token, "supervillain" made her think of figures dressed in dark colors, scheming behind closed doors, with dreams of world domination.

Part of that was true, but the real supervillain was much more than a parody the media portrayed them as. These were dangerous individuals with plans to destroy, and hurt as many people as possible. As more villains banded together, heroes around the world had done the same, each side forming teams to defeat the others. To help balance the scales, an agency was formed to work side by side with the hero teams. The United Law-enforcement Tactical Response Agency, or ULTRA, was born.

Recent events had led Kristin to believe there was more to the bad guys trying to take over the world. Did other heroes feel the same? She'd call the other teams to see if their leaders could meet with her to discuss the growing threats to the world.

She finished packing her notes and stood. The pictures of her teammates on the fireplace mantel caught her attention. The recently added wedding photos strengthened her resolve to never get roped into marriage. It was fine for her friends, but she didn't need a man to make her life complete.

This should be an easy trip. First the lecture, then picking up her friend, Jack McClennan at the airport. With luck, there wouldn't be any surprises waiting for her.

Chapter One

Where the hell could Jack be?

Kristin let herself be swept along with the crowd as they headed to baggage claim. She'd just made it to the Philadelphia airport right before her friend, Jack McClennan's flight landed. A click, a whir, a metallic groan, and the baggage carousel lumbered into motion as suitcases tumbled down the chute. She stood on her toes, but still didn't see him. He towered over any crowd so she couldn't have missed him.

She pulled out her cell phone and called him. Again. He should've answered before she called him five times. Once more, it went to voicemail. Her usual patience had been used up from the lecture she'd given at Temple University. She'd expected better from the assembled students, not the inane questions which bombarded her.

She dialed again. "Come on, Jack, pick up. I know your flight arrived on time," she murmured.

The crowd thinned and she pushed her way to the front, checking the tags on the last few suitcases. His bags trundled around so he must have gotten on the plane. Cold settled in her chest, spiraling out to seep its way into the rest of her bones. Yanking the bags off the carousel, she studied every person who passed her and prayed she would see him. Her phone remained silent, but she checked the screen anyway. Maybe she didn't hear it go off. *I'll have him paged. He should hear that.* She strode to the customer service desk.

"Excuse me. I think I may have missed a friend of mine. He came in on the flight from London. Would you page him to the front entrance, please?"

"Sure. What's his name?"

"Jack McClennan."

The woman scratched his name down on a piece of paper and reached for the phone. Kristin smiled her thanks and forced herself to relax the death grip she had on his suitcases. *Please, let him hear.*

She stood by the front doors, overwhelmed by the impulse to tap her foot. He'd been on the flight, so he must be in the airport. The page echoed over the speakers and she prayed he'd show soon. The cold feeling in her chest turned into full blown dread as the minutes dragged by. As an ULTRA field commander, Jack had made a lot of enemies. Powerful enemies. He'd been on the flight, though. She pulled out her cell phone and dialed him again. If he didn't answer or show up soon, she'd go back and check with security at the gate.

"He's not here," said a deep voice behind her.

She ended the call and turned. A well-built man stood there and stared at her. She had to step back to see his face, which put his height over six feet. He didn't look dangerous. He had short, black hair, gray eyes, and an angular face, but appearances were too often not to be trusted. In one short statement, he became an instant suspect.

"What do you mean?" Her shoulders tightened and she took a couple more steps away from him. "Where is he? What did you do to him?"

"Me? Nothing, but he's got a lot of enemies."

"Like you? Who are you?"

"My boss sent me here to find him. Give me your phone, Dr. Mentor. Yes, I know who you are. You're Dr. Kristin Mentor, one of the more well-known bio-geneticists in the country. You gave a lecture at Temple University then drove here to pick up ULTRA Field Commander Jack McClennan." He narrowed his eyes as he leaned closer. "You're also Proto, leader of the Angels team. Need I go on? Now give me the damn phone."

"I don't think so." She nodded to the case on his belt. "You have your own phone. Why can't you use it?"

He drew in a deep breath and released it. "The person I need to call may not answer if he sees my number. It'll be easier on everyone if he thinks you called him."

Kristin hesitated while he glared at her, then held out her phone. She watched him dial and waited. When the other person picked up, all he said were non-committal noises. Who he called and what the brief conversation entailed was a mystery. His gaze never left her as he handed the phone back to her.

"Kristin, are you there?"

A familiar voice startled her out of her brief stupor. Jack's teammate and longtime friend, Frank DiNello, echoed from the phone. Frank had been instrumental in clearing Jack of previous accusations of wrongdoing and had become a close friend of hers and the rest of the Angels team. How did this stranger know his number? And he hadn't pulled up her contact list, so he'd known it by heart.

"Yes, Frank, I'm here. Who is this guy in front of me?"

"His name is Grayson Styles. I know him from way back. Believe me when I tell you he can get the job done. He's got his own set of procedures, and it might not sit well with you. You may not want to trust him, but you'll need to try. He's one of the good guys."

Kristin frowned. "Can you please make some sense? Can I trust him or not?"

"The world isn't as black and white as you'd like it to be," Frank said. He'd never sounded so serious before. "Grayson is one of those gray areas. He has the resources to help you find Jack. Grayson's boss called me to let me know he'd been taken. The only other person besides me who knows is the ULTRA commander." He paused. "You need to get him back as soon as you can."

"I'll do my best. As soon as I have any information I'll be in touch, or if you hear anything, call me."

"Will do. And Kristin?" He hesitated. "Be careful."

"Count on it. Don't worry. I'll have Jack home before you know it."

She stared at Grayson as she hung up. "I don't like gray areas, Mr. Styles, and it doesn't make me too fond of you. I'm only listening to you because you know Frank, and he said you can get the job done. Would you care to fill me in on what you two don't wish to tell me?"

Grayson closed his eyes for a moment. When he opened them, he stared at her. "We have a past. There were…events…which happened between us. He forgave me, but it was after several years had passed."

"I think I'd better find Jack on my own." She took

6

a couple of steps toward the door. "There's a quality about you I'm not sure I like. Thank you for the offer, but goodbye, Mr. Styles. I don't need you."

His chest rumbled with a low, humorless chuckle. "Oh, you need me, all right. I have contacts in the area. I know who to talk to. I also partner with three other guys who have their own network. Trust me, doc. You need me a hell of lot more than I need you."

Kristin paused. He'd made a very good point. Her ego and mistrust needed to be shelved. For now. "Fine, but betray me, and you won't live long enough to regret it. Am I clear?"

"Crystal. Do you know the Atlantic City Expressway into New Jersey?"

Not one of her favorite roads, but at one in the afternoon, traffic wouldn't be too bad. "Yes, I know it."

"Take the Route 50 exit. Head north to Route 30. There's a fast food place at the corner. I'll wait for you there. My team should have some leads by the time we meet up with them later." He grinned. "Unless you want to leave your car here and ride with me."

"No, thank you. I'd rather take my own car. I'll see you at Route 30."

He reached for Jack's suitcases the same time she did. Their hands made contact and they stopped, staring at each other. "Do you need help with the bags?" he said.

His gaze captured hers, turning her well-ordered thoughts into a shattered jigsaw puzzle. There was something about him that drew her in. She could almost sense a primal pull at her heart, pushing her to him. She forced the sensation down and took a deep breath before speaking.

"No, thank you. I got them."

The warmth of his hand felt almost hot and rooted her to the spot. Pull away, she thought. It's easy. Apparently easier said than done. After a few minutes, he let go and took a step back. His mouth opened, then shut, his lips set in a hard line. Kristin wondered what he had left to tell her.

Her cheeks heated while he stared at her. What on earth was wrong with her? The way he stared at her, she could almost put stock into the fanciful tales of magic and soulmates. It happened to two of your friends, a little voice inside her taunted. She resisted the urge to duck her head like a shy teenager. She hefted Jack's suitcases to get a better grip and held them in front of her. Somehow, she felt safer with even that small barrier between them.

"See you at Route 30."

Kristin stashed the cases in the trunk, glad to put some distance between her and the stranger. Minutes passed while she stared through the windshield. Thoughts of Grayson Styles circled in her mind until every thought cascaded into a whirlwind of confusion. She found him to be incredibly handsome, but she admired the directness of his gaze. He never looked away, even with the uncomfortable reveal of his past association with Frank. She gave herself a hard, mental shake. She turned the key, and the car roared to life. Ridiculous daydreams wouldn't help to find Jack.

****

Grayson sat in his car, alone except for thoughts of Kristin. Shoulder length, light brown hair, brown eyes, and a figure that was way too easy on the eyes. Not tiny thin, but muscular thin and shorter than him by a good five inches. From the footage he'd watched of her and her team in recent battles, he couldn't help notice the power in her arms and legs through the form fitting, micro-flex armor she wore. The videos didn't do her justice. And her vocabulary certainly didn't contain the word tact.

An almost instant attraction slammed into him, and he put a little more stock into his mother's tales of soulmates and soul bonding. He'd always scoffed at the stories before, but after meeting Kristin, he wasn't so sure they were all fairy tales.

He shook himself out of his bemusement. He needed to get to Route 30 before she did. Yeah, the doc had a pretty face and could kick some serious ass, but he couldn't let his admiration go any further. Under no circumstances would he get involved with her. He started the car, determined to ignore the fact his soul recognized hers.

Another ache in his shoulders started, and he flexed his muscles to ease it. He pushed Kristin out of his thoughts, and the past he'd tried so many times to bury made itself known. He stiffened his spine as he ground his teeth and tried to banish the nervousness in his gut. When they rescued Jack, it would force him to come face to face with his former field commander.

The boss had told him he needed to lay old ghosts to rest. He'd never admit it, but she just might be right. Events of the past had chased him for a long time. Maybe the time had come to let them catch him. Now, if Jack would forgive him and not shoot him on sight, past sins might be forgotten.

Chapter Two

Kristin found the fast food restaurant right where Grayson had indicated. She spied him sitting on an outside bench and parked close by. Natural light let her see him better than the fluorescent lights of the airport. Sunlight showed dark brown streaks mixing with the black in his hair. Dark sunglasses hid his eyes. Unfamiliar disappointment filled her chest. How would the sun have changed his eyes?

A burger wrapper crumbled into a ball was tucked under his leg as he finished what looked suspiciously like a chocolate shake. It appeared even mysterious agents who worked in the disliked "gray areas" had an affinity for fast food.

She pointed to the empty wrapper "Have you been here long? I thought I made pretty good time."

He shook his head. "I got here a few minutes ago. I'm a fast eater."

"And a fast driver, too. But you appear more wary of brain freeze than the highway police." She pointed to the cup. "You are drinking a shake, aren't you?"

A small smile forced its way out. "Guilty as charged. Are you hungry?"

"No, thank you. I ate before I left the university."

He walked with her to her car, leaning against it while she held her keys. "My friend's house isn't too far, just down the pike in Galloway Township. We head east toward Atlantic City. After we hit the township limits, it'll be a short drive down a dirt road to his place. It's set back in the woods and out of the way because of the nature of our jobs."

All her suspicions slammed back into her mind. "If you wanted to allay my fears, you didn't. How do I know you haven't got some information on Frank to make him tell me to trust you?"

"I've seen you fight. I know you can handle yourself. You're perfectly safe. After I drive over, you can follow me."

She nodded, still unsure of Grayson Styles. And what of his friends? She could fight her way out of almost any situation, but if they got the jump on her, would she be able to defend herself? She took a deep breath and slid behind the wheel. Only one way to find out. She started the engine and waited for him to drive over.

****

Jack groaned and tried to roll over. His body felt like lead and didn't appear to want to move, no matter how hard he tried. With extreme effort, he forced his eyes open. Someone had chained him to the floor. Okay, then. He gave a weak tug on the bindings and couldn't move them. *This shouldn't be a problem to get out of. So why can't I?*

"Because I put a telepathic block in your mind. You can't access your cybernetics, Jack," said a cold voice from the doorway. "I've also given you a strong sedative to keep you compliant."

Bloody hell. He blinked several times to clear his vision, and a familiar face came into focus. Anita Haines, also known as Vertigo, and his teammate from his original team at ULTRA. Tall and leggy, she would be beautiful, except for the permanent hard glint in her ice blue eyes and the scowl on her lips.

"Bloody hell, Anita, why are you doing this?" Numbness had settled into his jaw, his speech slurred worse than after a trip to the dentist. "You can't still want revenge."

"Of course I still want revenge." She stood over him and glared. "My new boss pointed out revenge for past aggressions is beneath me. If I complete this mission, I'll be put in a position of real power. So it's a win-win situation. I get to pay you back and he gets to be rid of you. Besides, everyone needs a little revenge now and then."

"So do it and get it over with then." He closed his eyes as he let his head fall back. "Why are you waiting?"

Her lips curled up in an unpleasant smile. "Just because it's beneath me, doesn't mean I won't stoop a little to make you suffer. And you will suffer, Jack. Horribly. Painfully. And right before you die, you'll realize my plan. Then it'll be too late."

The door opened and a huge man walked in. Jack frowned. The man looked familiar, but he couldn't call the association to memory. If Vertigo hadn't decided to play literal mind games right now, he felt certain he'd recognize him.

"Mr. Trust is on the phone. He wants an update."

"He'll be happy to hear phase one is complete." She glanced at Jack. "Watch him while I go make my report."

He stood over Jack as Vertigo sashayed out. "What's the matter, commander? Can't remember where you've seen me before?"

"You look familiar." Jack frowned harder, but the man's name continued to elude him. "Do I know you?"

"Oh, yeah. You know me. Think on it. It'll come back to you."

He went to the door and stood there with his arms folded. Jack shivered. The man's hard stare stabbed him all the way to his soul. Yes, he'd think on it. He'd force himself to remember, and when he did, he felt sure the big man had caused him problems in his past too numerous to count.

****

Kristin shut the car off, not sure if the tremors in her hands were from nervousness or the ill repaired dirt road she'd just come down. The deep ruts jostled her hard enough to make her clamp her teeth together while her grip tightened on the steering wheel. The scattered gravel ricocheted off her car like ping pong balls, like someone shooting a BB gun at tin cans.

Trees sheltered the small, one story house and muffled any sound except for small animals as they scurried through the brush. Unseen birds sang their songs, but it sounded more eerie than pretty. The late September sun penetrated the thick canopy of leaves, and spots of light dotted the ground.

The whole scene reminded her of those ridiculous horror movies her friends watched. She shuddered, hating the uncertainty swirling around in her mind. Kristin Mentor didn't run from imagined threats. When Grayson knocked on her window, she bit back a scream as her hand instinctively reached for the short stun rod hidden between the seats.

"Should I help you out or are you going to sit in

your car and make us meet out here?"

"Mr. Styles."

As she looked at him from the driver's seat, he appeared taller than he had at the airport. He stood close, revealing the broad outline of his chest and the way his jeans hugged his waist. While he leaned on the roof of her car, his arms looked larger than she initially thought. Her heart pounded hard in her chest—from his proximity, from being startled, and from the whole strange situation. Add in the weird attraction picking at her mind, and the urge to go home overwhelmed her.

"I'm not sure if I'm safe here or if I should leave and try to find Jack on my own. I have no information about you or your people. You could all be in on it."

"Call me Grayson. A little mistrust is good for you. Too much, though, can cripple you."

She got out and slammed the car door harder than intended. "I might be able to trust you more if you would tell me more about yourself and your team."

As she stomped off toward the house, Grayson's presence loomed right behind her. She whirled on him. "I still think I would be better off if I tried to find Jack without you. If it wasn't for the word of a trusted friend, I wouldn't be here."

"I know, and believe me, I understand. As soon as we meet with my team, we'll give you some of the rundown on us and what we do. You shouldn't be too concerned afterwards."

She took a deep breath. "I hope so."

****

How could she command such an extreme effect on Grayson's mind? Kristin had a rare quality which pulled at him. It didn't matter right now if she trusted him. As he stood near her, his heart raced as if she'd taken it on a wild flight. Oh, he knew she fought hard, he'd seen it many times as she faced overwhelming odds. He shouldn't get involved with her, but that ship had sailed. She had to be connected to him, and it wasn't a road he wanted to go down. He eyed the sky, longing to take off, and stepped onto the porch.

He eased her off to one side before he knocked on the solid, light tan wood door. Seconds later, it opened a crack and a blue eye peeked at them before the door opened all the way. "I wondered what happened to you. I know traffic isn't bad for another couple of hours." He stuck out his right hand, a large handgun gripped in his left. "Jericho Black. You're Dr. Kristin Mentor, I take it?"

"Yes." She took the offered hand, giving it a firm shake. "Are you one of Grayson's associates?"

"Yep. There are two others on our team. One does all our computer stuff. You could call it his superpower. The other is a tracker of sorts."

"And do you have any powers, Mr. Black?"

"Me? Nope. Grayson has a power, though," he said, jerking a thumb toward his friend.

Grayson reached over his shoulder and scratched his back. "Don't say it, Jericho. I'm warning you."

Jericho laid the gun on the table and picked up a half empty beer bottle. He plopped down on the couch and his feet banged hard on the coffee table as he crossed his legs at the ankles. His eyes twinkled with a mischievous glint. "He can pull miracles out of his ass."

Kristin glanced at both men and smiled. "From the look on Grayson's face, you've said this more than once. If true, it's a very useful ability."

The left side of Jericho's mouth curled up in a charming smirk. "My thoughts exactly."

Grayson moved closer to her as he scowled at his friend. "Did Cole turn up any new information? Did you get in touch with Adam? McClennan's too noticeable for this kidnapping not to get some kind of coverage. Someone out there should know something by now."

"Not yet. Cole said he'd get in touch when his contacts called him. Adam got to Cole's about an hour ago. He got a slight psychic scent and started to track. Let's look at the map again."

****

Kristin looked over the man who let them in. Sandy blond hair cut short, the front sticking up like it didn't know which way to go. Square jaw, piercing blue eyes, broad chest, arm muscles bulging from his T-shirt sleeves, long legs with the same muscular build as the rest of him. He was almost as well built and handsome as Grayson. Almost. She frowned. Where did those thoughts come from?

If she kept staring at the two of them, she feared she'd look like a creeper. Instead she glanced around Jericho's small house. They'd entered the front door into the living room. Hipsters would call his mismatched furniture "trendy," but it more closely resembled what she would term as "thrift store chic."

Yellowed curtains covered the windows, the print on them faded with time. A threadbare area rug didn't do much to protect the scratched hardwood floor under the couch and two armchairs. Artwork of flowers obscured by layers of dust on the glass hung on the wall. A tall, locked, metal cabinet stood against the far wall. *Must be his weapons storage.*

Behind the living room, was a small kitchen, the appliances the avocado green of the early '70s. A small hallway off to the left had a door leading to the bathroom, and the door beyond should be the bedroom. What should have been a dining room had a desk and computer setup, with metal cabinets against the wall behind it. All in all, a standard bachelor pad, if you discounted the gun locker. And the large handgun on the coffee table.

She glanced over at them when Jericho chuckled at whatever Grayson had said. Jericho's easygoing nature made it easy to forget his dangerous side. Grayson had mentioned his boss. First chance she got, she would question them about their boss and the company they worked for. Once again, those complicated gray areas were in her way.

The two men discussed possible locations where Jack might be in low voices. The seriousness in Grayson made a perfect contrast to Jericho's casual attitude. He had a fierce determination, as though he couldn't stand the thought of failure. He pointed to a specific section, then pulled up the internet on his phone, stared at the area again before he double checked the map.

If he could be this focused on the mission to find her friend, he couldn't be all bad, could he? Her instincts told her these men could be trusted, and her teammates were fond of saying a person had instincts for a reason. However, logic dictated she needed more information before giving them the chance Frank asked her to give.

Chapter Three

Jericho's cell phone vibrated on the coffee table, and the three of them turned at the same time. He hurried over and snatched it up. "Hey, you got something for us? Uh huh. Yeah, we can be there in about twenty minutes, give or take. See you soon." He stuffed the phone in his pocket and pulled out his keys. "Cole thinks he has a possible lead, and Adam may have a fix on McClennan's location."

The late afternoon sun turned the sky the deep lavender of twilight. Kristin followed them to a standard size SUV, at least five years old with no noticeable external features. It blended well with the rest of the vehicles in the area. She slid into the back seat and let Grayson take the front.

"Where does he live?" she asked.

"Just down the pike in a small township. You think there's a lot of woods around my place? Cole is in a more rural area. The woods are thicker there and the houses farther apart."

More rural? Farms with huge fields blurred by. How much more rural could he get? Frank had told her she could trust Grayson. Did his statement hold true for the rest of the men on his team? Grayson and Jericho told her Cole and Adam were friends and teammates but didn't elaborate.

The occasional glimpse of Grayson's profile made

Kristin's concentration falter as she tried to focus on the mission, but he continued to intrude on her thoughts. How would it feel to be held by him? Would his kisses be hard and demanding or soft and subtle? How would she respond? Her hand curled into a tight fist and she clenched her teeth. With everything at stake, these were her thoughts? How much more ridiculous could she get?

She stared out the window and ignored the quiet scenery while she tried to sort her muddled thoughts. Would it be so bad to want to be more than the leader of the Angels and a top bio-geneticist? She wanted to be the woman her teammates were—fun, loving, and not obsessed with plans, bad guys, and working on new scientific breakthroughs.

What had Grayson done to tie her up in so many knots? Less than two hours in the company of one incredibly handsome man and fanciful, romantic notions filled her. She'd never entertained those types of thoughts before, and she certainly didn't want them now. If not now, the voice in her mind said, when? Three of your teammates are married. Who knows how much longer the rest will be single? Do you want to be all alone when you're older? She almost groaned aloud as those notions swirled in her mind.

The subject of her thoughts turned to look at her. "You okay back there?"

"I'm fine," she answered a little too quickly. "I'm anxious to know what your friend found out. I want to find Jack and get us both home."

"Understandable. Does Jack's wife know he's been picked up?"

Terrific. Of course, he knew Jack had a wife. "I

would expect so. Frank would've told her. I should've had him home by now."

Grayson faced front again. "Don't worry. We'll find him."

"Will we?" she murmured.

Jericho turned down a small side street. Then another. Then a smaller one, before he slowed the car to a crawl on a side road which looked like little more than a dirt trail. Kristin sighed softly. Well, they did say he lived in a very rural area.

She held the armrest in a tight grip as the SUV bounced over ruts, roots, and rocks, forcing her to clamp her teeth together. If she didn't, she feared she'd have a broken tooth before they reached their destination. The farther they drove down what could loosely be called a driveway, the harder Kristin wished for a quick end to the torturous ride. Jericho navigated the curves and managed to somehow miss the worst of the holes. She thanked whatever deity who listened when he stopped in front of a house smaller than his.

Grayson held out an arm to steady her when she tumbled out of the car. "I didn't think we'd make it here alive. This driveway is the definition of a serious trip through hell."

"Yeah, it's time for him to grade it again," Grayson said.

The heat of his fingers warmed her skin through her sleeve. As he held her, she resisted the temptation to lay her hand over his and keep the contact. *Stop being foolish. Act like the practical woman you are and move.* She forced herself to nod at Grayson, and he let her go before they followed Jericho to the low porch.

Jericho knocked on the door. After several minutes,

a chain rattled, then a deadbolt shot back, then another, and another. A tall man opened the door and dragged them inside. As soon as Kristin crossed the threshold, he slammed the door shut and shoved all the bolts back into place in one smooth motion

"You're a little more paranoid than usual. What happened?" Grayson asked.

"What I found is pretty bad so, yeah, I'm a little more paranoid."

Kristin looked at the man who let them in. Cole was yet another well built, handsome man with close-cropped sandy blond hair. He had a rounder face than Grayson's and a kinder look in his eyes. She sensed, like the others, he could kill her and not lose any sleep over it. As a hero, she'd worked with mercenaries and covert agents before. Their temperaments were iffy at best.

Cole moved with tight precision; every motion and movement served a purpose. His T-shirt stretched tightly over his shoulders and hugged his chest. Faded jeans dragged the floor, and he walked around in his socks. A pair of scuffed boots lay under what tried to pass for a coffee table. The leather sides had permanent creases, and from the worn look, he'd have them on and be gone in a matter of seconds if the situation demanded it.

"Dr. Mentor," he said. "I'm Cole Jamison."

"Mr. Jamison. Mr. Black said you had information for us."

He shot a glance at Jericho and raised an eyebrow. "*Mr.* Black?" He escorted Kristin over to a cluttered desk with a computer setup. It looked like it had been assembled by a deranged mad scientist. "And yeah, I do."

Kristin couldn't even begin to count the number of drives he had connected. There were three large monitors, at least two towers, and lots of different pieces she couldn't identify. It didn't look as sophisticated as the computer at Angel Haven, but she had a feeling he could do more with it than anyone, except maybe her friend, Amy. The handgun in plain sight to the right ruined the whole geek look.

"This is quite the setup you have here," she said. "Very impressive."

Cole gave her a lopsided grin. "It looks like junk, but I can access just about anything I want from here. I could list out all the pieces I have connected, but we're on a tight schedule." He tapped the keyboard and a paused video image appeared. "One of our agents got us some airport security footage. Do *not* ask how he did it. I don't know and wouldn't tell you if I did."

She leaned closer. "What did you find?"

"Check this out. I spotted McClennan right away. Between his size and the bright red, long hair, you can't miss him."

He started the video and pointed to the screen. Jack appeared as he walked through the boarding area. He stopped and dragged a hand across his forehead. He nodded to an airport worker and moved on. A little later, he stopped again and leaned against a column.

A security guard walked over at the same time a blonde woman approached. She smiled as she talked to the guard and patted Jack's arm. She waited while the guard called for one of the small, motorized carts. He had the driver take Jack and the woman to the main entrance, and she walked him out the front door.

"He acts like he's drunk, which means he may have been drugged before he even left the plane." Kristin noticed the time stamp in the corner. "I missed him by mere minutes. Can you go back and zoom in on the woman's face?"

Cole backed up the video and zoomed in. At Kristin's sharp intake of breath, he turned to her. "I know who she is. I take it you know her, too?"

"Yes. Her name is Vertigo."

He nodded. "I just needed confirmation. Her real name is Anita Haines."

"How do you know her?"

He stared at the screen and looked grim as he took a slow, deep breath. "I worked under her at HelixCorp."

She glanced over her shoulder at the sound of movement behind her. Another man entered the small living room. This third man stood as tall as the others with close cropped hair the same sandy blond as Cole and Jericho. He had a more angular face, but the same muscular build as the rest of them. It was uncanny how much they all resembled each other. He joined them at Cole's computer.

He shook her hand and gave her a small smile. "Adam Williams. Cole said Grayson had hooked up with you, doc."

"Grayson said he had three teammates. I take it you all work for the same company?"

He nodded. "Yep. Jericho got hired first, then Grayson. Cole and I were brought in at the same time."

"Jericho said you may have a fix on Jack's location. How did you find him?"

"I'm a telepathic tracker." He grinned. "I can find just about anyone."

Wonderful, she thought. If Adam tracked him and read his mind to get the location, Jack would be safe before he knew it.

"Stop right there, doc. I'm not a traditional telepath. I only track. There aren't any other abilities in my noggin. I can't do mind to mind communication."

"If you can't read minds, how did you know my thoughts?"

He shrugged. "I know the look."

Grayson looked up from the footage. "The Angels have a strong telepath on their team. Why don't you have her find him?"

The same question reflected on all their faces. "She's with her family right now. Her father's been ill, so she's gone home to help her mother. I could call her, but it wouldn't be fair. She would be too worried to concentrate."

"I see," Grayson said quietly. He glanced at Cole. "You said you used to work with this woman. Kristin, you know her also. You guys care to share?"

"I worked as her lab assistant at HelixCorp. Parents of kids with powers would enter them in the program there to help them learn control. Anita experimented on them. Sometimes they got better and stronger. Sometimes, they got worse," Cole said as he picked at the corner of a piece of paper on his desk. "Some never made it out alive."

He stared at the monitors. "When the program began, she told me these kids were there for help. I believed her because I wanted to, I guess. As time went on and I found out her real agenda, I knew I had to put a stop to the experiments. I started to help kids escape. There were two sisters there, twins. I almost couldn't save them." He jerked his thumb toward Adam. "There sits my last rescue."

"And it almost killed those two," Jericho said. "I found them and took them to our boss. She hid them, helped them recover, and trained them how to fight and shoot. They've been partners with me and Grayson ever since."

"I know Vertigo from when Jack and his wife broke the secret cabal at ULTRA," Kristin said. "We've had some recent run-ins. Every time we fight her, she appears to be more powerful. The only motive I can think of for her taking Jack is revenge." She turned to Adam. "How can you find him?"

"I got a faint telepathic signature when I tracked him earlier. If you'll allow me to get his psychic scent from your mind, it will give me a stronger trail to follow."

Kristin followed Adam as he walked to one of the chairs and sat, taking a few deep breaths. "Do what you need to. I'm ready."

As Adam's mind wrapped around hers, feathery static electricity brushed over her skin, and the hairs on her arms began to rise. She shivered as the light touch tickled her spine. It felt odd, but not unpleasant.

"Weird, isn't it?" Grayson asked.

"Very. It's a strange telepathic contact. I've never felt a psychic touch like it. Is it the usual response?"

He nodded. "Yeah. It happens every time he does it."

Adam's eyes drifted shut, and he lifted his head, turning left then right. "He's still in the area. He's a little more north from here. I can't get an exact fix but it feels like he's close."

"Finally, good news," Kristin said.

Jericho spread a map on the table and waved her over. "Not really. Come here."

She stared at the area on the map he indicated and her heart sank. The whole area was one giant state park. And Vertigo had hidden Jack somewhere in the middle of all those trees. "How big is the Wharton State Forest?"

Grayson looked up at her. "Over one hundred thousand acres."

"Adam sensed him nearby. This is your area. Where could someone be held and no one would notice they were there?"

Jericho laughed and Grayson scowled at him. "Anywhere," he told her. "Off the main roads, there's smaller roads. Some lead nowhere, some to mansions, and others to deserted houses."

She glanced at them, then to Adam. "If we drove down some of these roads while Adam scanned, could it narrow down where we need to search?"

"His ability works better when he stays in one place," Jericho said. "But it's worth a try. Adam, you up for this?"

"Of course." The tracker headed to the kitchen and grabbed a bottle of water. He grinned at them. "What's life without a rousing adventure?"

"We'll start tomorrow." Cole's voice drifted to them from behind the largest monitor. "I'd like to get a little more information before we head into any situations which could possibly get us killed."

"Agreed," Jericho said. "We'll go back to my place and be here at first light. With all of our resources, we'll get Jack back home in no time. After all, if we can't find him, no one can."

As they got ready to head back to Jericho's, Grayson scratched his back again. Kristin frowned. Did he have a nervous tic or something else? What secrets did he keep hidden? And did his team know about them?

Chapter Four

"You should stay here with me and Jericho," Grayson said. "I don't like the idea of you staying alone. That psycho telepath will have picked us up by now and knows we're coming after her."

"If she wanted to attack, she would've done so by now," Kristin said as she walked to her car. The two men followed her out and stood by the driver's door as she climbed in. "I need time to do my own research, and I would prefer you two be somewhere else. Vertigo won't bring attention to herself until she's ready. I'll be perfectly safe in a motel. I saw several on Route 30 as we came here. I'll call you when I'm settled."

"Fine. Give me your phone, and I'll put my number in."

Kristin took out her phone, but held onto it. "Tell me your number and I'll put it in."

A small smile curved his lips. "One would think you don't trust me."

"One would be right. You've already had my phone once today and I wasn't happy about it then either. I don't know you all very well yet. It's hard for me to determine if I should trust you or not."

She programmed in his and Jericho's numbers, then drove away.

****

"So, you like her?" Jericho said, a sly smile curling

up one side of his mouth.

"What? No. She's just another assignment." Grayson pulled his shirt off and large, feathery brown wings sprouted from his back. "What do you think she'd say about these?"

"She's the leader of a hero team. Why do you think she would care? I watched you dig at your back as soon as she got here. You know you get twitchy when you're nervous."

His fingers curled into his shirt and he stared at the ground. "It hasn't been this bad for a long time. I think the job is the reason. I didn't want this assignment in the first place, and you know why."

"I'm one of three people who knows the real reason why. You, me, and the boss."

Grayson flexed his shoulders and his wings extended out to their full span before he folded them against his back. "And the boss put me on it anyway. There's a good chance I'll have to use magic before this job is over."

"You can't still be worried about the North Wind Brethren? They haven't found you yet."

"Neither has the harpy tribe. Doesn't mean they aren't still out there. Each faction is as bad as the other. Tom's done what he could to cloak my presence when I've had to fall back on my magic, but these spells won't last forever. And the more I use magic, the weaker the cloaking spells get."

"Maybe." Jericho clapped a hand on his shoulder. "Maybe not. You know we got your back, right? Besides, you told me yourself both sides have abandoned the search for you. It's been a lot of years since you've heard from either tribe."

"I know, but they're out there. Creatures of magic don't give up easily." He glanced at his friend. "I wouldn't be this concerned if I'd stayed in New York."

"If you had, you would've missed out on my sparkling personality."

They walked toward the house, and Grayson shook his head. "You're not helping your case."

Jericho's mouth curled up in his trademark smirk. "As your friend, I'll tell you flat out, I'm not supposed to be any help."

In the kitchen, Jericho grabbed two beers from the refrigerator and tossed one to Grayson. "The boss is right, you know. It's time to lay the past to rest. This will haunt you for the rest of your life if you don't deal with it soon."

"Yeah, well, if everyone who's after me doesn't kill me, Jack will. I broke his trust when we worked together. It's the most unforgiveable of sins to him."

They walked to the living room, and Jericho dropped onto the couch. Once again, he put his feet on the coffee table. "Enough doom and gloom. I want to know what you think of the good Dr. Kristin Mentor."

"Have you ever watched the footage of her and her team? Her combat skills are well developed. She's a good team leader. She's always the first one into the fight and the last one to leave it. We're lucky she'll be fighting with us."

Jericho laughed. "How long have you been in love with her?"

"I'm not in love with her."

A deep frown creased his forehead. But that could change in an instant if what he suspected was true. He'd never wanted a soulmate. It had sounded like prison, being tied to one person forever. Maybe it wasn't the bad thing he'd built up in his mind. Not that he'd tell Jericho his real thoughts. The possibility his friend wouldn't understand about the deep emotional bond when two souls recognized each other hung over his head.

"I admire her. She's one of the most amazing heroes I've ever seen. Besides, it wouldn't work between us. She's all about science. I'm a man of magic. Science and magic are like oil and water. They don't mix."

"Or champagne and orange juice. They mix just well enough to get you drunk," Jericho said and gave him a huge grin. "If you like her, why not run with it while she's here? As soon as the job is completed, we'll be done and she'll go back."

"Will you drop it?"

"I'm sure the fact she's pretty hot hasn't escaped your notice."

"It hasn't escaped yours," Grayson mumbled. "All right, yes, she's hot. She's the complete package."

"So, what do you plan to do about it?"

Grayson laughed, but unlike his friend, his held no trace of humor. "Are you serious? Why would you think she's interested in any of us? Her focus is on the mission to find Jack."

"I don't think so. She glances at you when she thinks no one sees. Wings or no wings, magic background or not, you've got a shot with her. If you don't take it, you're an ass." Jericho stood, finished his beer, and set the bottle on the kitchen counter. "I'm going to bed. See you tomorrow, lover boy."

****

Kristin checked in and grabbed her small suitcase. The room had typical motel decor with the usual muted tan bedspread and heavy curtains the same dull color. A small bathroom with a shower stall, sink, and toilet was located at the back of the room. Right across from the bathroom stood a closet with a couple of hangers, sparkling in the low light. The smell of bleach and other cleaning products hung cloyingly in the air.

She opened the luggage stand and plopped her bag down. She needed time alone to gather her composure and do research on her temporary partners. Being so close to Grayson made her think and act in a very un-scientific manner. As she set up her laptop, Grayson jumped to the front of her thoughts. She dropped her head into her hands. Why would the man never leave her alone?

For meeting him a mere few hours before, inappropriate thoughts of him immediately occupied her mind. Could he be interested in her? He appeared serious and focused on the task at hand. Besides, he might already have someone. Then why did she always sense his gaze on her?

Why didn't she get more information on magical creatures from the wizard in residence at Angel Haven? She should've talked to her friends about it. Kristin's whole life was based in science. Magic and everything about it was an unknown commodity. There had been discussion about soulmates ever since two of her teammates had married in to the magical realm. Could Grayson be her soulmate? If so, was he a man of magic?

"Stop it," she told herself. "Yes, he's attractive and, yes, he acts interested in you at times. It's only a biological response to his good looks and the stress of the situation, nothing more. There are no soulmates in science. Now act like the team leader you are and not some teenage groupie."

The way he reacted every time Jack's name came up, there had to have been a big blowup between the two men. But what? As she waited for the internet to load, she wondered if she should dig into their backgrounds. Opening a new search, she hesitated. She couldn't go into a potentially volatile situation and not have any information about the men going with her. After typing in his name, she hit enter, and a list popped up. She had to make it her business to know.

****

Jack lay on the carpeted floor, thoughts of Vertigo's hired man on his mind. Where did he know him from? If the fog in his brain would lift for a moment, just for a moment, he'd have a clear thought. Bloody hell, his muscles ached. He needed to move around. Vertigo wouldn't let him stand, let alone walk.

The big man's face looked familiar, like a dream he couldn't quite remember. He'd called him "commander" so he must be from his ULTRA days. Jack mentally listed the members of his team before he'd been sent to prison. He thought he'd known all of the agents well, but the facts had proven him wrong.

He stared at the big man. "How do I know you?" he asked.

His guard dragged a chair over and sat. "I'm not surprised you don't remember me. You always acted like I didn't belong on your precious team. You ignored me, passed me over for promotion." He leaned closer. "I got to tell you, I laughed long and hard when you got

33

convicted. I prayed for your death when you were beaten in prison."

"What did I do to you to make you hate me this much?"

"Don't worry, Commander. It'll come back to you soon enough." He put the chair back where it belonged. "And you might not be too happy when it does."

The door opened, and Vertigo came in with a small bag. "Mr. Trust got me the supplies I needed, and I've had a wonderful surprise. I've telepathically picked up Cole Jamison and Adam Williams in the area. I've waited a long time to meet up with them again. If Cole and Adam are here, it's a sure bet the other members of their team are with them. There's also someone else with them."

She stored the new items for her experiment and turned to him. "I had Adam slated for this experiment at HelixCorp. Unfortunately, Cole interfered, and I never did get to finish with him. I want them both here, where I can keep an eye on them."

"Adam Williams is yours. What about Cole? Does Mr. Trust want him as a weapon, too?" he asked.

Vertigo's lips curved in a menacing smile. Jack couldn't stop the involuntary shudder from the frost in her eyes. "He hasn't said he wants Cole. Feel free to shoot him when I've finished with him. Then, I'll be done with both of them at the same time."

"They should be easy to find." He jerked his head in Jack's direction. "My sources told me they've already begun the search for him."

"I know."

Jack cringed as she stalked over to him. "How does it feel, Jack? Once again, your actions will lead to the deaths of five more people."

"What do you mean, 'five'?" Jack asked. "You've only mentioned two."

"Let's see," she said, ticking off names on her fingers. "There's Adam Williams, Cole Jamison, their partners Jericho Black and Grayson Styles, and then there's your Angel friend, Dr. Kristin Mentor. She's decided to join their little band. I will take great pleasure as you watch while I end her miserable life. However, right now, Adam and Cole are my priority."

As the two left, Jack closed his eyes. Of course, Kristin would be here to search for him. She and the men with her were about to be hurt and, once again, it would be all his fault. Bloody hell. Would the past never stay buried?

****

After a brief breakfast, her web search still yielded no clues about her temporary team. Kristin had never known this level of frustration. Ever. She found nothing on any site with information on Grayson Styles and his friends. Everyone had some sort of digital fingerprint. She'd seen Grayson with a cell phone. Jack had appeared in searches on the internet, even during his time as a renegade outlaw.

Every time she made some headway, the site would crash, or she would mysteriously get logged off. When she would get back online, all the sites she'd been on would be gone. She frowned as she drummed her fingers on the desk. It would take someone with incredible skill to wipe out every trace of them. Someone like Cole Jamison, an admitted tech genius. She frowned. Or someone like Jack's friend, Amy.

She didn't want to believe Frank and Amy capable

of duplicity, but as of now, she had no choice. She leaned back in the hard chair and grabbed her cell phone. Her patience with riddles and half answers had run out.

"Frank," she said, when he answered. "No more games. I need to know about Grayson Styles. Do *not* tell me to ask him. I'm asking you. Who are these men, and who do they work for?"

Chapter Five

"Good morning to you, too, Kristin."

"I'm serious, Frank. I need to know if I can trust these men or not. They live in the middle of the woods, like hermits. I must admit, I'm more than a little leery being in their company when I know so little about them. There's no information on the internet about them. Every time I get close, the system crashes or information disappears."

"Kristin…"

"Tell me the truth, Frank." When he still hesitated, her almost non-existent temper began to rise. "If there's something you haven't mentioned before, you need to tell me." She paused. "Now."

On the other end, Frank took a deep breath. "All right. I can't tell you too much about the men themselves, but I can tell you they work for Shade, Inc."

"Shade was investigated recently for extortion and running a protection racket in their neighborhood, weren't they?"

"Yes. The people called as witnesses wouldn't bad mouth the company. They say they make insurance payments and Shade always completed the claims in a timely manner. No strong-arm tactics involved. The prosecutor dropped the charges due to lack of evidence."

"I don't think Shade is an insurance company. What else?"

"All I know is Jericho Black and Grayson Styles work there. They've been teamed with Cole Jamison and Adam Williams for several years. They have a high success rate on their jobs. The only people who come out worse for wear are the people they're sent to stop. You have to trust they are the good guys." He chuckled. "Even if they are a little rough around the edges."

"Rough around the edges doesn't even begin to describe these men. Sandpaper isn't this rough." She paused to get herself under control. "Is Shade some type of covert agency?"

"Of course. They were the ones who contacted me about Jack's abduction. They knew before anyone."

"How? Who are their sources?" Once again, she had more questions than answers. "Am I safe with their agents?"

"I don't know how Shade gets information but, yes, you should be safe. You're in no more danger than usual. Watch yourself, though. A little extra caution can't hurt."

"You know I'm always careful. I'm hopeful, with their resources, we'll find Jack soon. I'll call you when I have news."

"Take care, Kristin. Keep in touch."

The phone went silent in her hand, and she sat back in the chair. He'd hung up before she'd had a chance to ask about his past connection with Grayson. She felt fortunate she got as much as she did. Frank had the uncanny ability to talk around any subject. You thought he told you what you needed to know, and then you realized you were still empty handed. Kristin had been taken in by him again. She rolled her eyes and realized she always would be.

****

Jericho's phone buzzed. "It's Cole." He snatched it up and put it on speaker. "Go ahead."

"Grayson, your girlfriend poked the internet for information about us, especially you. I blocked her, but I expect her to try again. How do you want to handle this?"

Grayson ran a hand through his hair. "Will you guys stop? She's not interested in me. I do think we have to give her the rundown on who we are and soon."

"I agree. I believe she's curious because she doesn't fully trust us." Cole chuckled. "Can't say I blame her. Look at us. We're not high society material, guys, and I can tell you, she is. Runs in some of the better circles of the scientific community, the upper class, and even the hero community. Right now, all she knows is the little bit we've told her."

"You've revealed the most, Cole," Jericho said. "You shouldn't have said too much. I'm sure it's the reason why she wants to know more."

Grayson stood and paced as his wings twitched with agitation. "More than likely, she's called Frank. He'll do what he can to cover for us, but he's had to give her some kind of intel."

"True," Cole said. "Think on it and let me know what you decide. See you tomorrow."

Jericho shoved his phone in his front pocket and stood. "I'm heading down to Pleasantville to see Sammy before lunch hour traffic starts. Want to tag along?"

Grayson almost said no but being by himself would

let the past and his current dark thoughts intrude. "Sure. Give me a minute to get ready."

Grayson pulled his wings almost completely in to his shoulder muscles and yanked his T-shirt over his head. He tucked his gun into his waistband at his back and grabbed his jacket while Jericho did the same. They climbed in Jericho's SUV, and headed toward the township of Pleasantville. As they hit Route 30, they passed one of the better motels.

"There's Kristin's car. Should we check on her?" Grayson said.

While they were stopped at a red light, Jericho turned to his friend. "You've got it bad. In our line of work, you can't do this. You can't end up with someone you care about."

"She's *in* our line of work." He turned to the motel again as Jericho moved forward with the traffic. "With Vertigo out there, who knows what could happen?"

"Fine. We'll stop. Maybe she'll want to come."

"I don't think so. My gut tells me she wouldn't approve of our methods."

As Jericho parked next to her car, Grayson pulled out his phone. He dialed her number, surprised when she answered right away.

"Grayson, do you have any new information?"

"No. We're outside by your car. We came by to make sure you were all right. We want to check with one of our contacts to see if there's any word on the street."

The door in front of them opened, and Kristin stood there. He hung up, and the two got out. She pushed the door open wider and allowed them to follow her inside.

She turned, crossed her arms, and stared at each of them. "Who are you? I called Frank and all he would tell me is you work for a covert agency. I want answers or I'll find Jack without your help."

They looked at each other, and Jericho shrugged. "We can't tell you about what we do unless the boss says we can. You should understand. You're a hero. Do you give everyone your life story who asks? Don't you have secrets you want to keep hidden?"

"Of course, but you've told me almost my whole history, and all four of you are still a complete mystery." She narrowed her eyes. "There's too much in your favor."

Grayson laid a hand over his heart. "I give you my word, we're on your side. We may walk a fine line between law and vigilante, but we are the good guys."

"I don't know why, but I believe you."

Jericho cleared his throat. "If you two are done kissing and making up, I've got a man to see about a kidnapped ULTRA field commander. Kristin, you can come with us if you want."

"No, I think I'll stay here and see what else I can dig up. Vertigo wouldn't risk her freedom to kidnap Jack for simple revenge. There must be a bigger picture. Stop by on your way back. Maybe I'll have found out what her real plan could be."

They walked out to the SUV, and Jericho had his familiar smirk in place. "You both got it bad."

"Have I told you recently to shut the hell up?"

****

Kristin waited until they left before sitting back down at the desk. What she wouldn't give to have someone to talk to right now. Her feelings for Grayson

41

confused her more and more. Maybe she should've joined in the conversations her teammates had about the dates they'd been on.

Well, she didn't. They all knew she had no patience for the foolish notion of romance. The romantic comedy movies they watched irritated her. When she pointed out the obvious problems with the couple and how they should be resolved, she'd been banished. Until now, she'd been fine with her movie exile. Then Grayson Styles walked into her life.

She'd been determined to stay professional, but didn't think she could. At times, she sensed a sadness in him. What happened in his past to make him so determined? She'd been trained to be practical, logical, and analytical. When he discovered her origin, he might not see her as anything more than a science experiment and not a true human. Then where would this silly attraction get her?

"Enough," she said out loud. "It's time to get to work."

She started her search for what Vertigo could want with Jack besides the obvious revenge. What could be the telepath's full plan?

Chapter Six

Jericho pulled into an overgrown parking lot behind a two-story warehouse. It stood alone and forgotten as the city's growth passed it by. The sunlight made it look forlorn against the brighter, newer structures. Dull gray wood panels covered the windows as yellowed paint peeled from the cinder block walls. Weeds grew high around unused entrances while vines tried their best to cover old bay doors and the metal stairs leading to a narrow platform.

As Grayson got out, he gazed around the area. "You get the feeling there's more people than just us here?" He kicked at trash the slight breeze blew in front of him. "This place gets worse every time we see it. Are you sure Sammy is still in the area? We haven't heard from him in a long time. It's possible he bailed when he heard Vertigo got into town."

"Precisely why I wanted to come here. I don't think he would've cut and run. The fact he didn't get in touch with us right away tells me he found something, or someone connected to the case found him." Jericho gestured to the bay doors. "Shall we?"

Walking around some of the taller weeds, they lifted one door a few feet, just enough to crawl under. The heavy metal door groaned as they slowly lowered it. Total darkness surrounded them until Grayson turned on the flashlight on his phone. Sammy's living area appeared more disheveled than usual. Jericho had a right to be worried. Unease settled on his shoulders, and his muscles ached as his grip on the phone tightened. They quietly slipped out of the bay as their hurried steps carried them deeper into the building.

Whatever company had owned the property in the past left no clue of what they did there. Empty offices lined the walls, with a large open area in the middle. Warped ceiling tiles barely sat in the metal frames. Where light fixtures used to hang were empty spaces, a telltale sign of scavengers cleaning out what could be sold. Most of the large windows behind them were boarded up. However, time and the elements had knocked a few down, and pale light trickled in to shine on the pale green walls. The presence of mold and mildew added to the already musty, damp smell assaulting their noses.

He put his phone away and pulled his gun. Jericho would use other methods before he'd draw his. While Jericho could hold his own in any hand to hand fight, Grayson liked having distance to get a clearer picture. If whoever they were after had the strength to run after Jericho's physical assault, Grayson would wound them. Jericho would then interrogate the prisoner while he'd stand guard. They'd fallen into this routine not long after they started working together.

Dripping water echoed through the empty hall and offices. Every room they checked gave no clue as to the location of their informant. A faint scuffle followed by a cry of pain stopped them. Their gazes shot to the ceiling as they heard it again. Jericho jerked his head in the direction of stairs at the end of the corridor. They treaded up the short flight to the next floor.

They hugged the wall and moved silently toward the soft noise. They reached the next level, and peered out at the second-floor hallway. Trash, leaves, and several small rodents scurried in their path. The cry sounded again, louder this time. Shadows moved in an office a few feet down on their right. Jericho nodded and they crept closer.

Grayson eased the door open a crack. Jericho wouldn't take time to throw any punches. The rage vibrated from his friend as he looked around at every detail. A large man had his back to the door, making it hard to identify him, but he was about to be in for a world of hurt. He wouldn't blame Jericho in the least if he decided to end this clown now.

Jericho's contact, Sammy, sat tied to a chair, his nose broken and bleeding. He sported a black eye and a split lip. More blood had soaked through his grimy T-shirt, and his right ankle twisted around. From the angle of his foot, Grayson recognized it to be a bad break. Sammy shivered and glared at the man in front of him.

His tormentor loomed over him, his fist poised to strike again. "Are you going to tell me who the men are asking questions about Vertigo?"

"I haven't yet, dumbass. Why do you think I'd start now?" Sammy spat blood on the floor. "You and your crazy telepath can go straight to hell."

"Have it your way."

Sammy squeezed his eyes shut and turned his head, but the expected blow never landed. He cracked one eye open, then opened them both wide. A small smile appeared on his face as he saw Jericho had the big man's wrist in a tight grip.

"You'd better have a damn good reason for why

you attacked one of my people," Jericho growled. "If not, you're going to have a real hard time explaining why your fist is in a very unnatural place on your anatomy."

The man pulled his arm free. "Well, well, well. Jericho Black. You never did know how to stay out of everyone else's business." He shot a quick glance at Grayson as his mouth curled up in an unpleasant smile. "And Mr. Grayson Styles comes with you. Or should I say ULTRA's former premier sniper, Agent Grayson Styles, also known as the Nemesis."

Grayson narrowed his eyes, recognition dawning. "Eddie Anderson. I'd hoped somebody would have put you in the ground by now."

"Not yet. People tried, though." He stepped closer to them. "I got a new gig now. After Jack ruined the inner circle at ULTRA, I got picked up by The Company."

Grayson and Jericho froze. They'd heard of The Company, but their team had never been able to dig up any information about them. Even their boss claimed they were a mystery to her, and she had many more resources than they did. All they knew, when The Company got involved, innocent people died.

Grayson grabbed him by the shirt and pulled him close, shoving his gun in Eddie's face. "Who else got picked up with you and Vertigo? Some of the other agents who betrayed Jack and the team?"

Eddie's unpleasant smile turned to a sneer. "If it were true, Styles, wouldn't you be an agent for The Company instead of for the weak woman who runs Shade? After all, you were part of the whole conspiracy, too."

Eddie threw a quick, surprise punch and caught him in the side of his face. The world tilted as his head rocked back. Jericho pulled his gun and snapped off a quick shot. Grayson hit the floor as Eddie charged at the same time Jericho squeezed off another shot. The big man cried out as he barreled through them. Soon, they heard the booming echo of the bay door as it slammed shut. Grayson pushed to his feet and started after him.

"Let him go." Jericho grabbed Grayson's arm. "His time will come. Help me with Sammy."

"Right."

Grayson pulled a small knife from an outside pocket on his boot. The sharp, thin blade made short work of the ropes. They pulled Sammy's arms across their shoulders and hauled him downstairs. Sammy's dead weight made them stumble several times as they eased him down the short flight of steps.

"If you were any larger, this would be really awkward, not to mention damn near impossible," Grayson said.

Sammy wheezed out a laugh. "Sorry. I'll work on my telekinesis, just in case there's a next time."

"You have to go to the hospital," Jericho said. "Your ankle needs to be set and so does your nose. Lord knows what else he broke in you."

"You worry too much," Sammy whispered.

They took him outside to the front and sat him against the wall. Jericho stepped away to call 911 as Grayson sat with him. "How did he grab you, Sammy? You're too careful to slip up. What happened?"

Sammy shrugged and tried to take a deep breath. He coughed and grabbed his side. "I'd heard word on

47

the street about some powerful drugs with a delivery address out near you guys. Some dealers have disappeared, but it's no loss to the people here. Good riddance. I wanted to call and let you know what I found out."

Jericho squatted down. "There's an ambulance on the way. How did he find you?"

"I called some people I knew, when there's this woman's voice in my head. She told me to go home and I would have a surprise. I tried to resist her, but she had a lot of power. She blew my psychic shields apart like they weren't there. I went home and found the big guy waiting for me. You know the rest."

Jericho's hands balled into tight fists. "He did this to you because you wouldn't tell him you work for me."

"Yeah. You know I'd never give you up, Jericho. You've protected me too many times to count. I owe you a lot. Both of you." He glanced at them. "He mentioned Vertigo and The Company."

"Yeah. Not exactly what we wanted to hear. The Company makes things a hell of a lot more complicated."

Sirens screamed closer to them. Jericho bounced his cell phone once in his hand. "I need to call the boss. She'll send someone to watch out for you and take you some place safe so you can recover."

"What about the telepath? Do you think she'll find me?"

"Don't worry. The boss has so many psychic shields in place, it would be impossible for her to pick you up," Grayson said.

"If Vertigo's been hired by The Company…"

Sammy started to say.

Jericho glanced at him. "Stop right there. Vertigo is psycho enough by herself. I don't even want to know why she's allied herself with The Company."

Grayson and Jericho stood back while the EMTs worked. When the ambulance pulled away, the sirens echoed the screams of rage the two men kept bottled up. Grayson felt Jericho's gaze on him but he stared at the ground. Eddie had brought up the one thing which made him try to refuse this job. His stomach clenched as he knew if Kristin found out, she'd never forgive him.

****

Kristin tried to search for any information on Vertigo, but the only links she found were for the medical condition. Even the computer at Angel Haven had very little on the telepath. She referenced and cross referenced for over an hour. Kristin discovered she'd been part of a minor villain team, then disappeared after the team broke apart. She couldn't find any mention of her employment at HelixCorp. The other hero teams might have more on her in their files, but then more people would know about Jack being MIA. Time to call Frank again.

When he picked up, the first words out of his mouth were, "Amy's going to get jealous if you keep calling me several times a day. Any news yet?"

The strain in his voice overshadowed the light tone he tried for. "Not yet, but I have a question for you. Does ULTRA have a file on Vertigo? She might also be listed as Anita Haines."

He paused for a long moment before he spoke again. "Anita's involved? How?"

"Jericho's friend saw her on airport security footage. She's seen with Jack, and then they're both gone. I know she'd been a member of your team back in the day, but what about recently? Do have any idea where she's been since ULTRA cleaned house?"

"Before she came to ULTRA, she worked as a lab jockey at HelixCorp. She's listed as the youngest person ever to be promoted to head researcher. ULTRA recruited her for field work. She did well and then, well, you know what happened with Jack. She went a little bonkers."

"A little bonkers?" Kristin repeated. She jumped to her feet. "The woman's insane and now she has Jack."

"When she escaped after Jack broke the inner circle at ULTRA, I heard she tried to go back to HelixCorp. They referred her to someone else, but we can't get any information about who offered her a job or where they're located."

"Keep your ears open, Frank. Let me know if someone comes up with anything."

"You got it. When you find her, do me a favor?"

"If I can. What is it?"

He paused. "I need you to end her. Permanently."

"You know I won't kill, but I will do my best to see she's turned over to ULTRA."

"Good enough."

The line went dead, and Kristin stared at her phone. For Frank to ask her to take a life, he must believe it to be the best solution to stop the renegade psionic. She dropped the phone on the desk and decided to see what she could find on HelixCorp. The more they dug into this case, the more the research lab came up.

The HelixCorp website loaded, and she read about

their history. As a scientific research facility, HelixCorp had a dedicated mission to understand and train people with paranormal abilities. Their main area of study had been, and still was, psionics. The lead researcher had been Anita Haines. She'd had complete control over the lab and all the subjects who stayed there.

After several successful years, her lab assistant, Cole Jamison, had gone rogue and destroyed a lot of her work. Not too long after, she'd been dismissed. After she joined ULTRA, the lab shut down for two years to put a new system in place. They were listed now as a fortune 500 company. The site listed Benedict Trust as the current chairman. His name rang a bell.

She'd met him several times at various fundraisers. He ran in circles more elite than she ever would. Women always vied for the attractive and charming man's attention. The few times she'd met him, he'd been polite, even gracious, but something about him sat bad with her. She'd never been able to pinpoint why, but her instincts made her want to keep a far distance between them.

She went to try another link when she heard a car pull up. She peeked out the window, and her heart beat a little faster when Grayson and Jericho got out. She glanced at herself in the mirror and decided she looked fine, then stopped. Did she really just check her appearance? She never primped because of a man. She allied herself with Grayson and his team to find her friend. That was all. Spiraling emotions needed to settle themselves down immediately.

Before they could knock, she yanked open the door. "Did your contact have any information?"

Jericho scowled and turned away. Grayson sat on

the bed and looked up at her. "One of Vertigo's men got to him before we did. If we hadn't showed, he probably would've been beaten to death. He's got some pretty serious injuries, but he should be okay. He did manage to find out a little bit more."

Kristin watched the two of them and waited. As soon as they took a few minutes, they'd tell her. Her emotions might have been put in a blender, but she refused to give up the tight grip on her patience.

"He said some high-end drugs were delivered somewhere near here," Grayson said.

"Did he have any idea where or what drugs were being shipped?"

Jericho shook his head. "No. He hadn't gotten very far in asking around. He could have been killed because of me. I should've known a situation like this would happen."

"He's got a limited range, and you're not psionic or clairvoyant," Grayson said in a low voice. "He probably sensed it right before it happened. Hell, maybe Vertigo blocked his power so he couldn't know."

"You're right. At this point, the possibilities are endless."

She looked back and forth between the two men. "Is your contact psionic?"

Jericho nodded.

"You say you have no power, and yet you're in contact with a lot of super powered people. Are you sure you're not paranormal?"

The now familiar smirk appeared, and the knot in her stomach loosened. "I've had several ladies tell me I am, but not the way you mean."

"The boss will move our guy somewhere safe,"

Grayson said. "Let's all head back to Jericho's and grab some food. I didn't realize lunchtime had passed." As Kristin grabbed her purse, he stopped her. "Have you ever heard of The Company?"

"No. Are they connected to this case?"

He shrugged. "Maybe. Let's get Cole and Adam and kick around a few ideas."

They got into Jericho's SUV and started the short drive to his home.

Chapter Seven

Cole and Adam sat in Cole's car with their phones out as Jericho pulled up. All five exited their vehicles at the same time and trooped behind Jericho to the porch. At the front door, he stopped them and pointed to the splintered door frame. He laid his finger on his lips and eased the door open.

They stepped in and Kristin eyed the damage. His living room had been torn apart. The couch cushions lay tossed across the room and the couch itself rested on its back. One of the armchairs had been cut open, the fluffy guts pulled out and resembling fuzzy, uneven snowballs. As they checked out the rest of his house, the other rooms had been trashed as badly as the living room.

Jericho glanced around at the carnage. "Far as I can tell, nothing's been taken."

"Who could have done this?" she asked.

Grayson and Jericho looked at each other. "We have an idea," Grayson said. He turned to Jericho. "If I'd reacted faster after we found Sammy, I could've ended this. Someone really needs to put that clown in the ground."

"Don't beat yourself up. If I'd gone in with my gun already out, I'd have had a better shot."

"Guys, it doesn't matter," Kristin said. "You can't stay here. Whoever did this could return. It would be wise if you were somewhere else."

"I'm surprised your computer is still intact," Cole said. "This should have been the first thing trashed." He booted it up, searched different files, and copied them onto a small flash drive. "Kristin has the right idea, but staying with me won't work either. Adam will be at my place until the job is done. When there's too many minds around, his ability to track gets harder. Is there some place you guys can go?"

Jericho's hands curled into fists. "I don't have to leave. This isn't a message to back off. This is someone who got pissed because he got shot. Kristin, you need to stay here. It's not a good idea for any of us to be alone. I can put some feelers out. I know a lot of the same people Sammy does. He's had to have told someone. He always makes sure at least one person knows his whereabouts."

"What if they come back here?" She gestured to the carnage around them. "We're after an incredibly powerful telepath with an agenda we still need to uncover. We don't want to put ourselves at an unnecessary risk."

"True," Grayson said. "But I don't see as we have any other option at this moment. If we all go to a motel, we'll be more exposed. At least here, the trees will give us some cover. At a motel, there's a greater chance of innocent people getting hurt."

"It's settled. Kristin, you'll have to stay here tonight. Tomorrow, you can go get your stuff," Jericho said. "Cole, you and Adam stay at your place. Keep up the search for any odd information on the computer. Adam, see if you can narrow down the places where Vertigo could hold Jack. The three of us will spiral out from here."

He presented a sound, logical reason and she couldn't argue with him. If her room was under surveillance, her appearance there might cause unnecessary problems. She could replace what she'd left, including her laptop. Since it was the one she traveled with, she didn't have any sensitive information on it. All the important files were backed up.

Jericho broke in on her thoughts. "I have spare toiletry items, and Grayson's T-shirts are big enough for you to sleep in. Since it gets dark earlier, I don't think you should leave. Vertigo may have people on the lookout for you."

"I've considered the same possibility. I don't need to go back to the room tonight. I cleared all my recent searches from my laptop."

Jericho's mouth curled up in a half smile. "And of course, you've backed up what you needed to."

"Of course."

Her close proximity to Grayson would be uncomfortable, even if Jericho was nearby. With all the new emotions eating at her nerves, she didn't trust herself. His complete focus, his concern for their contact, even his worry for her made him an irresistible temptation. And now she had to sleep in one of his T-shirts? Just thinking about the intimacy of wearing a piece of his clothing was almost too much to bear.

What would the consequences be if she acted impulsively? Would he accept her advances if she made them or reject her? This case needed to be wrapped up soon before she started something she didn't know she would finish.

Cole opened his laptop. "Adam and I waited for

you so we could show you what we discovered. There's been some drug deliveries to an address out near Smithville. Most of these drugs are experimental."

"Sammy found out there were drug shipments coming out to our area. He said a lot of the dealers involved have turned up dead or have vanished," Grayson said.

Kristin read the list on the screen over Cole's shoulder. "What kind of drugs are listed?"

"Strong sedatives, illegal street drugs, and some other experimental mind-altering drugs I don't think even the government knows about. There's a lot of components to Vertigo's formula."

"There are other components besides illegal drugs?" she asked. "What are they and how do you know about them?"

"Because they were all developed at HelixCorp." He turned to her. "I worked there when some of the compounds were made. I had a hand in some of the components. ULTRA requested the development of the drugs to help rehabilitate low powered criminals. Do you want to guess the identity of the lead researcher?"

"Anita Haines, now known as the criminal Vertigo?"

"Give the lady a kewpie doll. I worked on a low dose formula ULTRA ordered. Anita worked on a different project. Her formula is supposed to expand a telepath's power. She doesn't give a damn about people. For her, it's just about the experiment." He turned back to the screen. "I wish I could've blown the whole place to hell."

"You did what you could, Cole," Adam said. "You did more than anyone knows, except me. Don't beat yourself up over this." He grinned and clapped a hand on his shoulder. "I'm sure you'll get beat up enough before this is over."

Grayson opened the door and walked outside. Kristin left the three friends discussing the drugs Vertigo ordered and followed him outside. He stood on the porch and stared at the woods, a faraway look in his eyes. Past troubles and secrets he kept inside warred for dominance in his gaze.

She walked over to him and leaned against the railing. "What's wrong?"

He reached over his shoulder and scratched his back. "I'm worried about your friend. The ordered drugs are bad enough by themselves. Mixed together, they're powerful and could do some serious damage to the mind. With Vertigo's background, she knows how to make a toxic cocktail. It won't kill him, but there's a good chance it could alter him."

Kristin rubbed her arms as an internal chill froze her soul. "If I knew the other drugs Vertigo ordered, I could come up with an antidote to counteract it. How is it supposed to expand psionic ability?"

"Cole would know better than me. I know what some of the drugs are capable of doing. I also know Vertigo's an extremist. Whatever her plan is, she won't go halfway. I think she's got Jack for a test subject. When she's done with him, or if her experiment fails, she'll get rid of him."

"You're troubled by this mission. I can see it in your eyes. You and Frank have both hinted at a past association. I've gathered you were involved in some sort of incident. I don't know if you blame yourself for whatever happened, but I can see how it haunts you.

You need to come to terms with it and free yourself from the guilt."

He turned to stare at her. "And how would you know what I'm feeling?"

She laid her hand on his cheek. The warmth of his skin and the light stubble along his jaw made her palm tingle. A hurricane of emotions slammed through her, setting her blood on fire and encircling her soul to take it on a wild flight. This was more than a simple biological response to stress. A powerful force like she'd never felt in her life had begun to control her every thought and action. If she were forced to describe it, she would be forced to call it magical.

"My team telepath went through a rough time in her recent past also. She didn't start as a hero. She betrayed her sister and her team to warn us of their plans. I could see the guilt she felt. It took some time, but she eventually healed. I hope you'll also be able to come to terms with your past."

Taking her hand, he ran his thumb lightly over her knuckles. "I don't think it will be so easy for me. You see, except for my job and the guys inside, I don't have anyone in my life."

"Situations always change," she whispered.

"Yes, they do."

He placed a gentle kiss on her lips, and she deepened it, pleased when he responded. He pulled her tight against his chest, his heart beating hard against hers. She slid her arms around his neck, letting her fingers rake through his short, dark hair. Her heart began a fast, staccato beat as her blood surged through her veins. At this moment, she felt as human as the next person.

Light burst behind her eyes and, if she believed in souls, hers soared from her body to fly with the birds overhead. Grayson's lips were like a balm to her tangled emotions. The longer they were in contact, the more she felt him in her heart and mind. She could almost sense his presence inside her, bringing her mind and heart together.

How could a simple kiss take her on such a dizzy, whirlwind ride? His mouth gently moved against hers, his teeth lightly grazing her lip. A small moan escaped her as she pushed closer to him. The hairs on her arm stood straight up as static electricity danced over her skin.

He broke the kiss and stared at her. "I knew there was a powerful connection between us, but I didn't know how strong it could be. I'd really like to try it again."

"What's stopping you?"

He jerked his head toward the front door. "Them."

She turned. All three of his friends stood there, each one with a grin plastered to his face. Her cheeks flamed as she laid her forehead against his chest. "I do *not* believe this."

Grayson lifted her head. "You're not the one they'll feel obligated to give a large amount of grief to. I'm glad you'll be here. I plan to hide in the bedroom with you."

"Won't it be worse if you stay with me?"

"Oh, it will be worse, but at least I won't have to listen to those three."

As they went back in, Kristin considered what he said. He probably meant to tease her, but if the powerful kiss they shared made her want him, what about when night came? Would she want more from the handsome shadow agent? If she found the courage to make love to him, would one time be enough? A small sigh escaped her. Why did she think the answer would be no?

****

Jack watched as Vertigo bandaged the large man. From the sound of his shouts, she caused him more pain than she eased. He still couldn't remember where he knew the big man from. Who were the men they discussed?

"What were you thinking? You went to his house and trashed it? You were supposed to gather information, then report back. I had to beg for this mission, to prove I can handle a job of this magnitude. I won't get the funds for my research if I don't provide the results The Company executives want."

Eddie grimaced when she pulled hard on the thread while she stitched him up. "I'm sorry. He shot me and it made me angry."

She slammed the scissors down on the table. "Now they've gone on high alert. You need to learn to follow orders. No wonder ULTRA wanted to be rid of you. You're a disgrace. I'm surprised The Company took you in."

"At least now we have confirmation Jericho Black and Grayson Styles are involved."

"Oh, yes, what a big help," she said, her voice laced with sarcasm. "We already knew they were involved, and Black has contacts all over this area. Now he's seen you, and he knows who to look out for." She leaned close to him. "I should kill you myself and save Black the trouble."

"But you're a powerful telepath. Can't you wipe their minds?"

"Do you have any idea how much time and energy goes into erasing someone?" she shouted. "My schedule will not let me spend so much time on one insignificant man. I need to have full concentration on my formula. I wish The Company had never sent you to me. You're completely incompetent."

She stormed out and slammed the door hard. Both men cringed at the sound, and Jack almost felt sorry for him. As his guard took up his usual stance by the door, Jack's memory flooded back. Eddie something. He had it. Eddie Anderson.

He'd been added to Jack's team about a year before everything went south. His team didn't like the big man, and they didn't trust him. He'd had his own run-ins with Anderson, too. Anderson had pestered him at every opportunity for the squad leader job. His team told him it would be a bad idea to put Anderson in a leadership position. There hadn't been any need to convince him they were right.

Jack had been in the process of getting him transferred when his covert investigation blew up in his face—the frame up for the murder of his wife, the trial, going to prison, then the beating and the surgery where he'd been outfitted with experimental cybernetic parts. Could Anderson have been part of the plot against him? As Jack stared at him, he knew he had been.

Jack thought about the other two names he mentioned. He didn't recognize Jericho Black, but he remembered Grayson Styles. Grayson had been his team's sniper. When Jack had seen his wings, he'd given him the code name Nemesis. Rumors had abounded that Grayson had some magical abilities. Jack knew from experience magic existed. He'd seen evidence of it with his own eyes.

Grayson had earned awards and accolades for his marksmanship. The Gravediggers team accepted him right away. Then Frank had told him Grayson had been part of the conspiracy to frame him. Jack closed his eyes. And he'd never forgiven Grayson for his betrayal.

Chapter Eight

The next morning, Cole slid into the driver's seat as he and Adam headed out to check some of the smaller back roads. Jericho called them early and asked if they'd be up for an exploratory run. If they found an area that looked promising, Cole would call, and the others would meet them. The two agreed. They needed to start eliminating areas from the vast state forest.

Every so often, Cole would glance at Adam, checking for any changes in his friend as he scanned the area. Adam pointed to a small side street, and he turned. Then turned again. Then one more time.

"Do you have a fix on McClennan or are you trying to waste all my gas?" Cole said.

Adam shook his head, and frowned. "Could be one or the other. I had a hard fix on him when we left, but now things are confused." He pointed to a road off to their left. "Turn there."

A wide dirt road, packed smooth and flat from frequent traffic, led them to the front of a large house. The atmosphere around it felt empty and, from the look of it, had been for a long time. A For Sale sign sat crooked at the edge of the dry, brown lawn. They glanced at each other and got out.

"Can you still pick him up?" Cole asked.

Adam stared at the large house and frowned. "I'm not sure. This place gives me the whole horror movie 'we're not alone' feeling. I can't tell you why, though."

The door creaked open and they both stepped back. When Vertigo walked out, Adam glanced at Cole. "Now I know why this place has bad vibes. Look who's here."

Telekinetic force surrounded them and held them in place. They stood riveted as she glided closer to them. She smiled and stopped in front of them.

"Welcome, boys," Vertigo cooed. "I'm so glad you decided to visit me. I've missed you both so much. I wondered how I would find you, and here you are on my doorstep. We have unfinished business. It's a shame it may kill you. At least you'll go with the knowledge you helped advance a great scientific cause."

Cole saw muscles tighten in Adam's neck as his friend tried to speak. She laughed and waved her hand and moved him telekinetically to the porch. A large man walked out to stand by Vertigo.

"You have what you need?" she asked him.

He nodded. "Yes, ma'am." He pulled out a gun from a shoulder holster. "All I need is one shot to get rid of this guy."

"Now, now, Mr. Anderson. You can't put a bullet in his brain until I'm done with him. Mr. Jamison and I go way back. I owe him at least a chance to defend himself. I shall free him, and the two of you can have at it. Make sure he'll be ready to listen to me when you're done." She caressed her man's cheek. "Bring him with you. Do *not* fail this time."

He walked straight to Cole, stopped right in front of him, and aimed. "Oh, I won't."

Cole felt the field around him drop, and he went down with it, dropping to his knees as Anderson fired his shot. He landed a solid punch to Anderson's gut, thankful again to Jericho and Grayson for the lessons in how to fight. Anderson outweighed him by a good twenty pounds, and if he didn't end this soon, he wouldn't walk away. Anderson grabbed him and landed a hard right cross on his jaw.

Cole hit the ground hard, trying to will the stars circling his head to clear away faster. When Anderson reached for him again, he punched upward and got a lucky strike on the larger man in the crotch. He dropped and Cole hit him hard in the face, the familiar pop sound of a broken nose like music to his ears. He swung around behind Anderson and locked his arms around his opponent's neck. Anderson fell backward, and they landed on the ground. Cole struggled to draw a decent breath as Anderson climbed to his feet.

Anderson flipped him over his shoulder, and his meaty fists connected with every part of Cole's chest. Cole got his legs up and kicked out, forcing Anderson to back up. He rolled to his feet and stopped. His eyes widened when the black shape of a large handgun was leveled at his face. *I knew this wouldn't end well.* Then the muzzle flashed.

****

"Strange," Jericho said, as they pulled up to Cole's place. "His car is here but he's not answering his phone."

Grayson peered into the car and pulled his gun. "There's blood on the driver's seat."

"We've got to get in his house," Kristin said. She glanced in the car. "From the amount of blood, he's seriously injured. He must be here somewhere."

They hurried to the porch and turned the doorknob,

but it wouldn't open. They couldn't see anyone through the windows, and the house appeared in order. Jericho pulled out a key and turned all three locks. The door opened a few inches, then stopped as the chain held it in place.

"Damn him and his paranoia," Jericho said. "This is all wrong. Check around the house and meet me back here if you don't find anything."

They spread out and Kristin stayed close to the house as she headed around back. So far, the grounds were in order, but uneasiness coiled around her heart and made her hands shake a tiny bit. The silence surrounding the area raised the hairs on the back of her neck. Her fingers curled around her non-existent stun rod as she strained to hear anything out of the ordinary. The small, wooden porch creaked as she stepped up to the back door. She glanced in through the lower window pane and inhaled sharply.

"Grayson, Jericho, back here!"

They pounded around the corner of the house and crowded onto the small porch. Looking through the dingy glass, they saw Cole lying on the floor, blood puddled under him. Grayson used the butt of his gun to break the glass, then reached inside and took precious moments unlocking the two chains and the three deadbolts. They were lucky he'd never gotten around to installing the bulletproof glass he wanted. If so, they never would've been able to get to him in time. They pushed in, and Kristin grabbed dish towels from a drawer. Jericho's look turned dark when they turned him over, and the back of Grayson's shirt rippled.

Kristin pushed the two men aside and knelt next to Cole. "He's been shot twice, once at the base of his neck and once in the lower chest. It doesn't look like he's been hit in anything major. He must have turned away before the first shot." She ripped open his shirt to reveal ugly purple bruises covering his chest. "He's going to be sore after this fight. I have no idea how he managed not to get killed. If this second shot had been a little higher, it would've got him in the heart."

"He always had more luck than most," Jericho said.

Cole groaned before he grabbed her wrist hard. "Don't take me to the hospital. Do what you can here."

"Cole," Kristin said gently. "You have serious injuries, and you've been shot. You need medical attention. As it stands, I don't even know how you're alive."

He gave her a weak smile. "I ducked really fast."

She looked up at Grayson. "He needs a hospital."

Jericho glared at her. "No. Because of HelixCorp, hospitals are another piece of his paranoia. I don't think he'd be safe there anyway. Can't you fix him up here?"

"Yes, I can help him, but he needs surgery. The bullet in his neck passed through, but the one below his ribs needs to come out."

"Can you take it out?" Jericho growled.

"I've performed surgery before but…"

"Can you do it here?"

From his tone and Grayson's hard stare, she decided not to argue. She nodded her head. "I need anesthetic and some place a little more sterile. I also need instruments and implements to stitch him up. Do you have any type of medical or first aid kit?"

"Hang on a second." Jericho rose and left the kitchen.

Grayson grabbed some bleach wipes, cleared off the center island, and wiped it down. "Are you sure you can do this?"

"Of course. I've been trained for survival missions. I can do what I need to help myself or others survive."

Jericho came back in with one of the most sophisticated medical kits she'd seen outside Angel Haven. "You should have all the supplies you need in here. You've even got a strong anesthetic."

"Can one of you help me?"

Grayson looked at her. "I'll help. Jericho, go see if you can find out what happened."

"With all the doors locked, how did he get in?" As she prepped Cole, she looked at both of them. "The bigger question is, where's Adam?"

****

Adam hit the floor hard and groaned. Thank God for wall to wall carpeting. Vertigo let her thug beat the hell out of him before he'd been dumped in this room.

"Hey, are you all right? Can you hear me?"

Adam turned over on his back and groaned louder. "Yes, I hear you and no, I'm not all right. I think I'm dead."

"Jack McClennan. I'd shake your hand, but I'm a little tied up."

"Adam Williams. I'd shake your hand, but I can't feel my extremities." He turned his head and smiled. "I'm part of a team looking for you. Congrats. You've been rescued."

Jack stared at him. "How can you make jokes? You look like you've been through hell. Twice. What does she want with you?"

"I don't think I want to know." He pushed himself

up and laid his head against the wall. "Whatever it is, it won't be good."

Adam looked around the decent sized room where they were held prisoner. Of course, the restraints securing him and Jack to the floor ruined the homey look. From the size, it could be a bedroom or maybe an office. A solitary window above their heads had blinds lowered and closed. He'd been brought through the door across from where they sat, with a single chair next to it. Another door was on the wall to his right. From its narrow size, it had to be a closet. The walls, of course, were plain white.

The door opened and Vertigo walked in. "I see you two have introduced yourselves." She leaned over Jack. "Did Adam tell you he's one of your rescuers? Well, since he's been caught, I'd have to say he's not very good at it. As soon as the first batch of my compound is ready, he'll get to test it. I can't test it on you, Jack, as much as I'd like to."

"Why not? Why hurt someone else? Kill me and be done with it."

She laughed. "You're still quite funny. I can't use you because you're not psionic. Adam and I go way back. I wanted him to be my subject for this experiment at HelixCorp."

Adam glared at her. "I didn't want to do it then, and I don't want to do it now."

"Too bad. I hope my employee disposed of Cole Jamison. I wanted to kill him myself, but I may still get the chance. Cole always had more luck than most people." She tapped her chin. "I wanted to see what my formula would do to him."

"You must be so disappointed," Adam said.

"Well, we don't always get what we want. Thanks to Jack and what he taught me at ULTRA, I always have a backup plan ready."

"Anita," Jack said, "what are you going to do to him?"

She spread her arms wide and turned in a circle. "He's going to have a mind-altering experience. I'm very excited."

"You really are psycho, aren't you?" Adam said.

She held her forefinger above her thumb. "Maybe a little. You have to be crazy to get noticed. Mr. Trust will be so proud of me. I'll be rid of Jack McClennan, and Adam will be locked up as a weapon for his pleasure."

After she left the room, Jack turned to Adam. "I'm sorry you got involved in this. Once she expands your power and hands you over to whoever Mr. Trust is, you'll never get free."

"Yeah, I know. Sorry this isn't the rescue we had planned. She ambushed us. I'm not sure what happened to Cole."

"Who's Cole?"

Adam looked at him. "A friend. He got me away from her once. I don't think he'll be able to help this time. The big guy aimed a gun at him, last I saw. I don't know if he's dead or alive."

"Vertigo said you're psionic."

He nodded. "Don't get your hopes up. I don't do telepathy. I just track."

Jack laid his head back. They had no hope at all. "Bloody hell," he murmured.

Adam grinned again. "The good news is, I found you. You're officially rescued."

They looked at each other and burst out laughing.

Chapter Nine

"We need help," Grayson said. "We need to know if we can tell Kristin about Shade. We've gone into too many situations blind on this job."

Jericho rolled a beer bottle between his hands. "You want to hit the regional office in Hammonton?"

"Yeah. You stay here with Cole. I'll let the office know what happened to him."

Jericho stared at him. "If they don't already know. I don't think they've been honest with us. We should have been more prepared. Now Adam's been taken, Cole's lucky he survived being shot, and we still need to find Jack."

"Thanks for the summary."

Kristin dried her hands on a worn towel as she walked in. "You two sound like you've decided on a course of action."

"Our company has a regional office nearby. I want to take you there and see if we get a little more help. Jericho will stay with Cole and protect him from whatever. We can grab your stuff from the motel when we get back."

"Sounds good. He should sleep for the next several hours. He appears to heal faster than normal. I believe he'll be back on his feet sooner rather than later."

"Good to hear," Jericho said. "You two better hit the road. Bring back something useful." He paused.

"And lunch."

Grayson backed out of the driveway and turned west on Route 30. They rode in silence for several minutes before Kristin broke the silence "What kind of information do you hope to get from your company?"

"We want to be able to tell you about us." Grayson stared straight ahead. "We also want to know why they didn't give us more information. When we get handed an assignment, we usually get a complete background on the job. We've been almost blind on this mission since it started."

When Kristin didn't respond, he glanced at her. "It's okay. I brought you with me so you can ask your own questions. We're going to find Jack."

"And now Adam," she said. "Do you know why Vertigo would take him and leave Cole to die?"

He shrugged. "No. I'm hoping for a lot of answers, but somehow, I don't think it's going to happen."

They pulled into the farming community of Hammonton. Grayson navigated the narrow streets and parked in front of a building down a side street behind a bank. The dark interior of the storefront business didn't stop him from shoving open the door. He led Kristin around the single desk and into a back office.

"We knew you'd be here eventually," said a chubby man, the light shining on his bald head. "It's nice to see you're right on time."

"If you knew we would be here, then you know what we want. Why didn't you tell us Vertigo and The Company were involved?"

"I told them not to." A tall woman in a dark green skirt and jacket walked into the office. A hat the same green color perched at angle on her brown hair. A dark veil obscured the upper half of her face. "Grayson, you of all people know I have reasons for what I do and don't do. Why do you question me now?"

"We almost lost Cole today. Adam's been grabbed. Sammy's lucky to be alive. If you knew the situation, you should've warned us. Why weren't we told more? We've been blind since you gave us this case."

Her mouth turned down in a deep frown. "It's because you are one of my favorite agents that I allow you to speak to me this way." She turned to Kristin. "Greetings, Dr. Mentor. I am Grayson's boss. I run Shade, Inc. I knew you would be helpful on this job."

Kristin resisted the urge to fidget. "I haven't done much since I met your agents."

"Nonsense. You saved Cole Jamison's life. You will be very important the longer this case goes on."

"But who are you?" Kristin asked. "And what exactly does your company do?"

"I don't ever reveal my name. If I did, the people who knew it would be in danger." The chubby man got up, and Grayson's boss sat, folding her hands on the desktop. "I'm sure you're familiar with my area in New York. It has the lowest crime rate and the paranormal, let's call them troublemakers, know I won't put up with any disturbance of the balance I've created."

Kristin sank slowly into the chair in front of the desk. "Yes, I know it. No one knows why the crime rate is almost non-existent there."

"I'll tell you why. Everyone knows my territory is neutral ground. There are serious consequences for disturbing my peace. I have worked hard for many years to create a strict balance between right and wrong. My shadow agents help me maintain it. No one breaks my rules, and every team, good or bad, knows this."

"You were investigated recently on protection racket charges."

She nodded. "Yes. No one testified against me, not from fear, but from loyalty. My company may walk a fine line, but the people in my neighborhood know I will protect them from outside forces and petty criminals who wish to hurt them. What they pay varies from month to month. It depends on how their business goes." She leaned forward a little. "I do not charge them any more than they can afford."

Kristin paused. "I'm sure all your people are very grateful. But you've involved yourself and your agents in Jack's kidnapping. Why?"

"I am desperate to get Field Commander McClennan back. He is imperative to maintaining the balance in the city. Without him, evil will run rampant. You must retrieve him at all costs."

"Sorry. I have to interrupt," Grayson said. "You gave us the same speech before we got involved. Tell me something new."

"I have given you all I can. Events must unfold naturally. I knew Cole would be hurt, but one of my clairvoyants saw the good doctor here save him. All I can tell you is you're on the right track. Hunt down Vertigo. She is a danger to psionics everywhere. Stop her. You are closer to her than you think."

"Hang on a second," Grayson said. "We need to be able to tell Kristin about us. Can we have your permission to do it?"

"Yes. Dr. Mentor will be a strong ally. Divulge whatever you deem necessary." She stood and turned to Kristin. "You are a vital piece to this puzzle. My agents cannot do this without you. As of this moment, you are my shadow angel." She walked to the rear door. "I have to leave. I've stayed too long. Trust me, Grayson. You will succeed in this mission."

They watched her leave, and Grayson stood. "Come on, Kristin. What a huge waste of time." They got in the car, and he turned the key. "At least we know we can tell you about us."

"True." Kristin looked at him. "And I don't think we wasted our time. I know a little more about her and her company. She gave you permission to reveal what I need to know. I'm more confident about trusting you now. Let's get back. I want to check on Cole."

They rode back in silence and stopped to pick up fast food on the way.

****

Jericho balled up the burger wrapper and threw it toward the trash can, hitting it dead center. "And she didn't say anything else?"

"Nope. She won't give us any more than when we were given the job."

Kristin looked at them. "Are the two of you pouting? I had no idea shadow agents of a mysterious agency could act so much like spoiled brats. Is this how you respond every time you don't get your way?"

The corner of Grayson's mouth lifted slightly as Jericho laughed. "I think our Angel has put us in our place," Jericho said.

Grayson stared at her. "I believe you're right."

Kristin dropped her gaze and her cheeks grew warm. She cleared her throat. "What should our next step be? Cole can't be moved right now, at least not for another couple of days. Should we move somewhere else when he can travel?"

Jericho stood. "We'll come up with a new plan when you guys get back from your motel. We'll see if we can pick up Vertigo's trail while Cole recovers."

As Kristin followed Grayson to his car, she understood why her teammates taped a permanent list to the refrigerator. She thought about the now famous list of Men Not Going to Heaven Because What They Do to a Pair of Pants Is a Sin. When she got home, she knew she wanted to add Grayson's name.

They pulled up to her room when he turned to her. "You were pretty quiet on the way down here. Are you worried about Jack?"

"No, just lost in thought."

He watched her for a moment, then nodded. She didn't dare tell him where her thoughts had wandered to. How would it look for the logical doctor to admit to the fantasies swirling in her mind? He took her room key, and she waited while he unlocked the door.

He flipped her suitcase open. "Let's get your stuff."

"I'll follow you back to Cole's after I check out."

She sensed his gaze on her as she meticulously repacked her suitcase. He followed her to the bathroom while she gathered her toiletries. "You don't have watch me every second. What do you think could happen in a room this size?"

He pulled her into a tight embrace. "How about this?'

He kissed her, not gently this time, but harder, deeper, and full of passion. She didn't hesitate, returning his fire with her own. Every sensation she'd experienced before rushed through her again, but this time the intensity of it weakened her resolve. Her heart and soul were more in control of her at this moment than her head. No man had ever ignited her like this. His hands lifted up her shirt, and he trailed kisses down to the cleft between her breasts.

"I've wanted to see you for so long," he whispered.

"I don't understand," she whispered back. "We only met several days ago." His hands rested on her hips, the heat from them burning all the way to her soul, starting a fire not easily put out. "Don't we need to get back?"

He unbuttoned her shirt and ran his hands over her bare skin. "Soon. I want to make the most of the time we have right now."

Her head fell back and her legs trembled when her shirt slid down her arms. How could she be acting like this? She didn't know anything about him. He shouldn't be allowed these sorts of liberties. Hard, intense sensations started in her belly before they worked their way down to other areas. She didn't need science to tell her she was more than ready for him.

She shivered as his fingers lightly ran over her stomach before going higher. Her mind warred with her body, insisting she stop. When his thumb caressed her breast, her heart told her sensible, logical brain to shut up. She allowed the fire in her blood and the hurricane in her soul to consume her as she surrendered to his touch. How could she have never known such pleasure?

He raised his head and smiled. "Should we continue, because I'd really like to."

"Don't stop now," she said, her voice breathy with the passion.

He swung her up into his arms as he gave her a rare

79

smile. "You got it."

He sat next to her on the bed while the appreciation in his eyes shone. He lowered his head to kiss her again when his cell phone buzzed. His hand hovered over his pocket while he gazed at her.

"It's okay," she said. "Answer it."

"Jericho?" His head snapped up. "What's wrong?"

At his reaction, Kristin scrambled off the bed and fixed her clothes. She stuffed the few items left in her suitcase, then turned to Grayson as he ended the call.

Her heart skipped a beat when she caught the worried look in his eyes. "What's happened?"

"Something's wrong with Cole."

She threw her suitcase in the back seat of her car and ran to the office. After checking out, she yanked open her car door. "Go. I'll be right behind you."

What could have happened to Cole? She cursed herself for the delay, her nerves raw with guilt. Her thoughts had been of her own selfish needs and not of the men who depended on her. There would be no more interludes with Grayson until she accomplished her mission. If they never finished what they started and it drove her crazy, well, she would just have to live with it.

Frank had told her Grayson was a gray area. In spite of not liking gray areas, she'd jumped feet first into it, hadn't she? What would her teammates say? What could they say? They'd all been pretty mindless themselves when their men were involved. But being Dr. Kristin Mentor, bio-geneticist and hero team leader, she never gave into impulsiveness. She planned everything. She didn't fall for a man because of a simple biological response.

There had to be a rational, logical explanation, involving no magic whatsoever. Just because three of her teammates had fallen hard and fast, didn't mean she would. They had each found a wonderful man, which worked out fine for her friends, but she wanted something different for herself. She needed to keep her perspective. Emotions needed to be kept in check.

She didn't believe in soulmates or love at first sight, even though the evidence from her friends stated otherwise. She'd always wanted a better, more scientific, explanation. The sudden attraction between her and Grayson defied all sense and logic. This time, could magic be the real reason, not science? She stopped. Why was she even considering that? Because logic dictated that every possibility be considered.

The belief she'd held deep inside for years whispered to her that emotions always caused more problems than they solved. She touched her lips as she remembered Grayson's kiss. Maybe, just maybe, emotions weren't as bad as she first believed.

Chapter Ten

Jericho stood on the porch when they returned, beer bottle in hand, and a worried frown on his face. Kristin jumped out of her car and hurried over to him.

"What happened? Grayson took all kinds of chances to get back as quickly as possible. He lost me a couple of times."

"Not long after you left, Cole took a turn for the worse." He stared at them. "I didn't want to interrupt you. I had a feeling you two were, how should I put this, getting better acquainted?"

"It's all right. I should have hurried back. I knew he'd been targeted once already," she said. "We shouldn't have delayed our return."

Grayson walked up and nodded to Jericho. "Is he all right?"

"I'm not sure. I hope Kristin will have an idea on how to help him."

Kristin left them and hurried to Cole's bedside. She pressed her hand across his forehead. His skin burned her hand, and sweat rolled down his face in tiny rivulets. This illness made no sense. He'd been comfortably settled when she left.

"Cole, can you hear me? What's wrong? You were all right when I left."

"Vertigo," he murmured. "She's in my head. After the fight and getting shot a couple of times, I'm too weak to fight her. I don't know how she's doing it, but she's found a way to block my ability to recover."

"I'll try to help, but I'm not sure if this will work or not."

He nodded and fell silent. Kristin reached out with her mind. She'd only ever telepathically connected with her team. She couldn't be certain she'd make contact with Vertigo. Still, she had to try or Cole might not make it.

"Well, little Angel. You've connected with me. What do you want?" Vertigo said.

"Whatever you're doing to Cole, stop it. He hasn't hurt you. Leave him alone."

Vertigo's telepathic laugh echoed like nails on a chalkboard. *"Your big statement is to tell me to leave Cole alone? Don't you want to know where Jack and Adam are? They're right here, safe with me. And Cole Jamison has done plenty to me. I should've had him now along with Adam Williams. You don't know the whole story of how Cole ruined my life."*

"The only one who's ruined your life is you." Kristin pushed her determination through the mind link. *"And no one is safe with you. Don't worry. I'll find Jack and Adam. Then I'm going to deal with you."*

"My, my. You sound very dangerous. Fine. You be a good doctor and fix Cole's injuries." Her full power slammed into Kristin's mind, and she dropped to the floor. *"I'm not afraid of you. You and those morons in the other room can't hurt me, and you know it. First, I'll be rid of Jack and Adam, and then you. Sorry, Angel. You were doomed the moment you involved yourself in the search for me."*

Vertigo broke the connection, and Kristin pulled

herself up to sit on the edge of the bed. Frank had been right, as much as she didn't want to admit it. The telepath needed to be stopped permanently. She hoped, when the time came, she could force herself to take a life.

****

"So, you two almost got together," Jericho said.

Grayson nodded and stayed silent.

"Does she know about your wings yet?"

Grayson shook his head.

"Are you worried she'll back away because of them?" Jericho frowned at him. "Because you look like someone shot your dog."

Grayson glanced at his friend and pulled up his shirt sleeve. He revealed a large tattoo of the logo he and the rest of Jack's team had designed. They'd called themselves the Gravediggers and they'd gotten the logo as a tattoo. He'd never forget the day they went to the shop. The sight of over thirty ULTRA agents crowding into the tattoo artist's studio had taken the proprietor aback. Once they explained the importance of the logo, he'd gotten it done. Jack had looked so proud when they showed him.

"When she sees this, and a time will come when she will, she'll know what it is. She's Jack's friend. She's had to have seen it before."

"You have to come clean about your past. I know it." He tapped the bottle against Grayson's chest. "And you know it."

"It doesn't matter, all right? Until this job is over, I don't think she has plans for any more liaisons. After she finds out what I did, she won't want me anyway." He looked away. "I can't blame her. I committed a grievous crime against her friend. I broke the trust of my teammates. I can face her anger. I don't think I can face her rejection."

Jericho crossed his arms and stared at him. "It does matter. You need to lay out how it happened. Frank and the rest of the team forgave you once the truth came out. You weren't to blame."

"Back off, Jericho. You weren't there. I ruined so many people because of my damn weakness." He hung his head, his voice barely audible. "The only other time I showed weakness, it cost my parents their lives. They were ripped apart by the harpy tribe, and I couldn't stop it. I let doubt cloud my judgement against a man who treated me like I mattered." He stared at Jericho. "Then I failed him. Because of my lousy weakness. Never again. It won't ever happen again."

Grayson stormed outside and sat on the porch. He would have to make sure she didn't see the tattoo until he could fully explain. As much as Grayson didn't want to admit it, Jericho made a good point. He needed to come clean. If she found out on her own, all hope of being with her would be gone. Gone and wouldn't ever come back.

Several minutes later, Kristin came out and sat beside him. "Vertigo attacked Cole. I got her to back off, but it's reasonable to expect she won't keep her word. She admitted to me she plans to kill Jack and Adam. She wanted to have Cole with her now, too. I'm not sure how much time they have left."

He turned to look at her. "Where's Jericho? Did you tell him?"

"Yes. He's with Cole. I think it would be best if I stayed with him until he's better."

"Why are you out here?"

"I thought you'd like to know what I found out." Kristin turned to go back inside. "I know you have secrets. Remember, everyone in our line of work has secrets. Even me."

He turned and stared at her. "And what's your big secret? It can't be worse than mine."

"Are you sure? Well, here it is." She stood. "I'm not a real human."

As she walked back into the house, her cryptic statement rooted him to the spot. He knew his magical origin, but Kristin? He stared at the door. She had to be human. What else could she be?

****

Kristin headed straight for the bedroom to check on Cole. Jericho gave her a brief smile and left. Cole had his laptop on the bed, and his hand rested on top. His eyes were shut, and he frowned.

"Are you all right?"

He opened his eyes and smiled at her. "I'm good. I figured if I'm stuck in bed, I'd do more research into where the drugs are being sent. It's a long, convoluted trail but I think I've almost figured it out."

"Your laptop isn't even on." She pointed at the silent computer. "You were on the verge of death not thirty minutes ago. How are you this alert now?"

"I psychically connect with electronics. I use their energy to help heal any injuries and at the same time, I can search the web for information."

"I've never heard of this particular psionic ability."

He gave her a small shrug. "Welcome to another one of HelixCorp's genetic mud pies. I always had the ability to connect with machines. Then, the scientists upped my output. It took me forever to learn how to control it. They like to increase power in a person, but then they don't know how to control it once it's unleashed."

Kristin checked his wounds. They'd already started to close. At this rate, he'd be back on his feet within the next day or two. She sat on the side of the bed. "Do you have any leads yet?"

"Some, but not a lot. Almost every link goes back to the township of Smithville. We should start there."

"You're right. When you're better, we'll go. I'll let you get back to your research. If you need any help, give a yell."

"Only if it's you who answers."

She laughed. "You're quite the charmer, aren't you?"

His eyes twinkled with boyish humor. "I try."

She walked to the door, then stopped and turned. "I have to know. How did you get back in your house after you were shot? You had chained the front door and locked the back door. Would you care to let me in on your secret?"

"Not much to tell. After the big guy shot me, I managed to knock him out. I got in my car and drove back here. I made it into the house and threw all the locks when I got in. I dragged my poor, bloody carcass into the kitchen. I thought if I could at least slow the blood flow, I'd be okay. I had just reached for the kitchen towels when I collapsed. I thought my luck had finally run out. When I heard you and the others, I knew I'd make it." He smiled at her. "Don't you like locked room mysteries?"

"They're not my favorites. I thought maybe you

could teleport or have some other equally dramatic ability. I like the rare, simple explanations best."

His eyes drifted shut again. "Me, too."

Kristin left the room and quietly shut the door. She walked to the living room, her gaze drawn straight to Grayson. He and Jericho spoke in quiet voices, but both looked up when she walked in.

"Cole looks better. He might be able to move tomorrow, but he needs to take it easy. After the injuries he's had, I don't want him to overdo." She walked over and stared at the map. "He says Smithville came up in his research. He thinks we might get some good leads there on where Vertigo might be."

"He still logged in to the web?" Grayson asked.

"Yes. He said he's almost sorted out the tangled trail. I think we can get back on the investigation when we get to Smithville. How far is it from here?"

"About twenty, twenty-five minutes," Jericho said. "It's a little historic village with shops and restaurants. I don't think Vertigo would hole up there. It gets too many tourists."

Grayson stood and walked over to the map. "She might not be in the village itself, but there are a lot of woods and side roads near there. She could be down any one of them."

Kristin sighed. "Looks like we got our work cut out for us."

Chapter Eleven

"I'll say this about your Angel friend, Jack," Vertigo said. "She's quite persistent. I may have to deal with her sooner than I thought. Of course, it doesn't mean I can't have a little fun with her and the men with her." She rubbed her chin. "They may be good candidates for my experiment."

Jack jerked on the chains around his wrists. "Leave them alone. Take your revenge on me and be done with it."

She squatted next to him and ran a long fingernail down his cheek. "I am taking my revenge on you. You're helpless and so desperate to stop me. How does it feel? You want to save someone and yet, you can't. I hold all the cards."

She stood and glided to the other room. Time to wreak a little havoc on Kristin and her compatriots. She connected with Jericho's mind first and planted a few small suggestions. Then she did the same to Grayson. With a little nudge from her on occasion, they'd be at each other's throats in no time. If she did it right, their group would implode. This had to work. They were much too close for comfort.

"Vertigo?" Eddie said from the doorway.

She glared at him over her shoulder. He would have to be an unfortunate casualty in this project, no matter how much the higher ups liked him. He grated on her nerves. "What is it?"

"Mr. Trust is on the phone. He says he's worried about the agents on your trail and wants you to finish your mission and return to the office."

She took the cell phone and put it to her ear. "Hello, Mr. Trust. The situation is under control. My formula is almost complete. Yes, I have a test subject. I picked up Adam Williams the other day. If the compound works in the way I expect, it will break the barriers in his mind and pulse outward. You shouldn't be affected, but my calculations predict it will affect psionics in this area. I should be able to test the first batch tomorrow. No, Jack McClennan won't interfere. I've used sedation and my telepathy to block his access to his cybernetics. I have him under close watch. Yes, sir, I'll call with the results."

Vertigo stared at the silent phone in her hand. Damn him. Didn't he realize she couldn't rush the experiment? One small slip up could ruin the whole batch, and she'd have to start all over again. She'd killed off most of the dealers she'd bought or stolen from. There weren't many of those degenerates left to purchase the materials she required.

What she wouldn't give to be back in her lab at HelixCorp. Those were her glory days. All the supplies she wanted were at her fingertips with mindless lab assistants to do everything she asked with no questions. Except for Cole Jamison. He hadn't been mindless. He'd helped her, made some corrections on some figures, and fine-tuned the formula. They'd also had their nights together. He did things to her no other man had dared. He hadn't realized as they'd had sex, she'd probed his mind for information.

They'd been engaged in one of their more passionate sessions when she found out what he'd done behind her back. She'd been so certain they were on the same page with the project. Then he decided to get a conscience and interfere. He'd helped her subjects escape and hid them where she couldn't find them. His usefulness had come to an end soon after.

She never should've let Anderson attack Cole. If she'd just brought him back with her, she could've paid him back for the destruction of her experiment and her career at HelixCorp. She knew why she didn't. Cole's power couldn't handle the formula, but it would've been nice to see him die in agony. And keeping another person under surveillance would tax her powers even further.

Adam was a different story. He'd always insisted all he could do was track. He slipped on several occasions and demonstrated abilities proving he could do more. A slow smile curved her lips. After she expanded his abilities, he'd feel differently about being powerful.

She banged open the door and stalked into the room where her prisoners lay. A quick glance at Jack reinforced her new plan to rewrite his memories so he loved only her. It would be such fun to have him under her control. Maybe she'd have him kill Kristin. She tapped her finger against her chin as she considered it. Adam would be a weapon for her boss. Pity. She would've liked to have him under her control as well.

****

After he checked off the last location on their list, Grayson headed toward the small, historic village of Smithville. Trees blurred by and sunlight flashed in

Kristin's eyes. Why didn't she remember to grab her sunglasses out of her car when she got her stun rod? After lunch, there were a few more places to be eliminated, then they would head back to Cole's.

They just needed a few hours to search. They should be in and out before Vertigo would realize they were there. Jericho and Cole had blocked out a few neighborhoods to check and planned to meet them at the restaurant around noon. The tourist map crinkled in her hands as she opened it one more time. A bed and breakfast drew her eye again and again. As she glanced at Grayson, she wished they could stay there. To make the search easier, she amended. She had no other reason at all.

She rubbed her hands together, trying to soothe her jittery nerves. She had no reason to be nervous around him. When he'd touched her, and when he'd kissed her, a powerful, yet unknown, set of emotions slammed through her. The whole world spun as her blood ran hot through her veins. If her friends were right about soulmates, it explained the tickling tremors running through her at the oddest of times.

Every touch, every delectable kiss, ignited a fire in her which still screamed to be put out. These sensations and emotions were new, and uncertainty about whether she liked them rose up in her mind. They had no place in her logical life, but maybe she could make a little room for them.

"You've been staring at me since we got in the car," Grayson said, breaking the silence. "What?"

"Shouldn't we scout more places before we stop? We should have checked off more than three."

"Those few were all we had time for." He stopped

at a red light and gazed at her. "Jericho and Cole like this one particular restaurant in Smithville and there's always a crowd for lunch. The noise and all the people there may cause a lot of interference so Vertigo can't read us. From what I've read, telepathy is a tricky power."

"It is. My team telepath has an enormous amount of power but she can't control it." She glanced at him and suspected what he would ask next. "Yes, she's another of HelixCorp's experiments. She explained to me how hard it is for her to keep her thoughts separate from other people when she's out."

The light changed, and he eased the car forward. "I wouldn't ever want to be psionic."

"I've designed specific exercises for her, and her control is better, but I don't know how she keeps her composure."

He turned down what looked like an ordinary residential street, and a busy village came into view on their left. Grayson spoke to the lot attendant, who directed him to a spot at the far end of a row.

Grayson looped her arm through his as they merged with the crowd. "The restaurant is about halfway up the hill. It's got a good view of the lake."

People milled around, strolling in and out of the shops on both sides of the street. "Being around a crowd this size won't cause problems, will it? I don't want anyone to get hurt."

He shook his head. "I don't think so. From everything we've learned, Vertigo won't call a lot of unwanted attention to herself. At some point, she'll make us come to her."

The village had narrow streets, and Kristin

sidestepped children as they ran around. Some of the stores were converted homes with historical plaques next to the doors. Other shops had a more modern look. She wished she were here on vacation instead of a mission. Her friends would love this place. The late morning sun made jewelry sparkle in shop windows, next to stores with scented candles, movie memorabilia, clothes, and other numerous items.

Standing in the middle of the cobblestone sidewalk, they joined a long line which disappeared into the restaurant. Kristin checked out the front. Cream colored, wooden, slat siding offset the dark green trim around the windows and double doors. It gave the building a unique, quaint, homey look.

To her right, a low wall surrounded a small patio, with wrought iron fencing in between the short brick columns. Bistro style tables with bright red umbrellas were placed at regular intervals. It looked like the patio could seat approximately twenty patrons. With the bright sunlight and a slight, cool breeze, lunch outside would be very pleasant. As much as she would enjoy the sunshine and tangy air, it didn't feel comfortable today.

Kristin glanced over her shoulder. "I feel so exposed. It's like I can almost sense her nearby."

"It's because we're in the middle of a huge crowd. We've spent the past couple of days in a pretty isolated house."

"True." Another glance over her shoulder didn't reveal anyone paying them any attention. "When did you say Jericho and Cole would arrive?"

"Soon. I wish we could stay overnight. It would make it easier to be close by the areas we need to search. Cole lives near, but if she's closer to here than his place, we won't be able to react quick enough to stop her." He put his arm around her shoulders. "You're shaking. Are you always this nervous on an assignment?"

"Not usually." When he voiced the same desire she'd had in the car, it started those darn fiery trembles all over again. "I've never had an assignment hit this close to home before." She lowered her voice. "And I have no idea how much time I have to complete the job. Vertigo could snap any day."

"I get it, but you have to relax. I know your team always runs right into the fray, but with my team, you've got to act as a shadow." He pulled her tighter to him. "You'll draw more attention if you look like you expect to be jumped any second. Get ahold of yourself."

He made a lot of sense. She needed to get control or she would endanger herself, Grayson, and his team, plus the men who needed to be rescued. The warmth of his hand comforted her and calmed her frayed nerves. She never liked to skulk around in shadows or hide in the gray areas of ambiguous law. Now, she'd been thrust into both of those situations at the same time.

She strained to see into the dim interior of the restaurant as they inched closer. Were they ever going to get in? People around her voiced the same thoughts. To distract herself, she looked around the small town. The buildings were quaint and colorful, and a salty breeze blew the briny smell from the small lake to tickle her nose. The desire to explore hit her again.

Grayson caught her attention. The sun had turned his hair from black to more of a deep brown. The breeze ruffled it, and she longed to smooth it back into place. She studied the angular line of his jaw. She moved closer to him so she could see the hollow of his cheeks. He had a harder look to him than the men her teammates had married. She had to admit, she liked his look very much.

He didn't wear his sunglasses this time, and she gazed at his eyes. The natural light did them justice. In the airport, they were gray. In the sunlight, they seemed to change color from gray to dark blue, to green, to hazel, then back to gray. She wanted to stand there and just watch the sun play with the color in his eyes all day.

When he moved, it broke the spell she had weaved around herself. When he did, she saw the back of his shirt ripple. Did the breeze blow strong enough to make it move? No, she didn't think it did.

"Grayson, do you have problems with your back?"

He glanced down at her. "What do you mean?"

"Your shirt moved, and I don't think the breeze caused it. It's too light."

He shrugged and continued to scan the crowd. "Sometimes I have muscle spasms. I don't even notice them anymore. They're not painful, but they get looks." He smiled at her. "Like from incredibly astute people, such as yourself.

"I may be able to help with your spasms, if you like," she said. She reached out to run her hand over his shoulder blades and frowned when he turned away. "What's wrong? I thought you said it didn't hurt."

"It doesn't." He nodded toward the door. "It's almost our turn, and I thought I saw Jericho and Cole."

Funny way to say mind her own business. Fine.

She'd let it drop for now. "I didn't see them."

"I lost them in the crowd. I can't believe there's this many people here in the middle of the week. Usually, the big crowds come on the weekend."

She searched the crowd for the others, but spotted Jericho by himself as they made it inside. Grayson put their names on the waiting list. They sat at the bar and turned their attention to the game on the big screen television. Her current teammates each ordered a beer, but she declined.

She half listened to their conversation as they talked about the baseball game on the television and chatted with the bartender. She scanned the crowd. Could one of Vertigo's agents also be there, sent to keep an eye on them? Now she sounded as paranoid as Cole. She eyed the bartender. The woman hadn't moved more than five steps away from them from the moment they sat down.

She put her arm around Grayson and pulled his head down to whisper in his ear. "Do you think the bartender could be one of the bad guys? She hasn't left us since we ordered."

He had the nerve to give her a rare smile. "Nope. I think it's because she wants to catch the eye of our compatriot. For some reason, women think he's attractive."

She considered his answer. Oh, she'd noticed how handsome they were, but Grayson had her full attention. How could she have not noticed the others got stares of their own? The girl would lean on the bar and show her cleavage. With such an obvious display, Kristin rolled her eyes. Jericho didn't seem to mind, judging by his smile every time she displayed herself.

"Where's Cole?" she asked. "I thought you two would arrive together."

Jericho signaled for another beer. "He had something he needed to check out."

They stood when they heard Grayson's name. Kristin shook her head. "Come on, boys. Time to get some lunch."

She shoved them toward the dining room

Chapter Twelve

Where had Cole gone and what had he needed to take care of? Kristin thought back to her earlier assessment of him. He may have a kind face, but his friendly façade concealed an element of danger. All of them did. The longer she worked with them, the clearer it became.

They all looked up when Cole joined them. He wiped his hands on the hem of his shirt, and Kristin decided to ignore the red droplets on his shoulder. He inched around Jericho to the chair in the corner and sat with his back to the wall. The temptation to question him burned, but she might not like the answer. Turned out she didn't need to.

"Care to share what happened?" Grayson asked.

Cole glanced at his teammates. "The lot attendant seemed a little too interested in me and Jericho. I simply went to have a conversation with him. At first, he didn't want to talk to me, but it turned out he could be persuaded. He admitted he worked for Vertigo. She's in the area, but he didn't know where. His job was to let her know if or when we showed up."

Grayson banged his fist on the table. "She knows every move we make before we make it."

No one else mentioned the suspicious drops of red on his shirt either. Kristin cleared her throat. "Are you all right? You're not too tired, are you?"

"Not yet, but I can tell I'm not a hundred percent."

"I heard the attendant on his cell as we walked by," Jericho said. "He knew who we were."

Kristin glanced at Grayson. "Did you notice if he paid any attention to us?"

He shook his head. "He didn't look twice. Jericho, you're the one with the reputation. He had to be on the lookout for you."

"It's possible." His mouth curled up in a half smile. "After the threat I gave to the big guy who beat on Sammy, I'm pretty sure Vertigo gave my description to all of her goons. I guess I can't go unnoticed."

The waitress came by with their order and smiled at Grayson, Jericho, and Cole. She continued to stay at their table, even after she refilled Grayson's drink and set down two beer bottles. They repeated several times they were good. She gave them a last smile and left.

Kristin stared at them. "Did you have to encourage her?"

Jericho glanced over his shoulder where she giggled with the other servers. "We can't help it. It happens all the time."

She dipped a French fry in the ketchup. "Well, Grayson has pointed out you two draw attention anywhere you go because you are, apparently, attractive."

Jericho and Cole looked at each other. "Sounds like she doesn't believe women would throw themselves at us," Jericho said.

Cole grinned. "Women don't throw themselves at us. They lay calmly at our feet and offer themselves up to two of the sexiest men on the planet."

"Oh, please," she scoffed. "Contain your ego

before it pushes us out of the restaurant."

Jericho and Cole fist bumped. "When you got it..." Jericho started.

"Give it back," she completed for him.

The two of them laughed, and Grayson gave her a small smile. Her heart started a hard staccato beat, as if it wanted to let everyone know how he affected her. She hid her surprise at herself while she ate. If her teammates heard her make such a joke, they'd never believe it.

****

Jericho drank some of his beer and listened to the conversation. He tried to pay attention, but couldn't take his gaze from Kristin. They'd all been together earlier. She hadn't changed, so why the sudden interest in her? He glanced at Grayson and remembered his friend's admissions of admiration. He knew, deep down, they were serious about each other, even if they didn't realize it yet. Maybe she grabbed his attention now because she had become forbidden fruit. He swallowed some more beer and felt the need for another one soon.

Cole leaned forward and lowered his voice a little. "The other day, when Adam and I were out, we hit a small dirt road closer to the Garden State Parkway entrance. Looks like there's been a lot of traffic because it's been smoothed out. The trees are pretty close together, and we came up on a large house. There's a For Sale sign, and we didn't see anyone around. She ambushed us there."

"She may not have stayed or she never had her base there to begin with," Grayson said.

"Where do you think she might be?" Kristin asked.

"Jericho, this is your area. Where are the most probable locations for her to hide?"

He shook his head. "There's a lot of prime places for her to hole up. The trick will be to find the right one before she moves or has time to call in reinforcements."

Jericho watched Kristin toy with her food. Did her light brown hair feel as soft as it looked? He usually didn't like such round faces like hers, but when she became determined, the planes of her face would harden. His gaze dropped to her chest. There were some nice curves under those clothes, and he wanted to hold her. He wanted to feel those curves under his hands.

Now, she looked worried and more than a little lost. A sudden urge seized him, and he wanted to pull her into his arms and tell her it would be all right. He glanced at Grayson. His friend frowned at him. He suspected his thoughts showed plain as day on his face. He shrugged a little and stared at his lunch. He needed to figure out what started these strange thoughts, and soon, before he lost or hurt his friends.

Those future consequences didn't stop the direction his mind strayed to. He snuck a glance before he turned back to the lunch remains on his plate. He could picture what she and Grayson would do in the future. Why couldn't she have picked him? Grayson always had exceptional women flock to him while he always got the bimbos. For once, why couldn't one of those special women come his way?

Again, he glanced at her. He could picture her flushed with passion as he would make love to her. They would rise together as her body would meld with his. He saw her clearly in his mind. Her breasts would rise and fall as she said his name. The scene became so vivid in his mind, his body responded to the pictures in his imagination. His fingers curled into tight fist as he fought to suppress the images in his mind.

He stood abruptly and threw some money on the table. "I've got to get some air."

He pushed through the line to the outside and stumbled down the steps. He hurried over to a bench and plopped down. He closed his eyes and laid his head back. These thoughts weren't him. Yeah, he'd had fantasies in the past, but never about someone who dated one of his friends. He prided himself on his control. He took several slow, deep breaths to calm his racing heart. He vowed right then to watch himself and never be alone with Kristin.

"Are you all right?"

Great. I try to avoid her and here she is. "I'm fine, Kristin. When I'm in a crowded place too long, it makes me a little nuts. I didn't mean to worry you."

She sat next to him. "Grayson and Cole looked more than a little concerned. What happened?"

He couldn't tell her about the fantasy in his mind. The effects of the images lingered in his mind. If he could, he'd take her right here on the bench in front of the crowd in the street. How could he explain any of his thoughts? As he looked into her eyes, he didn't want to. He felt a hard lust for Kristin slam through him, making his gut clench as unknown fear settled into his heart. He stared at her throat and wished he could see where her skin disappeared.

"I felt...it just..." He stared at her. "I had a small panic attack," he finished lamely. A slight breeze ruffled her hair, blowing several strands across her face. He gave in to the urge to reach out to tuck them behind her ear. He briefly let his fingers linger on her cheek. "I'm okay now. Let's get the guys and try to work out a plan."

When he stood, she did too. "This came on quite suddenly. I think it's more than a simple panic attack. We're on the trail of a dangerous psionic who won't hesitate to play games with us."

He nodded and marched back to the restaurant. He hoped she saw the need for him to put some distance between them. He needed to talk to Cole about this. Could Kristin be right? Did Vertigo mess with his mind? If she did, how could he fight her? He'd never been this far out of his depth, and the thought made him sick.

****

When Jericho ran out, Grayson stared after him. Then Kristin followed. "Cole, please tell me you have some idea what just happened."

"Not a clue. I've never seen Jericho run before. Did he look uncomfortable around Kristin to you?"

"Yeah. He did. He also looked like he wanted her." Grayson glanced back toward the door. "Do you think he went far?"

Cole lifted one shoulder in a half shrug. "I don't know. Kristin will have caught up to him by now. Maybe she has a clue."

"Let's hope so. We've lost Adam. We almost lost you. We can't afford another hit." Grayson turned his glass in a slow circle. "This whole job is a complete disaster. We've never had so much bad luck on an assignment before."

"Well, there's a whole lot not to like. We started blind, and there's still no light at the end of this particularly long tunnel."

Grayson kept hidden the intense stab of jealousy that speared through him when Jericho stared at Kristin. He would have to let him know Kristin was off limits. If not, there would be severe consequences. As he drummed his fingers on the table, his stomach soured. These thoughts weren't him. He wouldn't be so hateful to his best friend, would he? A certain psycho telepath must be the reason.

Cole drank the rest of Jericho's beer as Grayson threw bills on the table. "Let's get out of here. We need to know if we can fix whatever the hell happened to Jericho."

They pushed out through the crowd to see Jericho and Kristin headed their way. They walked down the few steps and met them on the sidewalk. Grayson studied Jericho and his anger vanished as quickly as it spiked. All color had drained from Jericho's face, and his hands shook as he glanced around in every direction. Whatever had happened to his friend, it shook him.

"Why don't we take a walk down by the lake?" Grayson said. When Kristin moved to his side to wrap her arm around his waist, hot, bright anger flashed briefly in Jericho's eyes. Oh, yeah. Something bad had definitely happened.

The four of them ambled down the small hill toward the lake. Swans and ducks had gathered by the bridge where children pointed and laughed at the birds. Grayson kept an eye on Jericho, but, right now, he acted like himself. How long before his friend snapped again? They came to a quiet spot and stopped.

"We've eliminated some of the back roads which

led to places Vertigo wouldn't be caught dead in, so what area should we scout first?" Jericho said.

"I'd like to take you back to where Adam and I were ambushed," Cole said. "We might be able to pick up a lead or two. After all, nobody's perfect. She or her goon may have left some kind of clue behind."

"Sounds good," Kristin said. "When did you want to go?"

Grayson looked at the sky. "It's still early. We should have time to get out there and look around before it starts to get dark."

"Did everyone bring some kind of weapon in case there's a need for firepower?" Cole said.

When they all said they were armed, Grayson nodded. "After seeing one of Vertigo's agents here, I'd rather not be surprised."

They made their way back to their cars, noticing they parked close to each other. Cole walked up to Jericho's SUV and waited. Jericho lifted his hand, as though he wanted to usher Kristin into his car. She stared at him for a moment and hesitated long enough for Grayson to help her into his car. He and Jericho faced each other for a few seconds before they turned away at the same time to get into their own vehicles.

Kristin's muscles tensed under Grayson's hand. He'd read concern in her face in the few looks they'd shared. If she saw something off in Jericho, a definite change had occurred. First chance he got, he would talk to his friend. His eyes narrowed as he watched Jericho pull out. Yeah, they had a whole lot of issues to "discuss." He'd leave the outcome of the discussion entirely up to Jericho and his crappy attitude.

They rode in silence as they followed Jericho's

SUV to where Cole and Adam had encountered Vertigo. The car almost glided over the dirt road as it curved around. A large clear area opened up before them with a two-story house in the center. They armed themselves as they got out and stood by the cars, but no one made the first move.

Cole rubbed his side and leaned against the SUV. There weren't any indications of anyone else around, but they still didn't move. Signs of the recent fight still marred the otherwise smooth dirt. Small dots of blood speckled the road, testament to the assault Cole had taken and given in return. An eerie silence surrounded them, rooting them next to their cars as they all just stared at the empty structure.

Kristin voiced the thought on all their minds. "It feels empty. I don't think Vertigo's here. She probably used this location to bait you. I have to say, I don't like the feel from this place."

Grayson stood next to her. "Vertigo's been one step ahead of us the whole time. She must have picked this place because of its isolation."

"Vertigo has one major flaw," Kristin said. When they turned to her, she smiled. "Cole, you know what it is as well as I do. She's over-confident. She doesn't believe anyone can hurt her. As her power has grown, so has her ego."

Cole pushed away from the car and chuckled. "You're right on all points. She's so full of herself, it gives us a chance to take her down. It's a small chance, but it's there."

"Do you guys want to stand here all day or do you want to check this place out?" Jericho said as he stalked away.

Kristin started after him, but Grayson stopped her. "Does Jericho seem a little off to you?"

"Yes. I noticed it at lunch. He changed so quickly. I believe Vertigo has gotten into his mind. Have any of you been trained to know how to fight telepathic influence?"

"We've had the basics of building psychic shields. We've never come up against a situation like this before. If we had to face a telepath, we'd have a telepath with us. If she's got him, how do we free him?"

Kristin wrapped her arms around herself. "We're a little short on telepaths right now, so he'll have to do it on his own. He's got to find the strength and the will to fight her. It's hard to fight psionic power if you've never done it before. I bet he doesn't even realize she's there."

Grayson glanced at his friend as he walked up the steps to the porch. "Maybe Cole can help. He knows the most about psionics and their abilities."

"I hope so," she murmured.

By the time they crowded onto the porch, Jericho had picked the lock and opened the front door. He stood aside to let his friends walk in first. He shut the door and stood behind Kristin, then frowned when Grayson moved her to his other side

Jericho rubbed the back of his neck and turned to Cole. "When you were here, did you get to see inside this place?"

"No. She held us outside. Her goon kicked the crap out of me in the driveway. Adam had detected minds, but she must have led him here." He faced the others. "She wanted Adam to be the subject of her crazy experiment when we were at HelixCorp. Now she has him and can do whatever she wants."

"And that's the scary part," Jericho said. "Come on. Let's get this place checked out. Kristin, you take the upstairs. Cole and I will check out this floor. Guess where you get to go, Grayson."

Grayson scowled. "Sometimes, I swear you break us up like this on purpose, Jericho. Yeah. I'll check the basement."

Cole and Jericho grinned. "It's your turn. Cole had the basement the last time, Adam had it before he did, and I did before Adam. Sorry."

Grayson rolled his eyes and stalked off to check his section. "Whatever."

The house had been closed up so long, the musty air hung heavy around them. Grayson tried to shake off the pinpricks of fear as he watched Kristin head toward the stairs. He knew she could defend herself, but it didn't make it any easier to watch as she went off by herself. Had they already bonded with the first kiss they shared? An uncomfortable suspicion told him he knew the answer.

He walked into the kitchen and found the basement door to the right of the stove. As he eased it open, a loud creak made him cringe as it echoed through the house. He activated the flashlight app on his phone, grateful as the bright LEDs illuminated the dark maw of the basement. He tested each step as he headed down to the darkness.

"If someone's down here, they have to know I'm coming. If I get clobbered or bit by a rat, I'm going to do the same to Jericho."

As he started his search, his thoughts strayed to

how Jericho had acted at lunch. He'd recognized the look on his friend's face. He felt sure he looked the same way whenever he was near Kristin. She suspected the renegade telepath invaded Jericho's mind. Had Vertigo become so powerful she now affected them long distance?

He went over his limited knowledge of psionics. The accounts he'd read all stated a telepath had to see you to affect you, unless they were engaged in a mind scan. Vertigo appeared to be the exception to the rule. With as much power as she had, someone needed to end her. The sooner, the better.

He reached over his shoulder and scratched at his back. He would to have to fly soon. He'd never kept his wings contained this long before. Mold and mildew assaulted his nose and he wish he'd volunteered to scout the area instead. But then Kristin would have been alone in the house with Jericho. Those thoughts disturbed him more than the dank basement he currently searched.

"Of course, there's zilch down here," he muttered before stomping back up to the kitchen.

Chapter Thirteen

Cole searched the one bedroom in the back of the house. He cringed as Jericho made way too much noise while he searched the other rooms. Would searching this house give them a lead on where Vertigo might be holed up? And if they did find her, what then? Would they be too late? Would they be able to stop her? And how would they do it? She'd sense them before they'd get a drop on her.

Working blind always made him punchy and irritable. He missed Adam's limited power to keep a lookout for trouble. They'd used it as a major component to help so many psionics escape HelixCorp. Until now, he hadn't realized how much he'd come to rely on Adam's ability.

He started toward the front room when a low buzz began at the base of his skull. He rubbed the back of his neck as the muscles grew tight, a familiar sign of his rising stress levels. As the sensation continued, he felt it more in his mind than his shoulders. He grabbed the doorframe and his vision blurred as his stomach flip flopped while bile rose in his throat.

He took a couple of deep breaths to try and keep the nausea at bay. He ran for the bathroom, barely reaching the toilet as his lunch resurfaced. The subtle, quiet buzz increased to a full-blown scream. He threw up until his stomach convulsed with dry heaves. Pain lanced through his temples and his stomach lurched again, even though he knew he didn't have anything left to come out.

"Cole, what happened?" Jericho said from behind him.

He wiped his mouth on his sleeve and turned on the faucet. A trickle of water splattered the sides of the sink. "From my reaction, I think she just tested her formula." He cupped his hands under the water to rinse his mouth out. "So, I'm pretty sure my stress levels weren't involved."

Jericho grabbed Cole's arm as he stumbled to the front room and sat him on the floor next to the door. "Stay here while I get the others."

Cole put his head between his knees, taking huge gulps of air, hoping his stomach would quit tying itself in knots. He'd been through this before when Vertigo tested her serum at HelixCorp. The young telepath didn't survive, and it had been a fraction of what hit him now. This psionic blast punched through his mind with brute force. How far had the wave been felt? From the strength of it, he feared it rippled up and down the east coast.

"Are you all right?" Kristin asked as she sat beside him.

"Yeah. I'll be fine. I just need a minute."

She turned his head toward her and checked his eyes. "What are your symptoms right now?"

"Headache, dizziness, nausea. My power feels like it wants to punch its way out of my brain. Whatever Vertigo's added to enhance the effects of her formula, it's stronger than the compounds she had at HelixCorp. I knew the crucial piece she needed and I hid it." He glanced up as the others came in and stood over him. "For all the good it did. I think she found it."

Grayson walked over and squatted next to him. "For all of us non-scientists, can you tell us what this mysterious formula does exactly?"

"It opens the neural pathways. Psionics are vulnerable to drugs like these. When the pathways are opened, there's a surge in ability. The mind's natural psionic blocks are destroyed and then it taps into what could be unlimited power. Whoever is dosed with the compound would be damn near unstoppable."

"So why doesn't she use the formula on herself?" Kristin asked.

"When she first developed it, the components were unstable and unpredictable." He laid his head back against the wall. "This is why I hid the one vital element from her. I knew what it could do. From the force of the wave, she's finished it and the damn thing works."

"What piece didn't you tell her about?" Jericho asked.

Cole hesitated, then said, "LSD. It allows the mind to relax and accept the other drugs in the formula. There's not enough for addiction, but there is enough to expand the telepathic awareness."

"And you helped develop it." Grayson glared at Cole as his grip visibly tightened on his gun. "Is there a reason why we shouldn't think you're as bad as she is?"

"I told you. I tried to stop her. I don't blame you for your reaction." Cole rested his head on his knees. "You don't know how many years I've regretted my part in her crazy ass scheme."

"Grayson, enough," Kristin said, her voice hard.

She checked Cole over one more time. "After your recent injuries, I think you'd better rest for the remainder of today. If you keep up your current pace, you won't have the strength to fight her."

He glanced up at Jericho and grinned. "I think we should always have a doctor on the team. Especially if she looks like Kristin."

She smiled as she stood. "Now I'm sure you'll be fine."

"Did anyone find any clue to tell us where she might be?" Jericho said.

They all shook their heads. Cole kept Grayson in his peripheral vision. After his comments, Cole couldn't be assured of his own safety. He worried about the sudden shift in Grayson's attitude. Would his teammate try to take him out when their friends' backs were turned? God, he hated this assignment more and more.

Cole's legs shook as he stood and they decided to return to his home. After the psionic tidal wave rolled through his mind, he needed to lie down. As much as he didn't want to admit it, Kristin had been right. He pushed himself too hard after his battle with the man who took Adam.

"When we get back to my place, I want to boot up the computer and try to find her trail again," Cole said. "She's disposed of a lot of the dealers who supplied her what she wanted. I'm not sure if I'll be able to track her through those connections anymore, but I'm sure I can find something."

"Do what you can," Jericho said. "I've got some contacts in the area I can call. Grayson, do you have any leads you and Kristin can check out?"

Grayson stared out the window. "I think we've got bigger problems."

Jericho moved to stand next to him. A group of men trotted in tight formation across the yard toward the house. "You might be right. You realize, of course, this counts as a lead. What say we try to convince one or two to talk to us?"

Grayson ran for the stairs and took them two at a time. Kristin headed for the back of the house to check for a planned simultaneous attack from there. Cole staggered to a window with a view of the side lawn, while Jericho stayed by the front door.

Cole tapped the com link in his ear, glad he'd given Kristin their spare unit. "Everybody on? Looks like this could be one hell of a fight. Who needs firepower?"

"I'm good," Jericho answered.

Grayson checked in next. "Same. Kristin, what about you?"

"All set."

"Don't forget, I need at least one of them alive for me to talk to," Jericho said.

Cole nodded. He'd planned to keep a prisoner or two. Jericho had a reputation as a master interrogator. As a shadow agent, he employed stronger tactics than regular law enforcement. Those tactics had helped them save plenty of lives over the years.

Chapter Fourteen

Adam struggled against the telekinesis Vertigo used to hold him in the lone chair in the room. He knew he wouldn't get out of testing her weird concoction this time. Cole had done everything he could when they were at HelixCorp, but this time, there wouldn't be a last-minute rescue coming.

He eyed the clear liquid swirl around as it filled up the narrow syringe. It looked too small to do any real damage, but he knew better. How could something used to heal have such a sinister look? He frowned. Because Vertigo held it and she didn't care what happened to people, only her results. Her formula had killed a lot of psionics, and really, he didn't want to be another statistic.

"Give it up," he said. "The formula is a bust. You've had failure after failure with every variation. What makes you think it will be successful this time?"

She cradled the syringe like a precious gem and sidled up to him to stroke his cheek. "Because I discovered the piece Cole hid from me, and now it's been perfected." She leaned closer. "You were always my favorite, Adam. I only wanted to make you stronger."

"You want a weapon and a mindless slave. Not my idea of a good time."

"Do you know what I could do for you?" She let

her hands drift over his chest and down his stomach. "I can make you rich, famous, and very happy."

He jerked his head away. "Your price is too high. You can keep all your promises."

"Are you sure?" she purred in his ear. "I can give you whatever you want."

A sly smile curled his mouth as he stared at her. "Then give me and Jack our freedom."

She straightened up, mock sorrow in her eyes. "Sadly, you ask for the one item I can't give you. You always were a fool, Adam. You thought you could deny me what I want. It's my hope this formula will give you a dependence on me." She walked over and leaned close. "I'm not sure about you, but I know I'll enjoy it."

Finding the vein in the crook of his arm, she injected the serum. Adam felt the effects almost immediately. The carefully constructed walls he'd erected in his mind years ago shattered faster than children's building blocks. His power exploded out as thoughts slammed into his mind as the effect radiated outward. His back arched. He couldn't stop the scream tearing itself from his throat.

He knew what he could do and had locked away this power years ago. He didn't want to hear people's thoughts all the time. The power surge slammed Vertigo against the wall, and he fell to the floor as another scream burst from his throat. Sweat poured off him as his power increased in mere seconds. He got a swift telepathic impression of Cole, Jericho, Grayson, and Kristin. Cole appeared to be the only one affected by the pulse.

Vertigo stood over him, a maniacal gleam in her cold, blue eyes. She appeared to take great pleasure in his pain. The click of her heels echoed like gunshots as she walked over to the table and made notes. Of course, she'd use the one room without carpeting for her experimentation. He developed a sudden hatred for hardwood floors.

"Why aren't you affected by this?" he ground out.

She laughed, actually laughed, at him. "I have more power than you or any of those fools you work with realize. You can't hurt me. Your power is still too new for you to be able to control it well. Now, while your system processes the first dose, I need to begin on Jack's mind. You'll stay here, like a good boy, won't you?"

Adam's body jerked as another spasm hit. "Oh yeah, sure. I'll wait here while my brain shrivels to the size of a raisin and pops out of my ear. Take your time."

He curled into a ball and prayed the madness would end quickly.

****

Jack heard Adam's cry through the closed door. What did Vertigo do to him? She had mentioned her formula. Her experiment and Adam's distress were obviously related. She'd mentioned she couldn't test it on him because he wasn't psionic. If he was, would he have felt any effect? He gave a hard yank on the chain and felt it give a tiny bit. If he couldn't get free, the two of them didn't stand a chance. He pulled harder before being shoved hard against the wall.

Vertigo walked into the room and scowled. "You never had a chance. I don't know why you persist in this ridiculous idea you'll escape. Leaving me is not an option for you. Your rescuers will never find you. You and I have all the time in the world to get reacquainted."

"Vertigo," he said. "Anita, we were teammates. We were friends. I don't understand how we came to this point. Whatever you think I did to you, I'm sorry. How can I make it right?"

"I can't believe you don't remember." She used her telekinesis to pull the chair over and sat. "Think back. You and I were quite the item. Everyone on the team thought we'd end up together." Her eyes narrowed as she glared at him. "But then you went and married that black haired tramp who weaseled her way onto our team. She stole you from me. I've never forgiven you for your betrayal. You humiliated me."

"Whatever you think we had between us you built up in your mind. We were teammates, nothing more." He scowled. "Then you decided to ally yourself with the criminal inner circle at ULTRA. You tortured me when they took me prisoner. Even if there had been something between us, it would've ended when you became a turncoat to me and our team. You made your choice, like I made mine."

Anger blazed hot and bright in her eyes. "You might not have recognized my worth, but the Council did. They knew my potential. They were a balm to my shattered soul. And now you have another wife." She jumped to her feet, her power flinging the chair hard against the wall, cracking it and leaving a large hole in the plaster. "Why do you always pick everyone but me?"

Her fury left him speechless for a moment. "Anita, I felt friendship for you, nothing more. I tried to tell you on many different occasions, but you didn't want to hear it. We never had a future together. You've built up this whole relationship in your mind."

With her fists clenched tightly at her sides, she glared at him. "I know you loved me, Jack. I'm a telepath. I know you did."

"I admired you. You're a brilliant scientist and a powerful telepath. You were a great asset to the team. I never had any other feelings for you, I swear. I'm sorry if you think I hurt you. I never meant to."

"I'm going to fix it so you do remember. When I'm done with you, the only woman you'll ever love is me. This time, things are going to be the way they're supposed to. I *will* have the happy ending owed to me."

Her eyes began to glow, a telltale sign of her power. As she invaded his mind, Jack's heart sank. The force of her telepathy always felt like a sledgehammer pounding in his brain. She had the ability to back up what she said. She would rewrite his memories and he really would love only her.

****

Grayson fired off a couple of quick rounds in succession before he ducked out of sight. He needed to be out in the open to get clearer shots. His aim was much better than this. Vertigo could be affecting his abilities, but would he know it? More troops stormed from the woods, and his hope floundered.

He cursed under his breath as shots pelted the wall close to his cover. His muscles tensed as the agents advanced closer to the building. These weren't the usual thugs he and Jericho met up with on an almost daily basis. These were trained troops, moving with a tight, military precision. They had to be part of the force Vertigo had assembled to stop them.

He tapped the com in his ear. "Jericho, what's it look like down there?"

"Not good. More agents just circled around to come at you." Gunshots echoed through the link. "And I've got a crowd who decided to ruin my day."

"Who the hell sends armed troops to south Jersey?" The gunfire increased and he ducked back out of sight. "Cole, you got any thoughts on this?"

"If Anderson told you the truth, they've got to be Company forces. It stands to reason if Vertigo is here and thought she needed more protection, she'd ask The Company to send troops ahead to clear us out. She'd want them to end us before we could affect a rescue."

"My range is limited with my stun rod," Kristin said. "I need to get outside to do any real damage."

"Stay put," Grayson ordered. "If they grab you, we might not be able to get you back."

"What's your location?" she asked.

"Upstairs back bedroom."

"I'm right below you. Give me some cover and I can take down the rest."

"Kristin, don't!"

He had a feeling she wouldn't listen. His shoulders tightened as the agents moved to surround her. She jumped into the middle of the group and swung the stun rod with deadly accuracy. Every time she connected, electricity showered the ground with bright sparks.

Not taking time to strip off his shirt, he leapt out the window, and the fabric tore as his wings unfolded to their full span. She may need to be up and close and personal, but he had a better shot from open air.

The opposition dropped to the ground when he dove at them. When they got close to Kristin, she shocked them unconscious. With more room to maneuver, his accuracy improved. He summoned a blast of wind to keep them pinned down while Kristin attacked. Sooner than he expected, the troops retreated with no regard to their fallen comrades.

Jericho and Cole came out of the house and joined them. "Anyone want to guess why they attacked for no reason?" Jericho asked.

"I expected them to try to take us prisoner but all they did was keep us pinned down," Cole said. "Even The Company knows better than to pick a fight just because they want to."

An agent groaned on the ground. Jericho grinned at his friends and cracked his knuckles. "Looks like we have someone who might have an answer for us."

Grayson grabbed Kristin's arm, pulling her away when Jericho leaned close to the agent. "You don't want to see him work."

She glanced over her shoulder. "What about Cole?"

"He's used to it. So am I." He looked at her. "You don't want to get used to it. He gets results, but it's hard to watch."

As if on cue, a scream reached them and she flinched before running to the front of the house. "I should stop him," she murmured. "I'm a hero. I'm not supposed to condone this type of thing."

"You can't stop him. He'll get what we need to know."

The gaze she turned to him almost broke his heart. "Will he kill the agent?"

"No." He jerked his head toward the house. "You don't get a reputation like his by killing the people best suited to spread the tale. The man he questions will hope Jericho kills him, but he won't. He'll go back and tell all the others about what happened, and the fame of Jericho Black will spread even more."

Kristin wrapped her arms around herself. "I forgot how dangerous he truly is, you all are, but I didn't believe he could be so heartless."

He pulled her into his embrace. "He has to be. It's his job."

They stood together for several heartbeats and when she pulled away, he let her go. She eyed the large wings arcing out from his back at least six feet in both directions. Large russet feathers faded to deep brown, then a dark tan with streaks of white and gray. She reached out and carefully touched one wing.

"Is this one of your hidden secrets?" she asked.

"Yeah. This is one of the bigger ones."

"Is this why you continuously scratch your back?" When he nodded, she continued. "Doesn't it hurt to keep them pulled into your muscles all the time?"

"No, but if they're contained too long or if I'm under a lot of stress, my muscles become irritated."

As she circled around, he sensed her study his back where his wings joined his body. He could tell from her silence she wanted to ask him a barrage of questions. He rubbed the upper part of his left arm, glad he'd kept enough of his shirt to cover the tattoo he still kept hidden

"I'd like to know more about your background," she said. "When this is over, I hope you'll let me collect some data."

"All depends on how you want to get it."

As her cheeks turned a delightful shade of pink, he

smiled. Score one for the home team.

Chapter Fifteen

Kristin found Jericho standing on his porch as he stared across the yard. A beer bottle dangled loosely from his fingers. The information he'd gotten confirmed their fears. Vertigo suspected they'd return to the house and had stationed the agents nearby. If Kristin and the men with her could be stopped, fine. If not, the troops were to bring back a report on their strength and weapons. Their mission was to detain them and delay their search for Vertigo and her prisoners.

Jericho glanced at her when she stood near him. "Cole's asleep right now. You have any ideas about dinner?"

After the brief firefight they went through, Cole had wavered badly. Kristin breathed a sigh of relief when they got him back to his house so he could rest. His wounds may have closed, but from experience, she knew strength would take longer to fully recover.

Kristin gazed at the sun as it appeared to descend in record time. "I'd like to stay here. We can do delivery or you two can go for takeout. What else can you tell me about Adam's power? I know he tracks, but what will this formula do to him?"

Jericho shrugged. "I know about as much as you do. All I know is she had specific psionics in mind when she created it. Adam's abilities are limited but he has a potential to do a whole lot more. From what

Cole's told me, she became obsessed with his other abilities."

"I guess she succeeded today?"

"Looks like it. It's possible he affected every psionic on the eastern seaboard. Ones like Cole, who are closer, will feel it more strongly." Jericho stared at the beer bottle he held. "I don't know if Adam will be able to handle all the power she's unleashed in him."

"And what about you? Why are you suddenly around me all the time?"

He shrugged. "I don't know. When we were at lunch, I felt like I saw you for the first time. With the images I have in my mind, you should be glad I have a lot of willpower. You're good for Grayson. He's not as twitchy as usual. I think it's because of you." He turned to her and winked. "And as much as I like you, you're not my type."

Did he just say she made Grayson happy? If it were true, would Grayson agree? Every time she stood close to him or he held her, an odd, tingly warmth spread through her. And he had a determination she admired. Right now, he was solely focused on the rescue of their friends. He worked out plans and scenarios, covered all his bases to keep everyone safe.

She knew how she felt about him, but how did he feel about her? Could Jericho be right in his comments just now? With the strength of their attraction, there was also the strong possibility that soulmates were more real than she believed.

She smiled at him to ease the discomfort she sensed. "I understand. I suspect Vertigo has planted suggestions in your mind. Her secondary plan must be to drive a wedge between you and Grayson. If the team frays, she'll get what she wants."

"And what does she want?"

"What she always wants. Chaos. Revenge. It's her true motivation. She thrives on it."

"Have you collided with her often?"

"Only a few times. When I have, she's more powerful, more...hateful than the time before." She rubbed her arms when goosebumps ran along her skin. "I hope we come up with some viable leads soon. She can't be far from here, not the way Cole was affected."

"True. I'm heading out to see some people. I can grab some food for us when I come home. Do you want to come with me?"

She remembered what Grayson told her of Jericho's tactics and knew it would be a bad idea. "Thanks, but no. Grayson said he wanted to check with someone he knows. I thought I'd stay here and do some research. This way, I can keep an eye on Cole in case Vertigo should attack again."

He stepped back and spread his arms out. "Suit yourself, but you'd miss out on all this."

"I'll take my chances." She hesitated. "About what happened at the house after the attack? I know you got the information you wanted, but I don't like the way you got it. As a hero, I'm supposed to put a stop to those types of tactics."

"A lot of people don't like my methods, but they don't hesitate to use them. I'm glad you weren't there to see it."

"Grayson says he has trouble at times as he watches you work."

"He does. So does Cole. So does Adam. The agent I interrogated confirmed we're right. Those were

Company troops and they were sent to keep us occupied while Vertigo tested her formula. Now they know our strengths and a few of our weaknesses. They got a big clue when Grayson took off after you. He also confirmed Vertigo isn't far from here and she's perfected her formula. We've got the bad guys worried, doc."

"If they worry too much, I'm afraid of the consequences for Jack and Adam."

He lifted one shoulder in a half shrug. "It's a risk we need to take. I think our people will be safe until after she finishes whatever her cockamamie project is."

"I hope you're right."

He pulled her in for a tight hug. "I wouldn't have said it if I didn't believe it."

He walked over to his car and she sighed. He shouldn't act like this toward her. It also shouldn't be so easy for her to respond. Grayson had the uncanny ability to make her insides flame with desire. Jericho's easy manner calmed her rapidly fraying nerves, in spite of what she knew he could do. They had to find Jack and Adam soon. If not, the trouble which brewed on the horizon would slam into her current team.

****

Grayson watched the interaction between Kristin and Jericho from the living room window. Jealousy flared hot and bright, like a knife twisting itself deep in his soul, when she smiled at whatever his friend said. When he'd pulled her into his arms, it took all of Grayson's willpower not to storm out to the porch and wipe the smug look off Jericho's face.

Kristin appeared to want him and he knew she cared for him. He knew for certain he wanted her, but she always ended up alone with his friend. How did Jericho get her to respond to him all the time? Did she care for Grayson because of his determination to find Jack? He frowned. He needed to tell Jericho in no uncertain terms Kristin wore an "off limits" sign.

He turned when the door opened and Kristin walked straight to him. "I had a few questions for Jericho. I caught a glimpse of you at the window and you looked a little angry."

"Yeah. Why are you so attracted to him? Should I be worried?"

"Of course not. I'm not sure why you're so upset. Jericho has said he knows you like me and I know I like you." She stared at him. "I told Jericho I believe Vertigo has planted a mental suggestion to make him think he wants me. There's a good chance he's not alone. Odds are she's in your mind as well. It's also possible she's affected me."

As she voiced his own suspicions out loud, it made them more real. "It makes sense. We all appear to be a little off. We noticed Jericho's change. What if her plan for me is more subtle? I flat out accused Cole of working with her." As much as he wanted to allay her fears, he wouldn't lie to her. "We're not sure if she's gotten to you. If you're right and she's started to play her mind games, we might not sense her influence with us until it's too late. We need to strengthen our psychic shields if we expect to beat her."

"I don't have enough time to teach you what you need to know. She's so powerful now. I'm not sure if we can take her."

He pulled her close and stroked her hair. For the first time since they met, she sounded uncertain. "We can take her. I promise you. We'll end her and get our people back."

She laid her hand on his cheek. "I like a man with confidence. You said you planned to check with one of your contacts in the area. Do you think they'll have any information we can use?"

"I'm not sure. What will you do while I'm gone?"

She gestured toward her laptop. "I thought I'd check my own avenues of information. Somebody has to have some clue as to her final plan."

"I'd rather hold you all day."

Even though it shouldn't have, his admission surprised her. "Being held all day sounds wonderful, but it doesn't help our current situation."

"True." He planted a light kiss on her lips. "I'll be back soon. Maybe together, we can come up with another plan to find her."

"Be careful. You don't know who she's hired."

He nodded and hurried out before he changed his mind. He got in his car and headed east, toward Atlantic City. His main contact lived just outside the tourist city, so he'd miss a lot of the heavy traffic. When Grayson hadn't heard from him for several days, he'd begun to worry. Tom would have sensed Vertigo's presence the moment she hit town.

Twenty minutes later, he pulled up in front of a small one story house surrounded by a rusty chain link fence. Usually, kids ran amok in the yard while two small dogs yapped at their heels. Today, silence reigned and his stomach clenched as cold slivers of fear stabbed his spine. Bikes, balls, and other toys lay abandoned on the lawn, the horde of children absent from sight and sound. To see the toys there, untouched, scared him more than he wanted to admit.

The gate creaked as he pushed it open and he stepped silently up the overgrown walkway. No one answered for several minutes after the first trio of knocks. The door didn't budge when he pushed it. He reached behind his back, gripped his gun, and knocked louder. If Vertigo's troops were here, they'd already seen him. Pounding on the door seemed a good way to let them know he'd come ready for whatever they had planned.

Quiet footsteps could barely be heard and a few seconds later, the door creaked open. A short, stocky man stood there, his clothes thin and frayed around the edges. Brown hair fell over his forehead and the normally bright look in his eyes had been dulled. Despair rolled off him in waves, laying heavy in the unusually silent atmosphere of his home. He stepped to the side and let Grayson in, then shut the door and locked it.

"I knew you'd be around sometime soon," the little man said. "It's why I waited for you."

Grayson glanced around the small home. "Tom, what happened? Where is everyone?"

"We heard what happened to Sammy. After I talked to the boss, I sent the wife and kids to stay with her sister in Marlton Township. This whole job stinks to high heaven. People have clammed up or disappeared. I knew you'd be down today, but I didn't want to take the chance leaving the door unlocked. So after we talk and you leave, I have no reason to stay any longer."

Grayson followed him over to the couch. "Is there any information, anything at all, you can tell me?"

"Vertigo has taken over a new development out

somewhere between Smithville and the Garden State Parkway. It's down an unmarked road and surrounded by a lot of trees. She scared off the workers. You'll find her holed up there."

Grayson leaned back. "It fits with what we've found out. We went to Smithville and checked out some of the back roads around it. We were ambushed by Company troops. Vertigo's called in the big guns." He paused. "Did you feel the psychic pulse?"

Tom nodded. "Yep. Almost knocked my teeth out. I sensed Adam's power signature. What did Vertigo do to him?"

"Cole said she completed her formula."

They sat quiet for several minutes before Tom spoke again. "If she doses him again, it could fry his brain. He's always had a lot of power, but he's kept it buried for a long time. He doesn't have the experience or the strength to control the surge. Beware of her. I've had visions of her wanting to pick up Cole."

"Great," Grayson grumbled. "Did you get a clearer picture of where she is? There's major construction in a lot of places. It looks like they want to build up the whole area."

He shook his head. "Sorry. All I get is new houses and an unmarked road. The houses are large, so look for a nicer area, you know, one smelling of money." He pointed to Grayson's back. "You'll need to use those wings to take a look around from on high. You should get a better idea of where the more likely place is then."

Grayson nodded. "I planned on it. Thanks for the help. I can eliminate sites with one- or two-story houses. Get some place safe. You don't want Vertigo to find you."

Tom wheezed out a laugh. "She ain't caught me yet. I don't plan to let her start now. I won't be dragged back to HelixCorp again."

Grayson narrowed his eyes. "Can you tell me a little more about her? We know some, but there's a lot of gaps in what we have."

"Cole will be your best source of information." He walked to the kitchen and grabbed a bottle of water from the refrigerator. "Whether he talks or not is a different story."

Grayson followed him. "Tom, you took me in after my parents were killed. You taught me what I needed to know about how to hide from the harpy tribe and about my powers, and then you moved to south Jersey. Why? What couldn't you tell me? Have you seen what will happen to us?"

"You know I can't see all the futures, only the most probable ones. I knew you'd need me here." He shook his head. "I knew you'd be part of Jericho's team. It's why I told you where the family and I would be. You were destined to be here at this time." He took Grayson's hand, squeezing it hard. "You've turned into a fine young man. Your dad would've been proud. Get back to your team."

"Thanks. Give the family my love when you get to them."

Tom shuffled to the sagging armchair. He sat and raised the plastic bottle in a salute. "I will. Oh, when you marry the girl you got on your team right now, make sure you bring her by. I'd like a chance to chat with her."

Grayson smiled. "Why am I not surprised you know about her? She told me she isn't human. You have any idea what she meant?"

"Of course." Tom chuckled. "She's more human than she lets herself believe. Don't worry. She'll divulge her past to you soon enough. She'll have a hard time with your secret, but she'll come around. Be patient."

Tom's revelations gave them another connection to HelixCorp. The research center needed to be investigated, and soon. As Grayson got back in his car, he wondered what Tom had seen in his vision. He and Kristin were going to be married? If he decided to tell her, this would give her a huge shock. Maybe he'd better keep it to himself for now.

****

Adam shivered where he'd been dropped on the floor while Vertigo stood over him. "See? I knew you could handle it. The increase in your power is almost off the charts. I may have to wait an extra day to inject you with the second dose. We don't want to burn you out too fast, do we?"

He groaned and rolled away from her. Her voice sounded like nails being dragged down a chalkboard. Thousands of thoughts slammed repeatedly into his brain and he couldn't concentrate long enough to block them out. His telepathy had shifted to overload and he sensed people all the way into New England.

"I'll let you get used to being an actual useful psionic and check on you again in a few hours. Jack, you will keep him company, won't you?"

Adam frowned as her laugh echoed over and over in his mind. "I hate it when she mocks me. What I wouldn't give for a gun right about now."

Jack glanced at him. "Why a gun? Couldn't you

use a psionic blast on her?"

Adam forced his eyes open and he stared at him. "In my current condition, it would be like a baby trying to run a marathon. She's broken all the barriers I've built in my mind. It took years to get them as strong as I needed, but I did it so I wouldn't hear thoughts anymore. What I pick up usually isn't good."

"You locked your powers away?"

"Yeah. I can't handle it. It's bad enough when I psychically track someone. To be in another person's mind is the ultimate invasion of privacy."

"I get it," Jack said. "And now the floodgates are open."

Adam rolled to his back. "And the town will be washed away. If my team doesn't find us soon, we're nine kinds of screwed."

"I've had the same thought myself."

Chapter Sixteen

Kristin sat back and rubbed her eyes. Okay, so she'd been wrong and no one knew anything. Her computer skills were good, but she needed someone on Amy's level to find the backdoors. She briefly considered asking Cole, but would he help her find those particular doors? Frustration built as she vacillated back and forth between options and ideas.

She'd told Jericho she believed Vertigo had planted a suggestion in his mind. When she told Grayson she thought Vertigo could be in her mind too, she said it to ease his fears. Now she suspected she might be right. Indecision wasn't in her nature. Once she had a course of action, she stuck to it.

What if Vertigo had slipped around her psychic shields? She had enough power and absolutely no morals. The telepath did the most despicable acts and tortured people for her own personal amusement. Not physically, but in their minds, forcing them to see and believe the worst about family and friends.

He phone lay innocently on the desk and she considered calling the Angels in. She and Grayson's team needed more help. She closed her laptop and paced. Like the bad guys back home wouldn't notice if the entire Angel's team disappeared. She may as well advertise on a huge, flashy billboard about Jack's kidnapping.

"What is the matter with me?" she said to the empty room. "It has to be Vertigo's influence. I've got to get it together."

She decided to check on Cole. Yes, he carried a gun and had his own paranormal ability, but in his current state, he'd be more vulnerable to an attack right now. She wasn't fooling anyone. She wanted company. Troubled thoughts circled her mind and a small headache had started. If she talked to him, hopefully her thoughts would begin to make a little sense.

Cole's door stood ajar and she tiptoed closer. His eyes were shut and his chest rose and fell evenly. She debated on whether she should go inside and disturb him or head back to the computer.

"Come on in, Kristin. I'm awake." He turned and smiled at her. "I wanted to focus on the problem."

Kristin stepped into the room. "Do you feel any better?"

"I'm fine, just a little tired."

She pulled a chair over. "You can sit out the rest of the mission if you'd like. You've done so much already. Adam would understand if you stayed here and recovered."

He rolled his head back and forth as his eyes drifted shut. "I want, no, I need to be with the team when we take her down. If there's a situation I can prevent and I'm not with you, I'd never forgive myself. I can't sit this one out. I'm sure you understand."

"I do. I've been in the exact position you are now." She paused. "I haven't had any luck on my computer. Have you been able to access the internet for other information?"

"I've slept on and off since we got back. Currently,

the computer is not my friend." He glanced at her. "I'm not used to my powers failing me when I try to connect with the internet."

"You've had some pretty serious injuries. You haven't had enough time to recover. Wounds heal quickly. Strength takes a little longer to build up. I'm sure your power will be good as new as soon as you get some actual rest."

Cole closed his eyes. "I can't detect any sympathy from you, Dr. Mentor. I almost had my brains turned to oatmeal today. I would appreciate a little concern on your part."

It was hard not to be charmed by his boyish behavior, and she patted his shoulder. "There, there. You'll be all right. Better?"

He grinned. "It'll do for now."

"Where do you think Grayson and Jericho went?"

"I'm pretty sure Grayson went to check in with Tom. He's one of our contacts down here. He knows a lot but can't tell us all he knows."

"How does he get his information?"

Cole glanced at her. "How do you think? He's another psionic, a clairvoyant to be specific. He keeps a low profile so no one can find him. He hides in plain sight."

She thought about Grayson's and Jericho's cars and had to agree. "You all hide in plain sight. If the four of you weren't so attractive, it might be easier."

His mouth curled up in a crooked smile. "Why, Dr. Mentor. Did you just admit you find all of us handsome, charming, and a myriad of other compliments to balm our fragile male egos?"

"No. It's a proven fact. The general populace is

drawn to the more aesthetically pleasing members of the opposite sex. It's all science, my friend."

"Wow. Took the wind out of all the sails, didn't you?"

"My team has often said so." She stood and walked to the door. "Get some rest. I'll be in the other room if you need me."

Kristin walked to the living room and plopped down on the couch. If she liked the taste, she'd grab one of Jericho's beers. The fact she even considered alcohol, told her how desperate she'd become to get some answers. Well, they weren't at the bottom of a beer bottle.

Why couldn't this mission have been as simple as she'd hoped? A long sigh escaped her. Nothing was ever simple in the life of a superhero. The jobs which appeared to be the easiest were the ones with the most complications. And now she had the added stress of emotional turmoil because of her attraction to Grayson

It was a biological response, like she'd explained to Cole. So why did her heart turn cartwheels in her chest when Grayson looked at her? Every nerve in her body stood to attention when he was nearby. Her body responded in ways she had previously believed to be nonsense. It appeared all those romance novels her teammates were so fond of were right.

She rubbed her eyes. How much more ridiculous could she possibly get? She had no time in her life for such foolishness. She'd made the decision years before as a teenager to never get involved with anyone. Science made sense. Relationships didn't and were complicated, especially when she considered the magical element currently haunting her.

"More complicated than they need to be," she muttered.

A noise on the porch snapped her attention back to her surroundings. She rose and grabbed her stun rod from the coffee table. She crept to the door and kept her back to the wall to take a glance out the window. Men she didn't recognize were outside and prepared to break in.

She gripped her stun rod tighter and allowed herself a small smile. All of her frustration with not being able to find Jack, coupled with her problems with Grayson, had made her restless. Letting loose in a brief skirmish would be the exact remedy she craved. Three men stood on the porch. She'd handled more than this by herself as the Angels' leader.

They would be through the door in mere minutes, leaving her no time to warn Cole. She silently willed him to stay put and adjusted her grip on the stun rod. Right now, she had the advantage of surprise and moved to the other side of the door. They would have to come through one at a time and she could take them out as they entered. If the universe would be on her side, they'd be average, low grade thugs and not Vertigo's trained troops, or worse, supers.

The door crashed open and Kristin brought the shock rod down hard on the first man's arm, and electricity popped, jolting him as the bone snapped. His gun clattered to the floor and she brought her fist up hard into his jaw. He sprawled at her feet and didn't get up.

The second man had time to aim, but no more as Kristin swung the rod in a sharp arc. The crackle of electricity lit up his body as she smacked the side of his head. He dropped like a stone on top of the first as the third entered. Kristin parried his punch and ducked as he fired his weapon at her.

"Please," she said. "You must think we're fools not to have prepared for this." She smashed her fist into the man's face and heard the distinctive pop as his nose broke. She grabbed his jacket and pulled him forward to throw him in a chair.

"Kristin?" Cole shouted. "What the hell is all the noise out there?"

"Come see for yourself. We've had some uninvited guests." She smiled at him as he hobbled in before stopping dead in the doorway. "I believe Jericho will want to talk to them."

He looked at the two men in a heap on the floor. The third sat bent over in a kitchen chair, holding his face as blood dripped to the floor. He glanced at Kristin and grinned. "Will you marry me?"

She laughed. "Let me think about it."

****

"Do you want to talk to me, or do I break your arm? I'm good either way," Jericho said to the man he'd pinned against the wall. He hated this neighborhood in Atlantic City. Too many bad things had happened here. Too many bad memories haunted him. He refocused on the man in his grasp.

"Break it. Vertigo will do worse to me if I talk." The man turned his head enough for Jericho to see him smile.

"You know how much I hate it when my bluff is called." He pushed harder and the bone snapped under his hands, and the man in his grip cried out. "Now it's going to be harder for you to concentrate. What's

Vertigo's end game? You have five minutes to make me happy or your value hits rock bottom."

The man's eyes widened. "You wouldn't…"

"You know what it means, then, when people disappoint me. Don't worry. You'll be a fine example to others who think I can be played. Are you sure you don't want to share?"

The man slid down the wall to sit on the trash covered concrete while he cradled his arm. "If I tell you what I know, you got to protect me."

"I'll call my boss and someone will pick you up, but I need to know the information in your greasy, unwashed head. Everyone has fingered you as the man with the answers. I hope you are, otherwise I've wasted a full day. Where is Jack McClennan?"

Jericho could see the man knew full well he'd be disposed of with little thought. "He's in the area. Vertigo is holed up down one of the side roads, but I don't know which one. It's not around Smithville. It's closer to the other little historic village. You know, the one with the big manor house."

"Better." Jericho leaned close until their noses were inches apart. "I need more, or I'm done with you." When he still received no answer, he sighed. "You know I can hurt you and not even come close to killing you."

The man paled and shrank back. "All right, all right. She's rumored to be in a new community being built near the entrance to the Garden State Parkway. It's supposed to be for the more well off people. Price range starts in the high six figures."

"What else?"

The man looked up and down the deserted alley

and his voice dropped to just above a whisper. "Word is she's requested more reinforcements. You've gotten too close and she's worried you'll find her before she's ready."

"Who's she working for? Who's calling the shots?"

"Benedict Trust. His money funds this whole operation. Trust wants to use Adam Williams as a weapon. He wanted her to get rid of McClennan, but she won't. The latest rumor is Trust has a hidden agenda no one knows about, not even Vertigo. Don't worry about your friends dying. Worry about them if they live." He looked up and down the alley. "Now you got to protect me. They'll both know I talked."

Jericho froze for a moment, then pulled out his phone. He'd heard of Benedict Trust and what he knew wasn't good. Rich beyond words and a powerful business man, he presented a charitable face to the world. However, there was a whole other side no one in polite society knew about.

Jericho had seen firsthand what the man's mean streak had done to people. He and his team had busted up some of Trust's less savory ventures in the past. There needed to be a word worse than bad to describe Adam and Jack's situation. Maybe he'd invent one.

"There'll be a car here in," he paused to check his watch, "five, four, three, two, and one."

A dark blue sedan pulled up and two women got out. Both were tall and muscular. One had blonde hair and the other had dark hair. Both wore business suits and dark glasses hid their eyes. These two had always reminded Jericho of the mysterious Men in Black the conspiracy theorists always talked about. Except for the fact they were Women in Black and worked for his boss.

"We'll take him from here, Jericho," the blonde said. "He'll be safe. The boss said to remind you to end Vertigo and everyone associated with her. You are to take any measures necessary."

"Understood. Did she know about Benedict Trust's involvement?"

The dark haired woman shook her head. "I don't think so. He's a mystery she doesn't like. We'll relay this information to her."

Jericho ran his hands through his hair. "That nutjob adds a whole new layer of complication to this situation. Cole needs to be warned."

As he climbed in the car, the informant turned to him with an unpleasant smile. "One more point, Black. If you're here, who's watching the people you left behind?"

The blonde turned to him. "Get back. Defend your friends. Find Adam and Jack."

Before they had finished loading the informant in the backseat, Jericho ran for his SUV. This job had gone from bad, to worse, to absolute crap. He pulled out his cell phone and called Grayson. "Yeah. I talked to him. Get back to Cole's place, now. From what the little weasel just said, I think there might be trouble."

He jumped in and sped back to his team, worried about what he'd find when he arrived.

****

Grayson and Jericho pulled up at the same time. Kristin stood on the porched and waved. She didn't look worried or frightened. They couldn't see any wounds or any sign of distress. In fact, she looked downright happy.

"Are you all right? Did you have trouble?" Grayson said.

She glanced at each of them in turn and smiled. "Just a little workout. I handled it. There's a present for you inside, Jericho."

He stared at her before he pushed open the front door. Facedown on the floor, tied in with the most intricate knots he'd ever seen, were two men. A third sat bound to a kitchen chair. "Hey doc," he called. "Did you mean these guys?"

Grayson slipped an arm around her shoulders as they walked inside. "Yes," she said. "They tried so hard to be stealthy, but they weren't too good at it."

Cole walked out of the kitchen, a towel clutched in his hands. "I think I'm in love. She took them out all alone."

She shrugged. "After the armed troops we faced earlier, I expected this type of situation to arise. These men are low level thugs, hired by Vertigo. She wouldn't send Company troops. They're too noticeable. Jericho, are they familiar to you?"

He leaned close to the man in the chair. He grinned and cracked his knuckles. "Give me a few minutes and they will be."

The thug shrank away from him. "Jericho Black?"

"Yep. Vertigo didn't tell you I'd been put on this job, did she?"

The thug shook his head. "Whatever you want to know, I'll tell you."

Jericho walked over and dropped on the couch while Kristin sat on the arm and Grayson stood behind her. "By all means. Start talking."

"Every move, every thought you people have had,

she's known before you make it. She's herded you right where she wants you. She wants to turn your minds inside out."

"Wonderful," Grayson muttered. "Is there any good news?"

The thug stared at Kristin and smiled. "She's got a plan to make your buddy gut you."

Grayson frowned. "I'm sorry. I thought I asked for good news."

"Your other buddy is to be sent some place for more experimentation."

"Same song, different record. We're done." Jericho threw an empty bottle at the man and hit him square between the eyes, with enough force to knock him out. "I'll call the boss and have her pick these guys up."

Grayson had already pulled out his phone. "She'll have a car here in about thirty minutes. Tom said Vertigo's holed up in a new upscale community being built out by the parkway. He said to check the ones going for a higher price."

"Your information ties with what I found out," Jericho said. "The man I talked to said to check out beyond the other historic community with the big manor house. Batsto is the only community with a manor house out by the Garden State Parkway. The new houses out there fit with his information. Let's hope she's there and it's not another decoy. I'm real tired of this woman and her games."

"Then let's not give her any more chances. Let's go get her," Kristin said.

Jericho held his hand up. "Hang on, I'm not done yet. She's called in more reinforcements. She had a lot before. Now, we could face a small army. Adam is going to be used as a weapon. We don't know what she's done to Jack." The smirk appeared. "Now, you want to hear the bad news?"

The other three glanced at each other. "What's the bad news?" Cole asked.

"Benedict Trust is involved."

Cole stood and turned to go to his bedroom. "I'm done. As soon as I'm packed, I'm headed for a nice tropical island."

"I know Benedict Trust. I've met him at several charity functions. He has a dark quality about him. How do you know him?" Kristin asked.

Cole walked over to his front door, twisted the deadbolts, before he barricaded it with the armchair. "He's my former boss from HelixCorp. He stays in the background." He glanced at her. "I hope you kept your distance. You don't want to get to close to him. He's a nasty piece of work all wrapped up in Armani. He's got connections with a lot of the paranormal villain teams. He can make you disappear and never lay a hand on you."

"Then it's imperative we get our people back as soon as possible," Kristin said. "We need to scout the area and find out for sure where she's hiding."

Grayson rolled his shoulders. "Those were my very plans for tonight."

Chapter Seventeen

Jack sat in a chair while Vertigo smiled at him. The more she revealed about their life together, the more muddled his memories became. She insisted they were married, but it didn't feel right. He remembered a woman with auburn hair as his wife. Yet, Vertigo sat there, and stroked his hand to comfort him. She'd told him he'd rescued the auburn haired woman he saw in his memories.

"Anita, I can't remember our wedding."

She smoothed his hair back. "It's to be expected. You were the victim of a particularly vicious telepathic attack." She cradled his head to her breast. "It's okay. I'm here now to take care of you."

He hesitated, then placed his hands on her hips. "I can't think clearly."

"It's going to take some time before you're yourself again, but I'll be there to help you." She leaned close. "Every step of the way."

"I'm sorry. I need time to remember."

She stood back and smiled. "You take all the time you need. I only want to help you, Jack."

She took him back to the room where he spent most of his time. As Anderson refastened the cuffs to his wrists, he couldn't understand why his wife would keep him chained up like a dog. He leaned against the wall and saw another man on the floor near him.

He frowned, the man's name on the tip of his tongue. He knew him, or at least, thought he did. As he stared, the man's name popped into his mind. "You're Adam, right?"

"Yeah. I'm Adam." He jerked his head toward the door. "Don't let her in your head. She wants to rewrite your memories. You aren't married to her. Your wife has auburn hair, not blonde. She helped you clear your name. She's a hero and a member of the Angels team." He slammed his fist against the floor. "If I could get a handle on these new abilities, I'd be able to help you. Right now, it's like I'm trying to hold on to jello."

"You told me you can't control your powers, right?"

"Yep."

The fog in Jack's mind lifted a little. He remembered when he broke the hidden cabal at ULTRA. He could clearly see his wife and she did have auburn hair. She'd stood by him when he still had the outlaw renegade label attached to his name. Her face blurred and Vertigo's took her place.

Jack glanced at him. "Bloody hell, we're in a lot of trouble."

"I think maybe you're right."

They looked at each other and began to laugh.

****

Grayson waited until dark before he left. He stripped off his shirt and took to the sky. Hopefully, if anyone saw him, they'd fear they'd seen a glimpse of the legendary Jersey Devil. He missed being in the air for too long and turned his face to the wind. Next job, he would insist on reconnaissance.

He'd never been able to fly much as a child. The

few times his mother had taken him out, he'd called on his power to control the wind and used it to soar higher than he should have. When his parents found out about his abilities, they'd hidden him away from the tribal elders. He snorted. For all the good it did them. They'd been found out when the North Wind Brethren sensed his powers and came for him. He still blamed the Brethren for the vicious attack on his parents.

After his parents' deaths, Tom had taken him in and drove him out to the country. He taken to the sky as joy built in his chest to be able to fly and use his powers to push himself higher. He'd needed to strengthen his wings and learn about what he could do if he expected to keep both the harpy tribe and the North wind Brethren at bay.

After years of hiding in New York City, he'd gotten word both factions had given up the search for him. On his twenty third birthday, he'd joined ULTRA. He no longer feared either group. He had the skills to handle the magical threats. Right now, his biggest fear was the reaction of the man he betrayed.

The smaller housing areas were eliminated first as possible places for Vertigo to hide. It looked like the crews were still on site. He'd landed and walked around. Exhaust from the work trucks lingered and he saw trash in the strategically placed cans. A dead man couldn't miss the heavy ammonia smell as it drifted on the breeze from the porta-potties. The work here hadn't been interrupted, a clear indication of Vertigo's absence.

He launched himself into the air and soared over the trees as he turned toward the most likely place where she'd hide. He could see a cleared area up ahead.

Enough of the woods remained to afford the community some privacy and provide a noise barrier to the nearby highway. These houses were huge and he could see why they commanded such a high price.

A massive house stood alone at the end of an unfinished driveway. Lights bobbed around it and he swooped lower to land on a sturdy branch. The thick foliage hid his presence and he quietly whistled at the sight below him. Jericho had hit the nail on the head. Those weren't regular reinforcements down there. They were going up against a small army. It didn't look like they'd be able to take them out a few at a time.

They moved with the precision of trained troops with hi-tech weaponry on their hips and slung over their shoulders. They continually scanned the nearby woods. They'd walked close to the tree line but never went in. From what he could tell, they were ready for a full scale invasion. The fact Vertigo had called in so much firepower forced him to grin. She must be more concerned than they thought for so many men to have been brought in.

Time to get back and let the others know what he found. Despite the initial boost to his ego, this cemented the fact they were in a lot of trouble.

****

Kristin read while she waited for Grayson to return. They planned to stay at Jericho's for the night, then move over to Cole's the next day. She glanced at the clock. He'd been gone for just forty-five minutes. So how come it felt like he'd been gone for hours? She gave up and tossed the book off to the side to let Grayson occupy her thoughts. The abbreviated, although incredibly intense, make out session they'd done earlier at the motel had surprised her. She'd allowed him liberties denied to every other man she'd dated.

Every time she'd get her practical side back in place, he'd give her a rare smile or take her hand or initiate some other contact. When she remembered the look in his eyes when he gazed at her, all those rampant emotions rushed back. Apparently, a kiss could be as important as she'd been told. She stared at the window again and wondered if he'd been hurt. Had he been spotted or captured? She'd give anything to know what was happening.

These thoughts bordered on the ridiculous. She jumped out of bed and began to pace. He'd survived for many years without her and would continue to do so after she took Jack home. She stopped. It was the first time she thought about going back to her own life without him. How would he feel when she left? Would he miss her? Would she miss him?

She berated herself for her foolishness. Honestly, where was the logic in all these suppositions? They didn't give her the answers she sought. The simple, practical, logical solution would be to ask him if he wanted to come back with her or stay here. Did she want to be with him forever?

Thinking about his gentleness when he kissed her, yes, she wanted him for as long as she could have him. Would they make love soon? Deep in her heart, she hoped so. Their kiss had awakened all those crazy emotions she'd never had time for. His kiss seemed to be like the last piece of a complicated jigsaw puzzle. In his arms, she felt complete.

If they took the next step, the sex would be

explosive and she wanted to feel the passion burn through her. She wanted to feel what her married teammates talked about. Kristin had listened to them describe the glorious bond with the one person with whom they shared a very private part of themselves. Her friends were always fanciful and Kristin had kept a scientific perspective. Somehow, she had a strong feeling science was not going to be her friend when it came to Grayson.

A good, solid relationship needed more than sex to justify it. She needed more. She wanted a man who could keep pace with her, a man who respected her as a hero and a well-known scientist. She wanted a man who made her spirit soar. And all those thoughts circled back to Grayson.

She climbed back under the covers, to try and rest. Always a light sleeper, she knew she'd hear Grayson when he returned. Maybe when he got back, she'd make the first move to let him know how she felt about him. After all, they had to start somewhere. The thought left a smile on her face and she snuggled under the covers and dozed.

****

Grayson landed at Cole's house and folded his wings tight against his back as he stepped quietly inside. Jericho looked up from the map spread across the table and walked over to him.

"How's Cole?" Grayson asked in a low voice.

Jericho shrugged. "He looks all right, but I can tell he's not. You can see it in his eyes. Benedict Trust scares him."

"Cole might be paranoid, but he isn't scared of anything. He's usually the one scaring others." He glanced at Jericho. "You taught him that."

"Yes, I did. But now he's more than scared. I saw actual terror flash in his eyes, but only for a second." Jericho turned to him. "I know a little about Trust. Cole worked for him so he knows the most. I don't think he'll tell us too much. You saw him earlier. I've never seen him willing to run out on a job. I'm not sure what happened, but something tells me it was bad."

Grayson glanced toward Cole's bedroom. "Do you think we can get him to open up?"

"I'm not sure. Even I don't know the whole story about Cole. He's got more secrets than you and me put together. I don't even know how he managed to help people escape from HelixCorp and he won't tell me."

"How have we trusted him this long?"

"Because I'm the one who found him after his last rescue mission. I'd never seen someone so close to walking with the reaper and live." Jericho sat on the couch and stared at Grayson. "And because the boss vouched for him."

Grayson leaned against the door. "His paranoia has given him the biggest bloodthirsty streak. I don't think Vertigo will escape this time."

"I'm worried about him. He's been paranoid for a long time, but he keeps a tight lid on it. Now, it's like he's gone into full blown panic mode. I could barely talk him into staying. He only agreed because the boss called and told him he had to finish the job."

"Hang on a second. The boss called?" Grayson couldn't believe it. First, she met him personally in the regional office and now she called. How did she know Cole wanted to bolt? "We need to investigate our own company when this job is done. We've taken too much on faith lately."

"She's always done right by us before. Like all of us, she has her own secrets to keep."

Jericho gave Shade, Inc. and their boss his complete loyalty. She raised Jericho when his young, teenage mother couldn't. She trained him, set him up with almost everything he owned. No one talked bad about Shade or the woman who ran it to Jericho. Not even him, so he changed the subject.

"You were right. Vertigo has a small army at her disposal right now. I don't know if she's called any more in, but we'd better assume she did. We're not going to be able to sneak in."

"So, we're going to have one hell of a fight on our hands."

Grayson nodded. He'd wanted to bring better news, but like so many times before, he couldn't.

A mischievous twinkle appeared in Jericho's eyes. "When have the odds ever been in our favor? We got this and it'll give Cole a chance to let loose on some of Trust's troops."

Grayson smiled. "Very well put, buddy. Kristin and I will be by in the morning. We'll get together and discuss a plan at breakfast. Anything special you need from your place?"

"Nah." Jericho tossed him the keys to his locker. "Just make sure you grab enough weapons."

Grayson bounced the keys once in his hand and headed for the door. "Right. See you tomorrow."

He hesitated and opened his mouth, then clamped his jaws together. He needed to know Jericho's thoughts about Kristin. The last thing he wanted was a fight with his friend. There had to be a way to ask the delicate question. If he did, would it cause a blowup between them?

The two of them had been through a lot over the years. The thought that they'd fight over a woman was ludicrous. But Kristin wasn't any woman. She was his soulmate. He fully believed that now. She was his, no one else's. He'd keep a close eye on his friend. If the time came when he had to tell Jericho to back off, he'd deal with it then.

He leapt into the air and made it back to Jericho's house in a few minutes. Grayson slipped inside and shut the door with a quiet click. He entered the bedroom, where Kristin slept, moonlight bathing her in a silvery glow. The covers had slipped down and he smiled. She'd been waiting for him. The thin camisole enhanced the outlines of her body, but didn't conceal her curves. She may as well have been nude.

As a child, his mother told him stories of magical creatures like them, who had found their soulmates. She'd made it sound like the most wonderful experience in the world. He'd always dreamed about what it would be like to find the one special woman in the world who would be his alone. Now, she'd found her way into his heart and his bed. From the moment he looked in her eyes, he knew they were connected beyond the physical attraction they both displayed.

His willpower weakened and he crossed the room, brushing his knuckles over her cheek. Her eyes fluttered open and she smiled. What he saw in her expression, made hope swell in his chest. If he read the signs right, she wanted him as much as he wanted her.

"I'm glad you're back," she said. "I wanted to stay awake, but I got so comfortable."

When he turned back the covers, his willpower shattered. The satiny material had slid up and revealed the hard muscles of her stomach. Silk panties didn't cover her very well either, only outlined the secret area of her body he desperately wanted to explore. Not being able to resist the temptation she presented, he traced her bare skin. "If I had known how you were waiting for me, I would've come back sooner."

She watched as he removed his clothes and climbed in next to her. "I thought about you the whole time you were gone," she said. "I'd like to pick up where we left off the other day."

He ran his hand down her thigh and she moaned. "Glad to hear it. I remember how you felt when I held you. I had a hard time letting you go." He dragged his thumb over her lower lip. "I want to kiss you again."

"And maybe a little more?"

"Oh yeah. We'll do a lot more."

He eased her camisole off and bared her breasts to his hungry gaze. Like the rest of her, they were perfect, molding to his hand like they were made only for him. While his fingers teased her, tracing lazy circles around the sensitive buds, his lips left a trail of fire down her throat to her collarbone. She arched into his grasp, silently begging for more.

He moved his hands down, pleased his touch made her tremble. He skimmed over where he truly wanted to be and instead ran his hands down her legs. When he gazed at her, her eyes held a special light he knew would always be just for him. He smoothed a few strands of her hair back, surprised when his fingers shook. He wished he could see her a little clearer. The moonlight felt more appropriate, and she glowed with its ethereal light.

"You aren't stopping now, are you?" she asked.

Hooking his thumbs into the elastic, he eased her panties down her legs and threw them in the corner. "Sweetheart, the apocalypse couldn't stop me now. I just want to admire the view."

"You can admire all you want later. I need you. Now."

"The famous Dr. Mentor has an impatient side. I never would've guessed." He paused and cupped her cheek. "Despite your earlier claims, I think you're the most human woman I've ever known."

"Thank you." She ran her hands down his chest. "And I'm only impatient when it comes to you." She hesitated. "I'm a little surprised at myself. I never act like this. I mean, we met not long ago. This isn't too fast for you, is it? I don't want you to think I…"

"Stop right there," he said. "I think you're a beautiful, strong, fascinating woman. Ever since I first saw you, this is what I've thought about and not only the physical part. I've wanted to connect with you on a deeper level for a long time."

"It sounds a lot like you're talking about soulmates and true love. Do you believe in all those things?"

"I never used to, but I do now." Laying his hand at the top of her sex, he smiled when she shivered. "Now, if I've answered all your questions, I'd like to continue. We can talk more tomorrow."

"Deal," she said.

At his touch, her body jerked. As he settled into an easy rhythm, she opened wider, and let him do what he wanted. He delved inside her and her eyes drifted shut. He could feel her tighten around his fingers and grinned when she let go.

"You're good," she said. "My turn."

She pushed him back on the bed as her fingers drifted over his chest and down his stomach. She kissed him leisurely, copying the trail he left down her throat. Her tongue flicked his nipple and he groaned. When she found a sensitive spot where his neck met his shoulder, she focused a little more attention there.

She stopped above the stiff part of his body as it begged for her touch. She gave him a sly grin, she wrapped her fingers around him and slid her hand up and down. Her light touch started tremors in him and he arched his back. When she removed her hand, his eyes opened and he stared at her.

"I think you want to drive me crazy."

She laid her hands on his chest, and gazed at him. "I don't mean to. I have a better idea."

She straddled his hips and lowered herself as she took all of him inside her. He sighed and as she moved, his hands covered her breasts. Her hands rested on his chest while she increased her pace. As the fire in her built, white light exploded behind her eyes.

A shape rose with the light, its large wings spread fully out. The light folded around it and her release rushed through her, taking her soul on a journey with Grayson's. Their souls spiraled up to the heavens as their passion built. His cries mingled with hers and they came down together, while moonlight caressed their bodies.

She sprawled across his chest and smiled at him. "I had no idea making love to someone could be so intense."

"Thanks. You weren't so bad yourself."

She sat up as she continued to hold him prisoner inside her. "Are you always this good?"

He reached down to find the nub at the top of her sex. "Only one way to find out."

"Go for it," she whispered.

They got very little rest as the night deepened.

****

Bright sunlight splashed Kristin across the eyes. The weight of Grayson's arm made her feel uncharacteristically protected. She'd never needed a man to make her feel safe, but she had to admit, this felt nice. She turned to wake him up and her smile faded. A very familiar tattoo graced his upper bicep. She knew it immediately. The Gravediggers logo from Jack's original ULTRA team.

Grayson told her he and Frank had a past. Her heart sank as she now knew the past he had referenced. She jumped out of bed and grabbed her robe as he woke.

"Explain the tattoo on your arm." She pointed at it, the gesture accusatory. "I know it implicitly. It's the Gravediggers insignia. You were part of Jack's team."

Grayson rose and grabbed his clothes. "You're right." He pulled up his pants and turned to face her. "I'm a former member of Jack's team." He squeezed his eyes shut, then opened them. He stared at Kristin before he took a deep breath. "I'm the one who betrayed them."

Chapter Eighteen

Kristin yanked on her clothes and packed in silence. Her eyes burned and she wasn't sure who deserved her tears more. Her throat constricted, choking off her breath. An icy fist clamped itself around her heart. Jack and his team had lost so much because of the betrayal. She had given herself to him and, with one statement, he'd shattered her heart and her hard-won trust into thousands of shards.

He moved around behind her, packing his and Jericho's clothes, but she couldn't look at him. He walked into the bathroom and rattling noises drifted out to her. He brought the items out and put them in a small case, before shoving it into his travel bag. He grabbed all the bags and took them out to the car. He then methodically removed some of the weapons from the cabinet.

He'd finally told her the secret he'd kept hidden. Did it devastate him because he'd been forced to confess or because she'd found out? Blinking fiercely to hold in her tears, she wanted to run from him, but she couldn't. She still needed his help to find Jack.

A heavy silence followed them into the car, suffocating talk as they drove to Cole's. Grayson carried the bags into the house as Kristin stood by the car, trying to sort the emotions which currently slammed through her. A new day should bring hope and clarity, not this crushing weight sitting on her chest.

"You okay?"

She looked up and saw Jericho in front of her. "No. I don't think I'll ever be okay again."

"He told you, didn't he?"

"I saw his tattoo and recognized it. He betrayed his team. He betrayed Jack. To make it worse, he hid this very important information from me. How can I forgive him? How can I ever trust him again?"

Jericho draped his arm around her shoulders. "Only you can answer that particular question. If you need someone, I'm here."

"Thanks, but if Vertigo's in your head, I'm not sure I can trust you either."

He laid his right hand over his heart. "I promise, no hanky panky. I'm here as a friend."

She laid her head on his shoulder "Thanks. I'm in short supply of friends right now."

"Hey. You got me and Cole." He glanced down at her. "And whether you believe it or not, you have Grayson. It's hard for me to admit it, but I'm currently having brain issues."

Tears threatened to spill and she choked them back. "Jericho, how do we fix this? It's such a huge secret he kept from me. For the first time in my life, I don't know what to do."

"Did he tell you the whole story?"

Kristin shook her head. "I didn't give him a chance. I shut down the minute he told me he betrayed my friends."

He gave her shoulders a gentle squeeze. "There were plenty of extenuating circumstances. He always takes full blame, but trust me, he didn't have choice.

Don't judge him until you hear him out. He beats himself up enough."

She glanced up at him, startled when she saw a genuine smile. "You think very highly of him, don't you?"

"We've been through a lot together. I'd trust him with my life, and have on more than a few occasions. I depend on him to have my back."

Suspicion filled her as she listened to him talk. "You know all about this, don't you?"

"I'm one of a very select few who know the whole story." He held his hand up. "No, I can't and won't tell you. You need to hear it from him."

"All of you have conspired to drive me crazy, haven't you? It's not enough I need to save Jack from a vengeful telepath, now I have this to deal with. Can't you give me any clue as to what happened?"

He shook his head. "It'll be better if the two of you deal with this together, otherwise it will always be the proverbial elephant in the room."

Kristin frowned. Of course, Jericho had to be right. She should've thought of that solution herself. To tell the truth, she should've given Grayson a chance to tell her what happened. The practical, logical Kristin would've listened reasonably to what he had to say. *I miss the old me more and more.*

"Are you two having a good time?"

Grayson stood in front of them, a dark look on his face. If she'd been the nervous type, Kristin would've shrunk before the anger in his eyes. Her spine stiffened at his tone as she marched up to him. After what he'd told her, he had no right to be angry with her for seeking a little comfort from a mutual friend.

"Jericho just told me you weren't to blame for what happened and tried to convince me to give you a chance to explain. How dare you come at me like this? I'm the one who's angry at you. You committed an unforgiveable act. You're the guilty party here, not me."

She stalked into the house to check on Cole. What just happened? She'd decided to talk to him about the bombshell he'd dropped, when he'd walked up and accused her of doing something wrong. She got herself under control and knocked on the bedroom door.

She always knew emotions were more trouble than they were worth. She paused. Did she hear the echo of laughter in her mind?

****

"You want to tell me what's up with the attitude?" Jericho said.

Grayson stepped closer to him. "You want to tell me why you had your arm around her?"

"She looked like she wanted to cry. I tried to make you look like the wounded party so she'd give you another chance. You messed up my great plan, buddy."

Grabbing two fistfuls of Jericho's shirt, Grayson shoved him hard against the side of the car. "Don't let me catch your hands her again. Understand? If I do, I'll shoot you where you stand."

Jericho knocked Grayson's hands away and stepped closer to him. "You want to take a shot at me, go ahead. And you'd better make it count, because you know you won't get another chance. And one more thing, even though it's incredibly obvious."

"What?"

"This doesn't sound like you."

Grayson frowned and took a step back. Did he really threaten his friend? He and Jericho had been teammates for a long time. They'd had their share of women between them, but he'd never felt this blind rage before. "You may or may not be right. Stay away from Kristin and we'll be good."

"If she needs me, I won't ignore her. You need to back off." He grabbed Grayson's arm, trying to make him listen. "As soon as we take care of Vertigo, both of us should be back to normal."

He jerked his arm out of Jericho's grasp and stomped back to the house. A hard knot of uncertainty and guilt settled in his stomach. Jericho had to be right about this. He and Kristin had shared a special night. She gave herself to him completely, focusing all her attention on his needs and wants.

He had seen the light and the winged creature of his soul intertwine. It looked exactly like his mother had told him. He and Kristin had bonded on a deep, primal level. His heart kept dwelling on the fact Jericho was always near her. When she'd asked him to explain about the tattoo, he'd had to tell her. She deserved the truth.

But with that one statement, he'd destroyed what chance they may have had at a life together. Then, to make a bad situation worse, he had come out and threatened his friend. He glanced at the sky and wished his thoughts were as clear. He needed to fix this, and soon. Kristin deserved better from him. He stared at the ground. So did his friends.

****

The fog in Jack's brain thickened and brought a pounding migraine with it. He hadn't had one of those in years. When he accepted what Anita told him, the pain lessened. As soon as he tried to make sense of things, stabbing pain bored through his skull. He laid his arm across his face to block the light piercing his eyes.

"Jack, can you hear me?" Adam said.

He nodded.

"I know it hurts. I want to help you, but she's deep in your mind. Vertigo isn't only rewriting your memories. She's rewriting your brain."

Jack nodded again and wanted the man next to him to shut up. He needed quiet to try to make the headache go away. Maybe if he told Anita, she would give him some medicine to help with the pain.

The door banged hard against the wall as Vertigo stalked inside.

"Speak of the she-devil," Adam murmured.

"Anita," Jack called. "My head hurts so much. Can't you help me?"

"Just don't fight me," she crooned. "As soon as you do, the pain will stop on its own. I can sense you've tried and the pain lessened, didn't it?"

"Yes."

"Then, all you have to do is accept what I tell you. We're married and we're in love. You're no longer an ULTRA agent and now work for my boss. As soon as you're better, we'll take a long holiday."

"Back off, Vertigo," Adam said. "Leave him alone. If you continue to use your power on him, he'll be damaged beyond repair."

She turned to him. "You can now sense the changes in his mind? Excellent. Mr. Trust will be pleased to hear this. Eddie, take him to the other room.

It's been several days. It's time for another injection."

Jack watched Adam struggle as Eddie hauled him to the other room. "You won't hurt him, will you?"

She laughed. "Of course, I will. It's an unfortunate side effect of the serum. The good news is his power should increase again. Mr. Trust will be here soon to get him. He needs to be moved before he gets too powerful. Defiance in a strong telepath is not looked on favorably."

Jack watched her walk away. Who was Mr. Trust? The name sounded familiar. He swallowed hard. And why did it fill him with dread?

Chapter Nineteen

Cole ran for the bathroom and retched so hard, he just knew his stomach would follow every piece of food he'd ever eaten. When the dry heaves slowed, then ceased, he curled into a ball on the floor and pressed his forehead against the cool tiles. Sweat ran down his cheek and he shivered hard enough to rattle his teeth.

"I wish she'd stop injecting Adam," he muttered. "At this rate, she's going to wipe out every telepath on the east coast."

Jericho walked in, pulled him up, and helped him to bed. "It happened again, didn't it?"

"Yeah. With the second dose, he's getting stronger. This is as close to out of control as I've ever seen. If he can't get a handle on it, he'll burn out and take a lot of psionics with him, including me."

Someone knocked on the doorframe and Jericho turned. "Cole's not well," he told Kristin and Grayson. "He says Vertigo gave Adam another dose of the serum."

Kristin saw Cole stretched out on the bed, his arm over his eyes. "Already? Even Vertigo wouldn't be so reckless as to try to expand Adam's power so soon."

Cole lowered his arm and stared at them. "She would if she has a way to control him. She's got to be on some kind of timetable for her to have injected him so close to the first dose." He glanced at his friends.

"I'd bet every computer I own, Benedict Trust will be here within the next few days."

"Would he risk a public appearance?" Jericho asked. "I didn't think he's ever left his, I don't know, what would you call it? His sanctum?"

Grayson paced in the small room. "Adam and Jack are in more danger and have less time than we initially believed. If Trust is on his way here, we need to have some kind of a plan in place. We've got to rescue them before he arrives."

"What happens if we can't?" Kristin asked.

Jericho looked at each of them. "Then we'll never see them again. Jack will be disposed of and Adam will be a powerful weapon in Trust's arsenal."

"What arsenal?" she asked. "Do you have an idea of his plans?"

Jericho shook his head. "We don't have any concrete information. Word on the street is he's picked up some lesser known supers. Rumor says he can transfer their powers to himself. Adam might be part of his twisted equation. But like I said, it's all hearsay. The only hard fact we have is he wants to put together some kind of power base."

"I found their base of operations last night," Grayson said. "It's exactly like Tom told me. It's a high priced community out by the parkway. She's got to have at least twenty men, but there could be more. I don't know where they got their firepower, but I've never seen weapons like them before."

Cole sat up and massaged the back of his neck. "Trust has his own weapons designers. They probably came up with a lot of prototype guns to really hurt us."

Jericho handed him a wet washrag. "Like regular

guns don't hurt?"

Cole closed his eyes and held the cloth on the back of his neck. "Regular guns don't disintegrate you. I can almost guarantee you, whatever they have, probably will."

"Can this job get any worse?" Jericho asked. He pitched the used cloth into the bathroom and hit the sink dead center.

Grayson clapped him on the shoulder, giving him a conspiratorial look. "Sure it can. Remember Vegas last summer?"

Cole and Jericho both cringed. "You're right," Cole admitted. "So much worse."

Kristin looked at all three of them. "Do I even want to know?"

"No," they said in unison.

"What do we do now?" she asked. "We can't sit here all day. We've got to find them and get our people away from her."

"It'll be hard." Cole stood and walked to the window. "Anyone in this area could be one of her agents. If she decided to telepathically eavesdrop, we'd never know it."

"Cole, can you give us any more information about her or Benedict Trust?" Kristin said. "I know the memories are painful, but we need to know."

He stared at her for a moment. "I've given you everything relevant. I will tell you this. Don't show any mercy to either one of them. If you get a clean shot, take it. You won't get another."

Jericho glanced at each of them. "Then we try to get them out tonight. It's risky but it's the only chance we have. Trust will order the destruction of Jack and if

Adam is as powerful as we believe, we can't let Trust anywhere near him."

"It would be best if we go in around midnight," Kristin said. "Trained agents or not, everyone needs sleep. Hopefully, there won't be many guards on duty then."

"I don't know," Grayson murmured. "She's been one step ahead of us this whole time. It isn't unreasonable to think tonight will be any different."

"It's worth a try." Kristin looked at the others. "Do you guys have any thoughts?"

Cole and Jericho looked at each other and shrugged. "I say we go," Cole said. "I'm afraid of the power she's unleashed in Adam. One more injection and the backlash might fry my brain."

Grayson nodded. "It's settled. We'll go tonight at the time Kristin suggested. Maybe we'll catch a break."

****

Kristin and Grayson walked back to the kitchen. With the limited selection of food in the cabinets and refrigerator, she threw together a simple lunch. Every once and awhile, she glanced at Grayson. For now, he and Jericho acted normal, but she could almost touch the palpable tension between them. Could they work together to rescue their people or would Vertigo make their team implode? This whole situation had begun to spiral out of control.

After lunch, neither spoke as they went about what had become a normal routine. Kristin sat at her computer while Grayson called his contacts in the area. She remembered the passion of the previous night and all the little gestures from him. Those quick rare smiles, the solid determination, his defense of his friends, all made her want to be with him every second of the day and night. She had to make him talk to her. Not being able to stand the tense silence any longer, she stood.

"Tell me what happened in the past."

"I'll call you back," he said into the phone and ended the call. "What happened between me and Jack is none of your business. I told you the important part. There's nothing more to say."

"Jericho is under a different impression. I asked him and he told me to ask you. So I'm asking. What did you do?"

"Why do you always listen to Jericho?" When she stayed silent, he narrowed his eyes and stared at her. "Fine. I betrayed my field commander, my team, and my organization. Lives were lost and information ended up in the wrong hands. Are you happy now? Why won't you let this lie?"

"Why won't you tell me the truth? Frank told me the traitor on the team had been 'taken care of.' He didn't mention more than one person. It's been over a decade since this happened. Is there someone you still need to protect?"

"Me," he shouted. "I need to protect me. Don't you understand how hard this is to live with? Drop it, Kristin. I mean it."

"I can't. I need to know how to help you. Just tell me the truth. Don't shut me out."

"You can't help me. No one can."

He stormed out and her feet wouldn't move to follow him. His responses to her questions made her certain of one important point. He couldn't have betrayed Jack without outside influence. The true story of what happened would be known sooner or later. It had to be sooner, because secrets could and would tear a team apart.

Vertigo must have been behind Grayson's betrayal. She already surmised the telepath's role in their current round of uneasiness and mistrust. Grayson's temper exploded more often than not, Jericho had a strange obsession with her, and she questioned every thought and decision. Cole appeared to be the only one unaffected. Either his shields were stronger than he believed or Vertigo had planted him with this team. Somehow, she didn't think Cole would work with Vertigo anymore.

Jericho peeked around the doorframe. "Voices got pretty loud out here. Are you guys okay?"

"No. I demanded he tell me what happened between him and Jack. It didn't go too well."

He leaned against the counter and folded his arms as he crossed his ankles. "Shouldn't you be all scientific? Can't you use logic to con it out of him?"

"I've never used logic to con anyone in my life." She turned her back to hide her uncertainty. "Yes, I'm supposed to be the practical, logical, scientific person who never lets emotion cloud her judgement. Ever since I met him, I've started to make more emotionally based decisions. I don't even recognize myself anymore."

"I think a more emotional you is who you need to be. You guys are right together." He glanced at her and smiled. "As much as I want to push him out of the picture and try my chances with you, I won't. It's hard, but I know I'm being influenced." He stepped a little closer. "Grayson's my friend. I wouldn't move in on someone he cares for, no matter how much I want to."

She laid her hand on his arm. "You're a good guy, Jericho Black. You appear to be the glue holding everyone together."

He shrugged. "Maybe. I know how to take care of people who depend on me. Grayson and I have known each other for years. We're more than a team. We're friends."

"And then I came along."

"Nah. Vertigo came along. If she couldn't use you, she would've tried other ways to divide us. The fact we can still work together, and I mean all of us, isn't to be taken lightly." He jerked his thumb toward the door. "He'll be back when he cools off."

"I hope so." She hugged herself. "I didn't mean to upset him. I wanted him to get it out in the open so we could deal with it."

He headed for the refrigerator and glanced at her over his shoulder. "Did you reveal your secret?"

She shook her head. "How would he feel if he knew the truth about me?"

"Hey, you're as human as the rest of us."

She looked up sharply. He'd figured out her past? "How do you know about me?"

Jericho laughed. "I have a computer psionic in the other room. How could I not know? So what if you're an experiment? You weren't mutated from a banana, were you? No. You came from human DNA. You're a person." The grin faded and he stood in front of her. "Next time, don't ask him about what he went through. Tell him about you."

"Thanks for the advice."

His smirk appeared as he grabbed a bottle of water for Cole. "You're welcome. Remember, champagne and orange juice."

What on earth did he mean? More than ever, she wanted advice from someone who had been through the same situation. Of all the emotions jumbled up inside her, the confusion eating at her confidence was the worst. Her direction in life had always been crystal clear. Even with her suspicions about being telepathically influenced, the constant befuddlement irritated her.

The strong emotions Grayson stirred in her overtook her logic and sensible side. Unlike her friends, she didn't find love to be enjoyable. She needed distance between the two of them to sort out how she felt. If she did, she would put an end to any more nights like the one they'd shared. Was she sure she wanted to give up the way he made her body pulse with life and power? She sighed. She knew the answer should be yes, but her other parts screamed no.

Maybe she shouldn't have brushed off all those dates over the past few years. At the time, they didn't seem important. She'd had training exercises to plan, missions to be plotted out to avoid injury to her team, as well as her research and speaking engagements. Recently, every other day felt like another teammate walked down the aisle, so then there were weddings to plan. Love and romance couldn't be squeezed into her life right now.

The silent computer screen beckoned. She started her search for information again. If she wanted to be with Grayson, she needed to listen to what he had to say about the past and not judge him. She'd also better learn how to make time for the man who had begun to push science to the background in her life.

Chapter Twenty

Adam hit the floor hard. The blood leaking from his nose and ears showed Jack the severity of his injuries. The screams he'd heard earlier had come from the psionic currently curled up on the floor. Adam clutched his head and Jack wanted to tell him it would be okay, but before he got the words out, a sharp pain lanced through his skull.

He recognized the pain now as his will combating Vertigo's influence. As much as he wanted to end her control of his mind, he couldn't. He thought of his wife, waiting for him at home and grimaced as the pain increased. His eyes drifted shut and he laid his head back. All he had to do was accept Anita for what she claimed to be. The pain would lessen and he'd feel a little better. If he couldn't work around the pain, she'd win.

He turned to Adam. "Are you all right?"

"No. This is so much worse than the last time," Adam whispered. "I can sense minds from all over the country."

Jack knew Adam now had the strongest ability he'd ever heard of. Anita may have opened a literal can of whoop ass. "What did she inject you with?"

"I don't know, but it hurts." He looked over at Jack, as a tear dripped on the floor. "I felt psionics nearby. My power killed them. They were too young, too inexperienced to handle the sudden surge. How do I live with this? How do I reconcile myself to the knowledge I took innocent lives?"

Jack had been consumed by the same sense of loss and guilt. When he'd found the evidence implicating his superiors at ULTRA all those years ago, forces were set in motion, and a lot of his team lost their lives. Frank told him it wasn't his fault, but he'd carried the guilt all the same. His stubbornness, his unwillingness to look the other way resulted in too many deaths. Yes, he knew the guilt of having innocent blood on his hands.

"It isn't your fault. Vertigo killed those people, not you. She'll use what you're feeling to make you more amenable to her will. You have to fight her, Adam. You've got to get control of what she opened up, before this new power damages you. Then, we can beat her."

"I'm glad you're confident about this. It hurts and the worse the pain gets, the more I can't control these stronger abilities."

Vertigo walked in, shutting down their conversation. "Your power is off the charts, Adam. I've called Mr. Trust with the results and he's most pleased. He'll be here in two days to take you back to the lab, where you should've been all this time."

"Go to hell."

She stroked his cheek. "My poor Adam. You have no idea how special you are, do you?"

"I don't want to be special. I want my powers to be back to normal."

She stood and gave an unladylike snort. "How dull. You were so ordinary when I brought you back to me. Why would you want to be less than you are?"

"Because ordinary makes me happy."

"Leave him alone, Anita," Jack shouted. "If you keep up these insane experiments, you'll kill him. Let him go."

She turned, a look of complete indifference in her eyes. "All this concern for someone you've just met. You should've treated me with as much courtesy. After his interference to boost your defiance, I may kill him yet. We have work to do to clean out his influence. You do love me, Jack. You don't know how much yet." She turned to Anderson. "Bring him."

Eddie dragged Jack to the room where Vertigo tortured Adam. Blood droplets marred the light hardwood and he stepped over them. To tread on the blood, he felt, would be an insult to Adam. Vertigo's need for revenge made her nastier than most of the criminals he'd fought over the years, and he'd faced and taken down some of the worst. He couldn't have ever loved someone who hurt people and took pleasure in it.

Again, pain stabbed his skull and he bent over as he grabbed his head. A light touch soothed him and the headache receded as he listened to the calm, quiet tones of her voice. He didn't love Vertigo, did he? No. He loved Anita. He gazed up at her, thrilled when she smiled at him.

"Remember," she whispered in his ear.

Her breath tickled his cheek as he tried to call the memories of their time together to the front of his mind. Images formed in the fog which clouded his mind. He remembered. He relived their wedding night and all the nights since. She'd taken him to heights of passion like no other woman had before.

How could he have ever doubted her? Every word she'd spoken had to be the truth. The memories were all there, like she said. He took her hand and stood, the pain gone as he accepted what she'd said.

"I know who I am," he said. "I know who you are. I can remember our past. I'm so sorry it took me so long to see the truth."

She laid her hands on his chest as she gazed up at him. "I knew it would all come back to you."

He accepted the light, feathery kiss she gave him and watched as a slow smile came over her face. She said they were in love, so they must be. Or were they? As she smoothed his hair back, he banished all doubts. They would be together forever.

A quiet voice echoing in his mind reminded him about Vertigo's lies and the fact she'd killed people. Doubt clouded him for a moment and he wondered who said it. It vanished in seconds and he took his place at Vertigo's side.

****

Kristin glanced at the clock and wondered where Grayson could have gone. It had been a couple of hours since he stormed out. Should she call Frank? They hadn't spoken for several days. She picked up her phone, the small device cold in her hand. Would she get any more information from him? She sighed. Probably not.

A key turned in the lock and she jumped to her feet. Grayson had returned. Jericho walked in and threw his keys on the kitchen counter. She tried not to let the disappointment show on her face as she watched him take some items out of the plastic bags

"Have you seen Grayson?" she asked while he

placed a few items in the refrigerator.

"I thought he would've come back by now." He walked over to the couch and sat. "He hasn't called?"

"No. I'm concerned he might try to execute his own plan. Where do you think he could have gone?"

"Anywhere. He knows this area too well. Have you asked Cole to track him?"

"Not yet. When I last checked on him, he was asleep."

"Let's go see if he's awake yet."

He opened the bedroom door. Cole stared at his laptop, his fingers doing their quick, staccato dance on the keyboard. He looked paler than usual and had a deep crease between his brows. Every so often he'd stop and rub his side where he'd been shot.

The wound had closed, the skin almost completely mended. It must be a reflex action. "Cole," she said quietly, "are you all right?"

"I don't know. This whole situation is a complete disaster. Agents could be anywhere and I felt another strong surge in Adam's power. It killed a lot of young psionics." His fingers stopped their movement and he looked up at her. "The possibility Jack won't be himself when we find him is becoming more and more real."

Kristin tried to pull more air into her constricted lungs. "What do you mean?"

"I'm better with electronic devices and computers, but Vertigo's power is strong enough for me to sense psychic ripples. She's begun to rewrite Jack's memories. Soon, he won't remember his true past. He'll only know the memories she's planted. If we don't find him, we won't have anyone to rescue."

Kristin sank down on the edge of the bed. "We

need Grayson. Can you track him?"

"Yeah. If he's got his phone with him and it's on. It's a little harder if he's not using it, but not impossible." He picked up his phone. "I've discovered all phones share the same subtle, I guess you'd call it, frequency. I can use my phone to telepathically connect to his phone."

"Why don't you call him?"

Cole gave her a lopsided grin. "I can't take the chance he might be in a risky situation. A phone is too bright and makes too much noise, even on vibrate. I don't want him to have to talk to me if he can't."

"Very sensible and completely logical." She looked down at the floor. "I usually come up with those conclusions myself."

He held his hand up. "I get it. You don't have to explain."

Jericho turned to go to the living room. "I'm going to check around town. He might have just gone for a walk. You guys stay here and see what you can find."

Cole gripped his phone. "I'll see what I can do. Good luck."

Kristin wiped her clammy palms on her pants. The front door closed with a little more force than usual and she flinched. "I think they both need a little more than luck."

****

The sky turned lavender as the sun set behind the tall trees. Grayson walked around and took a deep breath while the cool air calmed him down. Why couldn't she let the whole situation stay buried? He'd confessed his shame. She'd rejected him. What more did she want? He didn't want to tell her the whole sordid story. Why couldn't she understand he didn't want to talk about it?

He yanked off his shirt and jammed into his waistband. His wings stretched out and he flew toward where they thought Vertigo might be holed up. When he arrived, he landed quietly. He glanced at the lights of nearby houses and hurried by to the woods beyond. The breeze ruffled his hair and he could almost feel Kristin's light touch. He never thought he'd find someone who'd accept him, wings and all. She wanted him for himself. At least she did until his shame became known.

There wouldn't be anything more than what they'd already shared. After they rescued their people, she would go back to her home in New York and he'd be here in South Jersey. Would she stay? He stopped. Would he follow her? More importantly, did he want too? Even more important, could he let her go? He sat on a tree stump and let his thoughts drift as he stared at the ground.

"So, here you are," Jericho said. "You must be preoccupied. I can never sneak up on you and this time, I wasn't even trying."

Grayson slowly lifted his gaze to his friend. "How'd you find me?"

"Cole. He tracked your phone."

"Of course. I should've known. Why aren't you with Kristin?"

Jericho walked over and glared at him. "Why would I be with her? You know I wouldn't make a play for her if she's with you." He paused and the silence grew heavy. "You want to talk to me?"

"I'm not sure what you want me to say."

"How about why you ran off and didn't come back?" Jericho folded his arms. "If we want to try a rescue tonight, we need to plan. You out here sulking by yourself doesn't help. Why can't you tell her what happened?"

Grayson stood and walked a few steps away. "I don't want to. It's bad enough I've lived with this for more than ten years. Why would I want to rehash it to someone I barely know?"

"You know her well enough to sleep with her."

In the blink of an eye, Grayson had taken two steps and connected a solid punch to Jericho's jaw, knocking him to the ground. Jericho pushed himself to a sitting position as Grayson stood over him, his hands curled into fists. He knew his friend wanted Kristin, but he refused to stand there and be insulted by this obnoxious upstart on the ground.

"You want more? Get up. We'll finish this right here, right now. I'm real sick of you, Jericho. You think because you're the boss's favorite you have some kind of elite power over everyone." He leaned close. "You don't. Why don't all of you go on this mission without me? It's obvious you don't want me here."

Jericho jumped to his feet. "What the hell are you talking about? Do you even hear yourself?"

When Grayson swung again, Jericho blocked and caught his arm. He twisted it around his back and held on tight. "You need to get a grip on yourself. Think, man. This isn't you. Come back with me. Kristin is worried about you."

Grayson rammed his elbow back, catching Jericho in the side of the head. When his grip loosened, Grayson pulled away. "The only thing she's worried about is me getting in the way of the two of you. Back off. If I want to come back, I will."

He threw his shirt at Jericho, stretched his wings, and exploded off the ground. Taking off so close to a busy neighborhood carried a certain risk, but he didn't care. He wanted to be as far away from Jericho as he could get. Running away appeared to be his best power.

Chapter Twenty-One

Kristin almost ran to the front door when Jericho came in. Her question about Grayson died on her lips. Jericho had a noticeable lump which hadn't been there when he left. The skin around it already showed the colors of an ugly bruise. Dirt and dust covered his clothes. Had the two men been attacked? Had Grayson been hurt or captured? If Jericho said the word, she'd be out the door.

"Where's Grayson?"

Jericho shook his head. "I don't know. He took off." He tossed Grayson's shirt to her. "And he did it before the sun fully set. He's always been temperamental, but now he's just unreasonable."

Her knuckles turned white as her grip tightened on the soft material. Once more, the python of fear coiled tightly around her heart as it constricted her lungs. "This confirms it must be Vertigo's influence. We have to break her hold on him somehow."

"Agreed. If you know how, clue me in. I didn't even realize she'd taken up residence in my head until you pointed it out to me." He shrugged. "I still have this desire for you, but it's not as bad as before. When it kicks up, I recognize it now as Vertigo's hand scratching my brain."

"You'll get better with practice. Grayson wouldn't act this way if all he felt was a casual attachment to me." Kristin forced herself to relax and analyze the situation. "The deeper the emotion, the stronger the hold she'll have on him. It's a Catch-22. His attraction to me and mine to him will help him fight her telepathic grip, but it also makes us more vulnerable."

"Don't you ever have good news for me?" Jericho said.

She shook her head. "Not until this is over. I've worked with my team telepath to understand the intricacies of mind to mind contact. I believe Vertigo might be easier to surprise now. Yes, she's powerful, but even a powerful telepath can be stretched too thin."

"Kristin's right." Cole limped out of his room to join them. "Right now, Vertigo's got her rewrite on Jack, the experimentation with Adam, and now she's decided to play mind games with you, and make Grayson crazy."

"Since Benedict Trust will be here soon, she needs to be prepared for his visit," Jericho added. He looked toward the window. "I wish Grayson would come back. We need him."

"I know you do," said a quiet voice in the doorway.

Kristin whirled around and she stared as he filled the doorframe. She rushed into his arms and squeezed him tight, then punched his shoulder. "You worried the heck out of me. I thought you'd been hurt or captured. Where were you?"

"I needed some time to think." His wings disappeared into his back and she handed him his shirt. He pulled it on and held his hand out to Jericho. "I'm sorry. I couldn't control myself. I can't believe how I've acted to you guys." He glanced over at Cole. "Sorry I'm so suspicious of your past association with

Vertigo."

Cole shrugged and Kristin looked at all three men. She hoped they could get through this and the future fight which loomed over them.

Jericho shook the offered hand firmly. "We've been through worse. We'll get through this, too."

"This is real nice, you know, hearts and flowers and all, but we need a plan for tonight," Cole said.

"True. There's a lot more of them than us," Grayson said. He kept his arm around Kristin, and she moved closer to his side.

"Can you fly close enough to see how far out the perimeter guards go? We may be able to take some of them out and then work our way in," Kristin said. She let her arm go around his waist and tucked her fingers into his back pocket. "We need to even the odds or we don't stand a chance."

"Point taken," Grayson said. "Cole, can you do your psionic computer distraction like we've done before?"

"You have to ask? Of course I can. It'll create a diversion long enough for us to get closer to the house to find Adam and Jack." He turned to his computer for a moment. "I don't know what shape the two of them will be in to travel. If they can't walk under their own power, it will make our job a lot harder."

"You're right," Kristin said. "I'm stronger than people realize, but Jack is heavy because of his cybernetic systems. We also have to consider how far Vertigo's gotten into his mind. If she's in deep, he may not want to leave. And if she's used a larger dose of her serum than we realize, Adam may be physically incapable to leave."

"We have to try," Cole said. "If you think it's bad now, Trust will make the whole situation worse. The increased security and the fact she's dosed Adam twice tells us he'll be here sooner rather than later."

"If we fail in this attempt, the next one will be harder." Grayson looked at the group. "If she doesn't decide to move to another location."

Kristin felt him grow tense under her arm. As she stood close to him, the small tremors she felt in his body made her worry more. "Do you think we should put off the raid?"

"No. I agree with Cole. We have to try tonight. We may never get another opportunity and you never know. We might get lucky."

Jericho grinned. "Or we might get Vegas-ed."

Kristin watched as they all flinched in unison. "When this is over, I want the story of what happened in Vegas."

"Sorry," Grayson said. "We made a pact to never reveal the shame of the Vegas mission."

"It couldn't have been that bad."

The three men looked at each other. "Yeah," Grayson said. "It could."

Sensing their need to change the subject, she gave Grayson a final squeeze. "We should get dinner soon. We need to be prepared for tonight."

"Grayson, can you whip up a quick meal? You know you're the best cook among us," Cole said. "I'll need to get my link established to my laptop before we leave. I can then psychically tap into the internet linked to their armor systems and confuse them for a few minutes so we can get in."

"Yeah, I can scrounge up a meal for us," Grayson

said. "Your web distraction is our ace in the hole. I don't think they'll be prepared for an electronic attack."

"We should leave for Vertigo's location at around eleven thirty. You should have enough time to scope the landscape before we go in," Jericho said.

Kristin followed Grayson to the kitchen. Fear had played havoc with her imagination when he hadn't returned. Now, she feared if she let him go, he'd vanish like a dream. She glanced at him over her shoulder to make sure he was still there.

Pots and pans clanged on the stove, drawing her out of her thoughts. She moved to help, needing to be as close to him as possible. The logical side of her brain called her a fool. The man stood right there at the counter. The knife clicked as he cut up vegetables.

She blamed the unfamiliar emotions churning inside her heart. She wasn't very fond of this whole love thing. She stopped. Did she love him? She hadn't known him very long, but yes. She could honestly tell herself she was falling in love with him. Maybe it was time to put more stock into the tales of soulmates her friends badgered her about.

"I don't want you to ever scare me like that again," she said. "How could you take off and then you hit Jericho? The only reason I'm not as mad at you is because I know Vertigo has exerted her influence over your mind."

He seasoned some pork chops, then shoved the pan in the oven and set the temperature. "You're right. I've never had to battle someone telepathically. It's hard to tell the difference between her planted suggestions and my own mind."

She laid her hand on his arm. "I know. It takes

years of practice to build psychic shields. I've been fortunate because my team telepath taught me how to make my shields stronger."

He pulled her into his arms. "And how do you make your shields stronger?"

"It helps to have a solid, emotional foundation on which to draw strength."

"Like this?" he whispered, his lips so close, his breath tickled hers.

As he lightly kissed her, he dissolved her fear and stress with the contact she craved. She'd always claimed she didn't need anyone and wanted her own personal space. How did this man she'd known for less than a week, worm his way so solidly into her heart? You know he's your soulmate, a small voice inside her taunted.

He broke the kiss and smiled at her. "We only have an hour. If we keep this up, we won't have dinner."

She stepped away from him. "I know, but when this is over, we'll have a lot to catch up on."

His mouth quirked up in a half smile. "I look forward to it."

****

As Adam's abilities grew more powerful, they became harder to control. If he didn't get a handle on it, neither he nor Jack would make it out of there. He'd almost had it when Vertigo had given him the second injection. Now, he'd been put right back where he started. He closed his eyes and focused on his abilities. Maybe not.

Yes, his mind had been expanded to the point he thought his brain would begin to leak out of his ears. And yes, all the extra minds he heard scared him, but he worked hard to reign it in and the fear had begun to lose control. He allowed himself a small smile. It would be bad for Jack, but if Vertigo kept most of her attention on him, he might be able to get some practice in before she figured out his plan.

The door to the other room opened. "Speak of the psycho bitch," he mumbled.

He frowned as he watched Jack's gaze follow her with total adoration. She'd almost completed the rewrite in his mind. She let Jack lie on the bed she'd had brought in and secured him there.

"It's only for a little while longer. It's for your safety in case those false memories return," she said.

Adam watched as Jack let her do what she wanted. He no longer defied Vertigo or fought her control. She'd ruined a good man and, because of her influence in his mind, he didn't care. He let his control go so she wouldn't detect the little he'd gained. He glared at her as she walked over to him and stood there to watch him.

"And how's my favorite experiment?"

He grinned. "Not bad. I just picture what you'd look like if your head exploded and it helps me sleep at night."

Rage flashed in her eyes before she cleared her throat and smoothed down her business suit. "I'm sure Mr. Trust will want to be rid of you. You can't control the power I've given you. You're more useless now than you were before."

"As long I can make you look bad, I don't care what happens."

Vertigo turned on her heel and stomped away. The door slammed and Adam's grin got bigger. Who knew you could surprise a telepath with a few jabs at her competence? Her over-confidence had grown to the point it pushed her ego out the door. Time to throw a huge monkey wrench in the works. He glanced at Jack. He'd start with creating a psychic back door into Jack's mind.

Adam looked out the window and watched the dusky twilight darken the sky. The time to make the attempt would be when Vertigo and Anderson turned in for the night. He needed better control to reduce the risk. Since they were doomed anyway, he'd take any chance, no matter how small, rather than no chance at all.

Chapter Twenty-Two

Kristin rubbed the back of her neck. A sharp ache started and had begun to grow. Maybe if she laid down for a little bit, it would go away. Even the pillow felt too hard to get comfortable. She turned her head from side to side and the pain flared for a second before it settled back to a dull throb. Her dinner sat like lead in her stomach. Even the thought of food made her stomach queasy.

Grayson followed her into the bedroom. "What's wrong?" He frowned as she laid her head on the pillow and groaned.

"I have a terrible headache. It came out of nowhere." She glanced up at him. "Are you all right?"

"I'm fine." Tablets clicked in a plastic bottle when he shook some into his hand. "Try these. They usually work pretty well for me."

Popping two tablets in her mouth, she took the glass of water he offered. "Thanks," she murmured. "If this keeps up, I don't think I'll be able to go with you on the rescue mission tonight."

He glanced at the clock. "We still have a couple of hours. Get some rest. I'll let Jericho know you're not well. Luckily, we always have a backup plan ready."

"I guess you guys are like boy scouts. Only taller and with non-merit badge skills."

"Interesting way of putting it. I'll back in a few

minutes."

She rubbed her head and prayed the headache pills would kick in soon. She usually wasn't prone to headaches of any kind. Could she be affected by Adam's power surge? Not likely. She had no psionic abilities, so she didn't think she'd be caught in the backlash.

What if Vertigo had activated a device of some sort to make non-psionics feel the telepathic burst? A thought struck her and she opened her eyes. What if this hadn't come from Adam or some diabolical device? When Jack had married into their team, he'd been included in the telepathic rapport. If Vertigo had tampered with Jack's mind, would she pick up a resonance of it? Could she pick it up? Did her teammates feel it too?

As these thoughts circled around, her head pounded worse than before. She prayed for Grayson to return soon.

****

Grayson walked into the living room the same time as Jericho, who looked more than worried as he walked out of Cole's room. His tough as nails friend looked afraid.

"Is there a problem?" Grayson said.

Jericho jerked his thumb toward the open door. "It's Cole. He got hit out of the blue by a migraine. I know he gets them sometimes, but not like this. It dropped him to his knees."

Grayson stepped closer and lowered his voice. "Kristin's down with one too. Is this an attack from Vertigo?"

"No. We know she's obsessed with her plan and

Cole thinks Adam is trying to stop her. But he hasn't been trained to handle this much power. The more his power bleeds out, the more people he affects."

Grayson frowned as he followed Jericho back into Cole's room. "But why is Kristin affected? She's not psionic."

Cole rolled his head back and forth. "I don't know. Even if we can't go, you guys have to try. Get our people back." He smiled. "And put a bullet in Vertigo."

"We'll do what we can," Jericho told him. He glanced at Grayson. "You ready to do this?"

Grayson glanced at the small alarm clock. "It's not even eleven yet. You sure you want to go this early?"

"We got to go sometime." The smirk came back. "We might even get back in time to see the late movie on cable."

He left Jericho to get ready and went back to Kristin. The fact she allowed him to not only hold her, but pick up where they left off said a lot about her. If they lived through this job, he'd come clean about his betrayal. Maybe then she'd tell him her secret about not being human.

When he held her in his arms, when he made love to her, she had more humanity than him. He branded himself a traitor, the lowest of the low. No matter what she said, it couldn't be worse than what he'd done. He opened the door and she'd turned on her side.

"How do you feel? Any better?"

"No. This is awful. How do normal people stand it?" She pressed her palms to her head. "I want to cry or scream. I just want to make the pain stop."

"Believe it or not, I get it. Migraines are nasty." He paused. "Cole is laid up with one too. He thinks it might be Adam's power."

"I thought that at first. I'm not psionic so I don't believe it would affect me like it does him. However, I am connected by a psychic rapport to Jack. My whole team is. If Vertigo has exerted a lot of power in his mind, this could just be backlash through the link."

Grayson rubbed his chin. "It's possible. Jericho and I still want to see if we can save Jack and Adam. Maybe if we get them away, we can get everyone back to normal."

"Be careful. You know the lengths Vertigo is willing to go. Don't let her into your head. Your battleground is not on the psychic plane."

He kissed her forehead. "We'll be fine." Someone knocked on the door. "Time for us to leave. We'll be back soon."

He glanced at Jericho and wondered if they could be trusted to work together. Because of Vertigo's influence, he'd hit and threatened his friend. Without the others to keep them sane, could they be successful? He sincerely hoped so. Otherwise, they were doomed before they even pulled out of the driveway.

He and Jericho strode across the lawn and climbed into Jericho's SUV. At the end of the driveway, Grayson caught a glimpse of someone at the edge of the trees talking on a cell phone.

"Did you see him?"

Jericho nodded. "Yep. Would it be too obvious to say he's probably one of Vertigo's agents?"

"Yes, it would. Could they have waited for us to leave so they could ambush the others? Should abort?"

"No. If they wanted to ambush us, they would've

hit the house before we left." Jericho glanced in the rearview mirror. "No, whenever we decided to do this, they'd always have someone who can warn them."

"Kristin and Cole should be all right, even laid up." Grayson gave him a small smile. "It's the whole damned if we do, damned if we don't Vegas scenario all over again."

Jericho hit the gas and they flew down the narrow roads. "We all agreed not to mention Vegas. Ever. Again. In our lives."

"Sorry."

The area blurred by as Jericho drove faster than the speed limit. Grayson never worried about Jericho being stopped. Jericho had the skills to drive any vehicle at any speed and knew too many cops to worry about tickets. He wasn't sure what hold his friend had over almost every officer in south Jersey, but he knew he didn't want to know.

Grayson recognized the area as they approached. "We're almost there," he said. "Find a place to pull over. I want to do a quick aerial check before we go in."

Jericho stopped short of a dirt road worn smooth by heavy equipment trucks before Vertigo took over the area. He glanced at Grayson, who nodded and stepped out of the SUV. He tossed his shirt on the seat before he spread his wings and took to the sky. He stayed low to the tops of the trees, knowing he'd be harder to spot against the leafy canopy.

He got closer to the house where he'd spotted the agents and stood on the thick branch he'd been on earlier. An eerie quiet settled over the property. Grayson stood close to the trunk and stared at the house. Nothing. No lights, no people, no sounds.

This couldn't be right. He knew he had the right location. Even with the head start the agent they spotted would've given the troops, so many men couldn't have had time to pack up and leave quickly. Not with two prisoners to watch. He made his way to the back of the house and took care to stay in the trees and use the shadows.

At the back door, he still saw no signs of life. He left the cover of the thick foliage and rode on a summoned breeze to the house. A flat roof covered the back porch and two windows faced him. He crouched and ran to the window on his right. At any moment, he expected to feel a bullet pierce his back.

His unease increased when the window he tested slid up with no resistance. If Vertigo and her prisoners were here, why would she leave a window open? His nerves jumped as silence drifted out to him. He stared at the window, then glanced over his shoulder. Should he go in or report back to Jericho? If he went in, he had a better than average chance of not coming out.

He hesitated for a second more before he shoved the window open and stepped inside. They needed to know the layout so he had to take the chance. If Kristin and Cole were with them, he wouldn't have been this desperate. Cole could've "seen" inside by psychically tapping into the security system. Since half their team was down, he needed to get the information they lacked.

He opened to door to the hallway and headed for the staircase. When he turned the corner, a glow came from the first floor. He breathed a quiet sigh of relief. Of course, Vertigo would've had the windows covered. Grayson had found this place originally by the amount of guards outside with flashlights.

Since they were still here, where were the guards and the small army she amassed? If they were all inside, he would've heard some noise by now. Eyeing the stairs, he started down. One way to find out, he thought, and descended lightly. He stopped where the short wall ended, and his chest grew tight when a familiar voice reached him.

"All right, Vertigo," Jericho said. "I did what you asked. Now give me back my friend."

"I don't see Grayson Styles with you," she replied. "Would you care to divulge his location?"

"How should I know? He took off with those crazy ass wings of his. He wanted to scout the area for your men. Why don't you send out some of those rent-a-cops to go find him?"

Grayson could almost hear the smile in her voice. "I don't think a search for him will be necessary. He's on the stairs." A shadow appeared on the floor at the bottom of the steps. "Come out, Mr. Styles. I know you're here. I knew it when you lurked about in trees."

Grayson descended the rest of the way and faced the woman they'd wanted to find. "What did you do to Jericho?"

He frowned when she walked over to his friend and draped her arm around his shoulders. "I had no hand in this. He came to me with this wonderful idea to exchange you for Adam. I immediately accepted his offer."

He looked at Jericho and his friend shrugged. "I had to or she would kill Adam."

"What about Jack?"

He tensed when Jericho took two steps in his

direction. "Jack is the one who got him and us into this mess. Vertigo's too powerful for us to take down. I decided to cut my losses." He smiled at her. "Besides, have you looked at her? She has every quality I want in a woman. Beauty, intelligence, and power she's not afraid to use."

"She's gotten in your head, Jericho. This isn't you."

Grayson watched as his friend frowned. "No, she hasn't. We made…"

Vertigo frowned. "Say it, Jericho Black. Tell him what the new plan is."

"The…new plan?"

Grayson knew then Vertigo had Jericho under her control. It explained why all the guards weren't to be found. She must have sent them somewhere else so she could use her manipulation on his friend. They had to get out of there and it left him with one option.

"Don't even think about it," she snarled. "I know your plans before you even conceive of them."

"I know." He whipped out the handgun he'd brought and fired five shots at her. They all pinged off the hastily erected telekinetic shield she'd thrown up. Jericho lunged at him and knocked him to the floor. Grayson twisted around, pushed to his feet, and pulled his friend with him.

He blocked the straight on punch from Jericho, grateful he knew his friend's fighting style. Asking silently for forgiveness, he slammed his fist into Jericho's jaw, knocking him out. He snatched his gun off the floor, and fired two more quick shots at Vertigo as she raised her shields again. He threw his friend over his shoulder, before he slammed into her shield and knocked her over. The front door banged open from the force of his kick. Outside, the tree line and the safety of its shadows beckoned.

Vertigo raged behind him as he adjusted Jericho to carry him in his arms. He needed his wings free. Using a strong wind gust to boost him off the ground, he flew straight for their SUV. He feared carrying Jericho all the way back to Cole's would draw too much attention. They needed the car. He chanced it wouldn't be guarded or worse yet, gone. He couldn't fight and protect Jericho at the same time.

The SUV sat right where they parked it, and Grayson couldn't stop the sigh of relief which escaped him. Kristin correctly predicted the telepath's over-confidence. He propped Jericho up next to the SUV and fished around in his friend's pocket for the keys. Grayson laid him across the backseat and Jericho groaned.

As he started the car, he shook his head. How did it all go so bad so fast? One minute, they had their plan and things were going their way. The next, the whole job had gone straight to hell and didn't even bother with the handbasket. He spared a glance to his friend. What would happen when he came to? Would Jericho attack him or be back to normal?

"God, I hate that woman more and more," he grumbled as he sped back to Cole's house.

Chapter Twenty-Three

Jericho groaned from the backseat. "What happened? My brain feels like pudding and why does my face hurt?" He sat up and glared at Grayson. "You hit me? Again?"

Grayson parked next to Kristin's car and shut the SUV off. "Vertigo had a deep hold on you. I knocked you out so you wouldn't let her convince you to shoot me or something else equally bad."

Jericho staggered out of the SUV and leaned on Grayson for support. "I don't think you needed to hit me hard enough to rearrange my teeth."

Grayson fought the rare urge to grin. "I had to make sure."

"Why do I get the feeling you enjoyed it a little too much?" Jericho leaned on the hood, all joking gone from his voice. "I could hear everything I said. It all sounded so normal, but I knew I wouldn't say or do anything like what she wanted."

The two of them walked up to the house and sat on the porch. "How did she get you? What happened?" Grayson asked.

"I sat there and waited for you to come back and tell me what we were up against. All of a sudden, I felt this weird compulsion to go to the house. When I saw her, I knew exactly what she wanted me to say. It felt like she sapped my will to fight her."

"We're way out of our depth here. We don't fight telepaths. Neither one of us have those abilities."

Jericho glanced at him. "I know. I can't figure why the boss wanted us on this assignment. We're not supers. Well, you might be with those wings and the control you have over air, but we've never had to go up against someone this powerful without the right kind of support."

"You always say, the boss has her reasons. I just wish I knew what they are for this disaster of a job."

Jericho got to his feet and waited for Grayson. "Let's go check on Cole and Kristin."

Grayson stopped at the spare bedroom while Jericho headed for Cole's room. He opened the door and walked over to Kristin. Her chest rose and fell as she slept, her face looked relaxed. After he took off his clothes, he sat on the side of the bed and she stirred.

"How did it go?" she asked, her voice thick with sleep.

"It didn't. How do you feel?"

She yawned. "The headache went away not long after you left. I hope Cole's better too. Tell me what happened."

He tucked the covers around her. "Tomorrow. Get some rest. Whatever we have to say can wait until then."

"Okay." She yawned as sleep claimed her again.

Grayson draped his arm across her waist. When she found out how badly they were screwed to rescue their people, she wouldn't take it well. Would she fly off the handle as her emotions would get the better of her, or would she take the team leader, practical, scientific approach?

As his eyes drifted shut, he desperately hoped it would be the latter.

****

Jericho leaned against the door, his head down as his grip tightened on the beer bottle in his hand. After what Grayson said, he couldn't stop the shakes racking his body. Being mind-controlled was a new and extremely crappy experience. Something stronger than beer would calm his nerves. He didn't want the team know how badly Vertigo had scared him.

They still had to rescue their friends. What would happen when they went back? Would Vertigo control him again? Had she taken up permanent residence in his thoughts? He'd never wanted to run from a job, but he wanted to head to the nice, tropical island Cole mentioned before.

"What's wrong, buddy?" Cole said from his bed.

Jericho swallowed some of the beer, but it didn't help. "We failed."

"Follow me." He got up and padded to the door. "I think I have something that can help."

Jericho walked behind him to the kitchen and watched his friend grab two short, square glasses from the cabinet and a bottle off the counter. He sagged down on the couch and Cole pressed the glass into his hand. The smell of whiskey burned his nostrils as the glass filled with dark, amber liquid. Cole set the bottle down with a deep thud in front of him on the coffee table.

"How'd you know?"

Cole grinned and flipped on the lamp. "We've been friends for too many years. You looked like you've seen every ghost and monster in New Jersey. And I've had this stashed in here for a couple of months now." He sat, staring at the glass in his hand. "For when my nightmares get bad. Tell me what happened."

Jericho tossed back the whiskey and the fiery liquid soothed him almost instantly. "Vertigo took me over. She had absolute control over my mind. I couldn't fight her. She made so much sense."

"What did she want you to do?"

Jericho hung his head. "She wanted me to hand over all of you to her." He looked up. "I would've done it."

Cole sat quiet for a minute, then nodded. "What stopped you?"

"Grayson. He laid me out with one punch and got me out of there."

"He did a good job matching the new bruise to the old one he gave you," Cole chuckled. He refilled Jericho's glass and poured another one for himself. "You've never been telepathically controlled before, have you?"

"No." He shuddered. "It's like an invisible enemy you know you can't fight and if you do, you sure as hell won't win."

Cole raised his glass in a salute. "And it's why Adam doesn't want his power expanded. He hates to be in someone else's mind. To know all their secrets, to be them, it unnerves him."

"Well, it sure as hell wasn't a picnic for me." Jericho returned the salute. "You look better. Headache gone?"

"Yeah, a couple of hours ago. It's been almost a year since I've had one that bad. We need to wrap this up sooner rather than later. If we don't, our survival chances will drop like a stone. For Adam, for Jack, and especially for us."

****

A new day dawned and Vertigo still raged as loudly as the night before. She'd gotten the miscreant, Jericho Black, under her control and his fool of a partner broke her hold on him. Then, Grayson Styles had the audacity to knock her over. If she hadn't been so shocked at the contact, she would've destroyed him on the spot.

Now Mr. Trust sent a message saying he would be delayed a little longer. She wanted done with this whole situation. Didn't he realize taking care of his prisoners drained her more than she wanted to admit? The rewrite on Jack's mind had been harder than she first believed. Every time she had him convinced they were married, he'd break the compulsion and she'd had to start over. She blamed Adam for her current round of problems. Maybe she should keep him sedated until Mr. Trust arrived.

Her hands curled into tight fists as she paced. She couldn't. Mr. Trust insisted on no sedatives until after he examined the subject himself. As much as she admired her boss and wanted his approval, he irritated her with all of his politics and red tape. Why couldn't he let her do her job the best she knew how?

She glared at the closed door hiding Jack and Adam from view. If she saw them right now, she'd be tempted to kill them and be done with all of it. She took a deep breath. Now she was being ridiculous. She'd put too much time and effort into both men to wipe them out because of a few problems.

She smoothed her skirt down. Maybe she should

see if she could get Jack to make love to her. It took very little prompting to get a man engaged in a physical activity. She smiled as the idea took hold. She could tell him they would reenact their honeymoon. He believed they were married. It shouldn't be too hard to get him in bed.

She opened the door. Time to try. "Good morning, gentlemen. I trust you slept well?"

Jack swung his legs over the side of the bed she had allowed him to sleep on. "Yes, thank you, Anita."

"Go to hell," Adam said from the floor.

Her smiled slipped a little as she walked over to him. "You need to adjust your bad attitude, Mr. Williams." She reached out with her telekinesis and pulled him upright. "You will watch your language with me."

Adam tried to laugh, but instead, it turned into a fit of rattled coughs. "Why? You can't damage me anymore than you already have or your precious boss will get angry. Back off, Vertigo. You can't touch me and you know it."

She tightened her psionic grip until his eyes bulged. Damn him for being right. Maybe she'd give him one more injection and make it a lethal overdose. She could make up some excuse Mr. Trust would believe. After all, she'd been her boss's favorite for a long time.

"You put too much stock in yourself," Adam said. Her eyes narrowed and he grinned. "No, I didn't read your mind. It's written all over your face. Don't ever play poker because you can't bluff."

She dropped him to the floor. "I don't need you anymore." She turned to Jack. "You're the one I came to see. Did you hear we had visitors last night?"

He nodded. "I heard them. They sounded angry."

"They were, but I got rid of them. They wanted to hurt you."

Jack took her hands and kissed her cheek. "Thank you."

She moved closer to him. All she had to do was make another small push to cement her hold on his mind. "Would you like to show me how grateful you are?"

Adam faked puked from the floor. "Don't do it, Jack. She's probably got some weird disease she can pass onto you."

At the interruption, her concentration faltered and he frowned. He became confused and started to shut her out again. Damn Adam. He always ruined her plans. "We can talk later," she said to Jack.

She used her telekinesis to slam Adam's head against the floor several times. "As for you, get in my way one more time and I'll kill you no matter what the consequences are."

She turned on her heel and slammed the door on her way out. Damn both of them. What a terrible start to her day. Maybe she needed to have a heart to heart with a certain woman named Kristin Mentor, leader of the Angels.

Chapter Twenty-Four

Kristin yawned and stretched. Every muscle in her body ached from the headache she'd had the night before. It appeared migraines had the ability to hurt more than just the head. Grayson stirred next to her. She traced the tattoo on his bicep. His skin felt smooth and warm under her fingers, the muscle underneath hard and unyielding. He'd betrayed his team. How could she still let him into her bed and her heart?

He had yet to tell her the whole story of what happened. Jack's team had to know he didn't willingly betray them. If so, they would've delivered their own harsh justice. They did to the other traitor they captured. What redeemed him in their eyes? Even Frank hadn't condemned him outright.

The planes of his face may be hard and angular, but she remembered the kindness in his eyes when he held her. The heat of his arms when he'd pulled her close ignited into white hot flames when their bodies connected. She almost giggled. When did she become such a fanciful romantic? Being with him made her knees go weak and her heart race, as it was doing now.

She shifted in his loose, yet somehow heavy grasp and his eyes opened. He smiled and those odd flutters returned. "Good morning," she said. "Did the mission go as planned?"

"No." Grayson stood and yanked up his pants. He

pulled his shirt on and turned to her. "Things are about ninety nine percent worse than we believed. We don't know if we'll be able to free Adam and Jack or not."

Ice engulfed Kristin's heart, chilling her blood and stabbing her soul. This job had turned out to be more difficult than it first appeared, but she'd never once contemplated failure. She left the bed, put her robe on, and walked over to him. "What happened? Did she have more men than you saw? She didn't already dispose of our people, did she?"

"No." He paused before he forced the words out. "She telepathically controlled Jericho. She slipped into his mind so quickly. Even if he'd been trained, I don't think he could've stopped her."

Kristin paced while she considered what he said. "Okay, so now we know how much power she has. We'll need some kind of protection to block her. I'll put in a call to Frank and see if ULTRA will let us borrow a particular device in their arsenal. If she slipped into Jericho's mind as fast as you said, our people are in greater danger than we initially feared."

Grayson stared at her and she glanced down. Her short robe did little to hide her from his heated gaze. She smiled. "If you don't stop with those looks, we won't accomplish any of our goals today. Our focus needs to be on the mission for now."

"For now," he agreed. "When the job is done, we'll concentrate on more important things."

She grabbed her clothes and headed for the bathroom. "Go check on Jericho and Cole. Tell them to get themselves ready. If we're going to confront Vertigo soon, we need a better plan."

He walked to the door, then stopped. "How soon

do you think Frank can get the equipment to us?"

"No later than this afternoon."

****

Kristin stepped out of the shower to an empty room. The guys' voices drifted to her, but Grayson's deep tones were crystal clear. Even his voice made her tremble. These emotions needed to settle down and soon. She dressed and dried her hair before she grabbed her cell phone.

"Frank, I need a particular piece of equipment from you," she said when he answered.

"How can I help?"

She walked over to the window and stared out. "Does ULTRA have any extra telepathic blockers? If so, I need four units, and I need them today."

"Yeah. We've always got extra units. Let me get to the armory and I'll send you what we have. The package will be small. You should have it no longer than it takes to drive there."

"Thanks, Frank."

He paused. "Is this your way of telling me the situation isn't good down there?"

"More or less." She walked back to the desk and sat in the chair. "Vertigo's gotten so powerful. I'm not sure we can defeat her."

"The Kristin I know never lets unbeatable odds stop her." His voice grew hard. "I'll do what I can to help. Text me the address and you'll have what you need."

"And if you and your team aren't busy within the next few days, I need another huge favor."

"Tell me."

After outlining her plan, she hung up and texted

him the address of Cole's house. The odds were stacked higher and higher against their success. If the small army Vertigo had gotten didn't give her the upper hand, her increased power was the clincher. Failure had severe consequences for more than just Jack and Adam.

Her cell phone buzzed. An unknown number flashed and Kristin let it go to voicemail. As soon as the thought hit, she reached for the phone.

"Hello?"

Vertigo's voice sliced through her. "Sorry about the mental nudge. I wanted to speak to you and I had to make you answer your phone."

"I have nothing to say to you," Kristin said.

"Oh, please. You have plenty to say to me," Vertigo laughed. "I want you to meet me at a small restaurant. It's not too far from Cole's house. Will you grant me this small courtesy?"

So, Vertigo knew their location. The one agent they'd captured did say she'd known every move they would make before they did. "I don't want to meet you. It's in your nature to attack and you know I'll retaliate. If I do, I'm pretty sure you'll dispose of Jack and Adam as soon as you return."

"I give you my word those two are safe for now. Besides, they'll have a very important visitor soon. I need to keep them more or less healthy."

"You know I'll tell Grayson, Jericho, and Cole about this."

Another laugh. "Go ahead. You'll be unharmed while we meet. I promise."

"I noticed you didn't say you wouldn't mess with my mind."

"Honestly, Kristin," Vertigo said, annoyance

creeping into her voice. "Unharmed means no harm. I only want to talk. No more, no less."

"Fine. What time and where?"

"How about around noon? By then, I'll be ready for some lunch. I'll telepathically send you directions."

"Just text me…" The line went dead. Kristin sighed. "The directions."

She stared at the now silent phone in her hand. Had she been manipulated? She closed her eyes and turned her focus inward. She couldn't detect an outside influence. It appeared she'd wanted to meet with their enemy. Time to let the guys know and her gut told her it wouldn't go well.

****

"Are you crazy? She'll get in your head," Grayson said. "You can't go."

As much as Kristin wanted to shout back at Grayson, she'd heard the worry in his voice. She worried about her, too. "I'll be fine. Besides, a package will be delivered from Frank. I need you here to get it."

"I agree with Grayson," Jericho said, his voice quiet. "You can't meet this woman. Her word is worthless."

"I know you're all worried, but I have to go," she said. "If I can get her to slip up, it will help. I haven't done very much this mission. I need to take the chance she'll tell me at least part of her plan. Besides, I've been trained for psychic attacks. My shields aren't as strong as hers, but they're better than yours."

Cole stood. "I'll go with her. If she tries anything, I'll be backup for the good doctor here. Besides, I'm pretty sure she'll be too overconfident to care I'll be there."

"And while Cole and I deal with her, you two can come up with a plan. She'll need to concentrate on us, so she should leave you alone while we're with her."

Grayson and Jericho looked at each other. "I still don't like it," Grayson said. "It's a risk you shouldn't take."

"I'll be all right. When the package from Frank comes, if she does plant a suggestion in my head, the frequency of the device should disrupt her telepathic signal."

"It's a real comfort to have a scientist on the team," Jericho said.

"Hey," Cole interrupted. "I'm a scientist and you never called me a real comfort."

Jericho gave him a not quite so innocent look. "She's prettier, therefore, more comforting."

Kristin hid her smile by looking at her watch. "Do you guys have any clue at all on how we're going to beat her?"

"We've kicked around a few ideas, but I don't want to tell you until you get back. She might think you'll have a plan she can pull out of your memories. Why let her ruin the surprise?"

"True. Cole, shall we go get the lay of the land?"

He held the door open. "After you, pretty scientist lady."

As she followed Cole to his car, Kristin hoped this wouldn't be a huge mistake.

****

"We shouldn't have let them go," Grayson said. "We could end up with four people to rescue instead of two."

"I know." Jericho poured the remainder of the

whiskey into a glass and drank it in one gulp. "But she's a grown woman and Cole knows what Vertigo is capable of. He used to work with her, remember? I think they'll be okay."

"They will, but what about you? I've never seen you drink this early in the day. Hell, I've never seen you drink anything harder than beer. You want to fill me in?"

Jericho stared at the glass in his hand. "I can't shake what she did to me. To be me, and yet, not me. I've never been through anything like it before. I can't explain it. You know what you're doing is wrong but you can't stop. I've never felt so…helpless."

"You've never been helpless, have you?"

Jericho shook his head. "Not once in my entire life. I learned early on how to be strong, how to take care of myself."

Grayson remembered his parents' deaths. He could still see his mother being torn apart. His father's screams continued to haunt him, a painful reminder of the one time in his life he'd been helpless. He felt for his friend, but if Jericho didn't snap out of it, he'd never shake the fear and he'd be close to useless in the final fight.

He took Jericho by the shoulders. "You've got to pull it together. I know she freaked you out, but if you can't bounce back, not only does she win, we'll lose more than the fight. Vertigo knows you're the heart of this team. By taking you out, she's damaged us, more than when she took Adam, more than when her goon hurt Cole."

Jericho threw his friend's hands off and stalked to the other side of the room "Don't you think I realize this? You have no idea what it felt like. I would've sold you out in a heartbeat. I did." He upended the bottle and a small trickle dripped into the glass. "Sorry, but you aren't the solo traitor in the room anymore."

"And Vertigo is behind both betrayals. More than anyone, I know how you feel. You know my background. I'm all too familiar with helplessness."

Jericho raised his glass in a silent toast. "I know. Sorry. I shouldn't have dumped on you." He cleared his throat. "Now, what kind of a plan do you have?"

Grayson laid out the map and grabbed a pen. "Let's come in from the main drive. She'll already know we're there, so why be quiet? We'll scatter into four different directions so she'll have to split her attention between us."

"Where are her troops and about how many has she got?"

Grayson pointed to the map. "From what I saw, there's somewhere around twenty troops who patrol around the house. They stay close to the tree line and avoid the woods. We may be able to pick a few of them off before they get wise to where we are."

"This confrontation needs to begin and soon. You have your usual plan in mind?"

"Yep. If I stay in the low to middle branches of the trees, I'll get some pretty decent shots. I'll also have more maneuverability when I get airborne."

Jericho glanced at him. "You know they'll have body armor, right?"

"Yeah. If they're Company troops, and I'm sure they are, their body armor will be augmented. If I take my time lining up my shots, I should be able to take most of them out." He straightened up and summoned a tiny whirlwind in his hand. "Don't forget I've got some extra surprises in store if they don't go down easy."

Chapter Twenty-Five

Kristin refused to acknowledge the nervous tick dancing along her nerves. Yes, Vertigo was powerful, but as her power grew, so did her one major flaw; her over-confidence. Vertigo saw it as strength, displaying it like a badge of honor. The telepath actually believed no one could touch her. Let her believe she was untouchable. When they started their rescue mission, Vertigo was in for a huge dose of reality.

People hurried across the parking lot, walking in and out of stores. Cars drove up and down aisles, as drivers checked for a coveted close spot. Traffic whizzed by on the main road behind them. All in all, a perfectly normal, and yet, surreal day. Here she sat, ready to meet someone who could kill her with a thought, while people laughed and shopped. It didn't feel fair somehow.

"You okay?"

She glanced at Cole and smiled. "I'll be fine. It's a quiet lunch. No ambushes. No world ending battles. Even Vertigo isn't reckless enough to call unwanted attention to herself in a busy strip mall."

"I'm not too sure." He stared at the restaurant and the connected stores. "She's got a lot of weapons at her disposal. You said you've fought her before. She knows you won't endanger innocent people. She'll use your ethics and whatever else she can against you."

"I know." She took a deep breath, holding it for a moment before releasing it. "I hope all she wants to do is talk."

"Kristin," he said. "If she tries to hurt you and I get a clear shot, I have to take it. Don't hang me up because of your hero's code. She needs to be stopped and soon."

"Understood. I don't approve of excessive force on anyone if there's another way. This time, though, I'm forced to agree with you. If a chance presents itself or if she tries anything, take it. I won't stop you. I always hope these situations will end peacefully, but I'm practical enough to know when events have spiraled too far out of control."

He gave her hand a quick squeeze. "You saved my life. I don't want you to think less of me or the others if it comes down to a permanent solution."

"Cole, you will always have my friendship. You, Grayson, Adam, and Jericho. I still know so little about all of you, but I'm a good judge of character. You're good guys and from what I can tell, all of you use extreme force when the situation calls for it and not before."

"That means a lot." He nodded toward the restaurant. "Shall we confront the dragon lady?"

"Did you want to wait in the car? Just in case she's got something up her sleeve?"

"There's no point. She'll know I'm here, so I may as well come in. If I'm out in the open, one of her goons could shoot me. Just the thought of the possibility doesn't give me the warm and fuzzies. I'd rather be inside."

"Good idea." She smiled. "Even if it does sound more like paranoia."

He simply shrugged and got out of the car.

They pushed on the restaurant's heavy wood and glass door and stood near the hostess station. Immediately, the heady aroma of cooking food with pungent spices and the bitter scent of beer filled the air. The mingling smells made her stomach growl. Kristin took a deep breath, savoring the tangy scent surrounding her.

A long, rectangular bar took up the middle of the floor, a polished mirror behind the rows of bottles of alcohol at the end. Low light gleamed off the lacquered wooden tables. Conversations, silverware as it clinked against plates, and music from hidden speakers raised the noise level as more people filed in behind them.

Kristin spied Vertigo in a corner booth and gave Cole a slight nudge with her elbow. The hostess hurried over and Kristin pointed to the back. They were led to where Vertigo waited, her fingers twined around the stem of a wine glass. The waitress laid menus on the table and hurried away as they slid into the booth.

"I didn't think you two were ever going to show," Vertigo said, her voice smooth as silk. "I'm not surprised to see Cole with you." A pout pursed her lips. "And he brought a gun. How disappointing. Firearms are so pedestrian. I knew those men wouldn't want you alone with me. I wanted us to have some girl talk. I hope you'll be willing to listen to reason."

Kristin moved her menu to the side. "We didn't want to come. You're the one who wanted to meet. Cole is with me and armed because this smells of a setup. So say your piece and then we'll all leave."

Vertigo sipped the white wine. "Cole and I used to work together, you know. We had such good times in the lab." Her eyes shone with a predatory light. "And out of the lab. You were such an enormous help to me with my experiments."

Cole snorted. "Don't remind me. You turned a way too young and inexperienced college kid into your own personal puppet. When I discovered your real purpose, I knew exactly what kind of research you were engaged in. You had to be stopped then and you need to be stopped now. Just give us our people. No one has to get hurt."

"No one has to get hurt," she mocked. The smile disappeared, replaced by a small frown. "There's a line I haven't heard for a long time. You still think you can stop me. Of course, people have to get hurt. Mr. Trust will be here in a few days to take possession of the prisoners. I'd like to give him you, too. He still remembers what you did to him."

Cole stilled beside Kristin. His left arm brushed hers and she could feel his muscles grow tight and hard. Whatever he'd done to Mr. Trust, it had to have been incredibly violent. If Trust wanted revenge, there was a very real possibility he'd get it. She spoke up to stop the smug smile on Vertigo's face from getting bigger.

"Why did you want us here? If you wanted to waste our time…" Kristin let the sentence hang.

"Of course not. The whole time we've talked, I've scanned you. Your supposed powers are laughable. The men with you are beneath my notice. The only one who might be worth my attention is Grayson Styles. I've never had a winged super to experiment on. It will be quite delightful to see what I can pull out of him."

She held her hand up and stopped their replies before they said a single word. "If Cole surrenders to me now, I will release Jack McClennan. Mr. Trust has no interest in him. All he wants is his property back. That means Adam and Cole. He's invested too much time and money into both of them."

Kristin kept her face neutral while her rage built deep inside. She didn't doubt Vertigo picked it up, but losing her temper in such a public place would cause an unnecessary scene. Cole laid his hand on her shoulder. She could feel the slight tremors in his touch.

Kristin glared at her. "You have no chance to take or keep any of my people. If one of them doesn't end you, I will."

"Poor, arrogant, little hero. I know your limits and how far you're willing to go to stop me." Vertigo smiled and sipped her wine. "You have no idea what I'm capable of. If I wanted to, I could make you fall in love with Cole right now and have you dump Grayson. Or, and I like this much more, I could have Cole shoot you outside. There is so much I could make you submit to."

Kristin leaned forward. "Why don't you?"

"Because as fun as it would be for me to watch, my plans are bigger and better than you know. You'll get to see it firsthand when you try your failed attack. Yes, I know, all about it. Your partners were right to plan it after you left. I'd read them to find out what it is, but I have so few surprises left to me anymore." She sat back and stared at them. "I hold all the cards, not you. And I already knew you would reject my offer to release Jack."

Kristin and Cole looked at each other. Vertigo's plan wouldn't be pretty for any of them. Would one of the men with her be hurt? No. Not while she had the power to protect them.

"You can't watch them all the time," Vertigo said. "I can't wait to destroy the lot of you. It might even satisfy me more than sex with Jack." She walked over to Cole and kissed him on the cheek. "And Adam will be the one I use to kill every last one of your team."

They watched her sashay out of the restaurant before turning to each other. Kristin knew Vertigo's barb about sex with Jack would upset her, but she knew her friend. Even mind controlled, he'd never touch her. The kiss she laid on Cole could have been a cover. What could her statement have meant? Did she slip into his mind? Could she have planted a tracer of some kind on him? Kristin ran her hand over his shoulders and up under his shirt collar.

"What are you doing?" he asked.

"I just want to be sure she didn't plant a device on you. Can you detect her in your mind?"

Cole closed his eyes for a few minutes, then shook his head. "I can't find her power signature anywhere. She truly believes we can't stop her."

Kristin sat back in the booth. "So, this was just a waste of time. Why would she call us here and not give us any information?"

He shrugged. "With Vertigo, it could have served some other purpose, one she's hidden from everyone involved."

"It would figure," she muttered.

Cole got out of the booth and offered his hand. "It doesn't give me any comfort either. I wish I knew what she has planned."

"I think everyone who knows her wishes the same thing." She paused. "I'm worried about our chances."

They walked outside and Cole hesitated when they reached his car. "I'm sure she wanted to undermine our confidence. I think she wanted to demonstrate how much she can do and how little effort it takes. She may not have gotten in your mind, but she sure as hell got in your head. Since you've been with us, I haven't seen you lose confidence yet. You've got to press on."

"Keep the faith," she said in a low voice. She looked up at Cole. "My friend's husband always says keep the faith. I guess we need to now more than ever."

"Sounds like a smart guy."

"He is. He's got ties to the magical realm." She smiled. "As a scientist, I never thought I'd believe in magic or faith."

"Even scientists need a little faith once in a while." They got in the car and Cole twisted the key. "I'd like to pay you a visit one day and meet this magical guy."

"We'll arrange one when this is over."

"Deal."

He turned onto the road and headed back to his home. When they pulled up and Cole shut the car off, she turned to him. "Can you give me any information about this Mr. Trust? I've met him a few times and only for the briefest of moments."

Cole laid his forehead against the steering wheel. "It's too long of a story to get into here. The short version is he headed up HelixCorp when I worked there. When I started my rescue attempts, I found out he had sanctioned every experiment done to the kids who were kept more as prisoners than patients. I went to his office to demand an explanation and he had an older teenage girl there. He beat the crap out of her and made me watch. I managed to save her and her sister. They do say turnabout is fair play. Benedict Trust has wanted my head on a plate ever since."

Kristin sat back. The more she learned, the more tangled things became. It started as a rescue mission to save her friend from a kidnapper. Now, a man whose name scared these tough as nails men could possibly be involved. And Benedict Trust gave them another link to HelixCorp.

"There needs to be an investigation into HelixCorp. Too much leads back to them."

"Let's rescue Adam and Jack first. We'll revolt against the evil overlords second."

She glanced at him. "Joke all you want, but I can hear fear in your voice. I promise you, I'll take care of Benedict Trust and his company. Then you'll have no reason to be afraid."

"Good luck. When this is over, I'll tell you why it will be damn near impossible to take him and his company down."

Chapter Twenty-Six

"And she said nothing else?" Grayson asked. "Didn't she give even one clue as to what will happen when Trust gets here?"

"She said he wants his property back, meaning Cole and Adam. My thoughts are he'll have Jack disposed of soon after he arrives." As she sat on the edge of the couch, Kristin gazed at each of them in turn. "She said she'd trade Jack for Cole. I declined her offer."

Cole leaned against the doorframe with his arms folded. "She wouldn't have given up Jack anyway. She's got plans. I don't know what they are, but she's got them. Even when she only went by Anita Haines, she always had an ulterior motive."

Jericho snorted. "I wouldn't be surprised if she planned a double cross on Trust along with everyone else."

"Let's hope, if she does, they'll kill each other and save us the trouble," Grayson said.

The shadow agents were too nervous to stay in one spot for long. Benedict Trust had already wreaked havoc on her current team and he wasn't even here yet. Kristin wanted to know how much power Trust wielded. Did he have a "super" ability or was it more like mob power? Either way, she didn't like it or him, and she hadn't even collided with him yet.

Grayson held a small box out to her. "This came about thirty minutes after you left."

"Thanks. This should be what I called Frank about."

She opened the box and saw the exact piece of equipment she'd wanted. She held up one of the devices for them to see. It had the size and look of a large hearing aid. An ear bud dangled at the end of a short, plastic coated wire attached to a curved, rectangular unit.

"These are the great devices you told us about?" Jericho sounded less than convinced.

"Yes. These were created by some of the best lab techs at ULTRA. My team telepath also had a hand in the design. Most of the agents wear these into battle situations as an added defense measure. I can assure you, they do work."

Cole picked one up. "If I wear this, I won't be able to use my power. It'll block Vertigo, but it will also block me."

Kristin laid the device back in the box. "You are more than your abilities. All of us are. We need any and all advantage we can get."

He eyed the small box as though he feared the devices would leap out any second and bite him. "You'll effectively blind me with these."

"Cole, I know you're worried, but if they can help us stop her, you have to."

"I know."

Grayson took one out and examined it. He found a tiny switch imbedded in the bottom and used his fingernail to push it over. A green light began to blink. He settled it on his right ear and turned to the group.

"What do you think?"

"Looks good," Jericho said. "Will this knock her out of our heads if she's there?"

"No," Kristin said. "These will keep her from exerting more control. If you sense her in your mind, you can increase the frequency and it will help stop her influence."

Jericho frowned, then his smirk appeared. "Well, as you said, it's better than nothing. Let's hope she stays out of our brains until this is over."

"When should we try to get back to where she's locked up our people?" Grayson asked.

"The sooner the better," Jericho said. "She's had them too long as it is."

Grayson walked over to the window, staring at the late afternoon sun. "My guess is she's expecting us to show up there tonight. How about tomorrow?"

They agreed on the time and Grayson followed Kristin to the other room. Jericho and Cole kept two of the ear pieces, so they could get used to how they felt. The door clicked shut and Kristin turned to Grayson.

"I can't allow you the luxury of secrets any longer. You have to tell me what happened with Jack and his team all those years ago."

He raked his fingers through his hair and turned away. "I thought you'd dropped this subject."

She stepped closer to him. "How can I? The secret you've locked away is huge and we need to get it out in the open. If not, Vertigo could find some way to use it against us. Is this a chance you're comfortable taking?"

"No, but you don't understand. I've tried so hard to bury what I've done. If I tell you, it makes it all real again. Can't you see, I don't want to remember anymore?"

"Grayson, I told you I wasn't human. Would you like to know what I am?"

He faced her, the question in his eyes. The muscles in his arms tensed and he stayed silent. When it became clear he wouldn't ask her to explain, she sighed.

"I'm a genetic experiment, created in a lab and designed to replace humans for space travel. My hero name is Proto, because it's what I am. I'm a prototype experiment. I'm human, and yet, not human at the same time."

His eyes widened, but he remained silent.

"The man who created me, Dr. Caspian Mentor, worked in a top secret research facility. It had a small staff and another man worked with him. As I grew older, he became like a father to me. He received orders to turn me over to begin the next phase in my development and he refused. He basically kidnapped me and took me to his home. My father insisted I still train, but to be a hero here on earth."

"Did he tell you what you are?"

"Yes. ULTRA took over funding the space exploration program I was designed to take part in. The board of directors decided to scrap the program after Jack broke the hidden cabal in the organization."

"Why?"

Goosebumps broke out on her arms and she shivered. She didn't think it would be this hard to reveal her past. "The public took a harder look at ULTRA and its funding. Because of what investigators were searching for, and subsequently found, the ULTRA director had been told to clean house and close any unnecessary programs."

A hard laugh escaped him. "And you can thank me for that fiasco, too."

She wanted to rail at him, tell him to close down his pity party, but instead, took a deep breath. "No, it wasn't your fault. The corrupt leaders wanted the planted evidence to be found. When I turned fifteen, my father began being contacted by friends and colleagues. Their children had developed their own powers and needed to learn control in a safe environment, which he provided."

"And he just decided to put together a hero team?" he said, his sarcastic tone setting her teeth on edge. "How noble of a man involved in genetic experimentation."

"Will you stop with the interruptions?" she snapped. "He extended the invitation to help people whose powers had emerged so they could learn how to use them. Three of our members didn't come from his friends."

"I know those two of your team. You have an alien and a person from another dimension, but who's the third?"

"Our telepath. From what Cole has said, I believe she may have been one of HelixCorp's experiments. She fought in a criminal organization with her sister. When her powers had gotten too far out of control, she came to my team for help. She's been with us ever since."

He folded his arms and leaned against the door. "And you forgave her. Why would you take in a known criminal? Weren't you afraid of betrayal?"

"When she first arrived, yes, and she wasn't instantly forgiven. It took a lot of time. She's proven herself time and time again to be an invaluable member of the team." She looked away. "If she didn't need to be with her family right now, she'd be here, finding Jack and fighting Vertigo. All of the Angels would be here if I called them."

They stared at each other. So many long-buried emotions simmered in Kristin. Grayson stared at her and she worried she might have revealed too much. The silence between them stretched into long minutes. They faced each other, and her words hung heavy between them.

"You don't have much faith in my team, do you?" he said.

"If I didn't, I wouldn't still be here. I would've cut and run and gotten every agent in ULTRA down here in the blink of an eye. Why can't you understand I'm afraid for all of you? I'm afraid of the worst possible scenario. If you've never gone up against someone like Vertigo before, there's no way I can properly prepare you."

"What about your magic devices? Aren't they supposed to give us an edge?"

"They will, but they won't stop every power she possesses."

Grayson pushed away from the door and sat on the bed. "Tell me. What else can she do?"

"Can you please put a hold on your sarcasm? Where do you think she got her code name from?"

He gave her a half smile. "Hitchcock fan?"

Her gaze shot to his face but her retort died when she saw his smile. "It's her main ability. She can give you vertigo. The whole world spins and you can't tell up from down. If she attacks you while you're flying, you could hit the ground hard enough to seriously injure yourself or worse. Add in her telepathy, mind control, and telekinesis and you've got a very strong package of power, vengeance, and hate."

After a few minutes, he spoke. "So, let me get this straight. If I understand what you're saying, we're screwed nine ways to Sunday."

She answered his grin with one of her own. "Interesting phrase, but yes."

"We already knew the danger we would be up against, my dear."

She held out one of the devices. "These will help, but if she harnesses Adam's power, he could burn them out. Without them, we'll be vulnerable."

"Especially Jericho. He's still freaked out about what she did to him. I expect her to go after him first."

"That's a safe assumption. However, you aren't safe either. She's been in your mind. It will take very little for her to convince you to hurt one of us."

Jericho's eyes still flashed with fear when he talked about Vertigo. She would catch glimpses of the same fear in Grayson. Her own team had gone through similar situations with the telepath. After the first few battles, they'd learned what to expect and had been able to prepare better. This time, though, Kristin didn't have any telepathic backup. She resolved to get them through the coming fight and home safe.

"You look like you've come to a decision," he said.

"I have. I promise, I will get all of you out of this and back here in one piece. I've done it before. I can do it now."

He stood and gathered her into his arms. "I believe you. We know you got our backs, Kristin. You're our guardian angel tomorrow night. "

As he held her, it dawned on her he still didn't tell her about his past. Looked like Frank wasn't the only one who had mastered the skill to talk around painful subjects.

Chapter Twenty-Seven

Jericho stared at the small device in his hand. He didn't believe the small earpiece would help keep Vertigo out of his head. The new, sour feeling took up residence in his stomach again, making him question why he and his team were even here. The boss knew they didn't have the power to match with a renegade telepath and yet she'd sent them anyway.

"Don't let the doubt control you," Cole said from behind him.

"I'm trying," he snapped. "I've never not been in control of myself or a job before. Now I've lost control of both. I want to know why the boss sent us here. You and Adam are the psionics on this team and even you guys don't have the power to beat Vertigo. We needed to have a full blown telepath with us and we got Kristin."

"She's powerful in her own way and she's fought telepaths before. For not being psionic, she came out okay."

"The telepath on her team helped her and gave her the proper backup. Kristin's the hero, not us." Jericho squeezed his eyes shut. "Not me."

Cole handed him a beer. "Just because you're so freaked out, I have a secret you need to hear. I haven't told anyone this, not even Adam and we've been friends longer than you and I."

"What?"

Cole popped the top off of his own beer and leaned on the countertop. "Everyone congratulates me for being so brave, so resourceful, getting those kids out of HelixCorp and I was, up until one particular point. When Trust discovered what I'd done, he kicked the crap out of me."

Jericho sat on the back of the couch as his friend took a long drink from the beer bottle. "While I lay there bleeding, I thought he'd watch me die. Just watch me bleed out right there on his expensive carpet." He gave a quiet snort. "But I didn't. He had worse plan in mind for me."

When he failed to continue, Jericho glanced at him. He'd gone pale and his hands shook. From Cole's reaction, whatever he'd been through had been bad. Cole had survived a nightmare worse than bad. He knew the psionic harbored a lot of paranoia. Now he would get the answer why.

"What did he do?"

"He had this girl there. I've never seen anyone so beautiful. She had long red hair and a perfect figure. I never saw her eyes because she had to wear these dark glasses. She worked with the light spectrum, but she couldn't look at it." Cole picked at the label on the bottle in his hands. "She, uh, she had a twin sister, a telepath, who couldn't control her power. I knew Vertigo had caused the sisters' problems."

Jericho said nothing while he waited for him to go on. Cole finished the rest of his beer and took several deep breaths before he spoke again.

"I'd been beaten almost senseless. I couldn't do anything to help her, so Trust beat her. She tried to use her power. When she couldn't, I gave it a shot. I thought maybe I could fry him with a quick electrical strike, but I couldn't summon even a tiny spark. It didn't dawn on me he'd have power dampers in place. So, I fought off the guys holding me, grabbed a knife from one of them and plunged it into his chest."

"He obviously lived. What happened?"

"I sucked at hand to hand combat at the time." Cole opened another beer, and drank half before he lowered the bottle. "I guess I didn't hit any vital organs. The next week, they slipped me enough poison to kill me. When I couldn't stand on my own, or fight back, they threw me in the street."

"Where I found you on the verge of death."

"Yeah. Being poisoned ranks right up there at number one on the list of things that suck. The newspapers were leaked information about how I sabotaged HelixCorp and wanted to blackmail the board of directors for money. Of course, the rest of the story said I'd been fired and vowed revenge and all the rest of the crap corporate stooges feed to the media. They wanted the news to read I'd committed suicide instead of going to prison. After I'd recovered, I thought I could go back to saving people. I didn't realize my mind had gotten so messed up.

"I barely got back in to save the sisters. My hands shook the whole time and my heart pounded. I'd saved kids for months, but after the one incident with Trust, I knew I'd never be the same. If he caught me again, he would've killed me or some innocent kid. I got Adam out before it all went to hell." He stared hard at Jericho. "My real shame is this. I couldn't go back to try for anymore of the psionics. I couldn't convince myself to take the chance."

"There's no shame in protecting yourself."

Cole snorted. "Are you sure? I knew how to get back in without keycards. With my power, I could've bypassed the security system any time I wanted. But I knew if I went back, it would put me near Trust again. I didn't want to be within fifty feet of him." He stared at the floor. "There's so many kids who suffered, and are still suffering, because of my cowardice."

"This isn't the whole story," Jericho said. He stood in front of Cole and folded his arms. "What else did he do to you?"

As he eyed the now empty bottle, Cole turned back to the refrigerator. "I'm not drunk enough to tell you. Let's just say I know what it's like to be physically and psychically tortured. When I tell you I know the fear and doubt you feel, I want you to understand I mean it."

Jericho rubbed his hands on his jeans. If Cole could find the strength to face the people who had damaged him, he could do the same. He'd always known deep down he'd overcome Vertigo's influence. Now, all he had to do was remember what his friend had been through and he'd have the strength to fight anyone or anything.

Thoughts of Vertigo made him come to one grim conclusion. The psycho telepathic bitch from hell wouldn't see another sunrise.

****

Jack flinched every time Vertigo's steps brought her close to him. Once again, he'd almost broken her hold and now she grown angrier than ever. She'd thrown Adam around the room, blaming him for Jack's defiance. He couldn't deny how Adam talked to him, told him of Vertigo's manipulation.

He squeezed his eyes shut, wishing both of them would be quiet and leave him alone. He could figure this all out if he could have some peace. But the more Vertigo tried to get him to believe her, the more Adam pushed back.

Adam wheezed from his spot on the floor. At one point, he coughed so hard, blood trickled from his mouth. Jack glanced at Vertigo as she stood over him. He had to try to get her to cease her assault or Adam would be seriously hurt.

"Anita, you have to stop. He'll die if you beat him any longer."

"Ha!" She turned to glare at him. "I've telepathically checked him. He's not in any danger. Besides, Mr. Trust needs him alive, which is the reason I allow him to remain so. As for you, I fear we may have company soon. I need to make sure you're on my side when the supposed rescuers come for you."

"Vertigo," Eddie said. He stood in the doorway. A silver briefcase dangled from his right hand. "I got what you wanted. Mr. Trust said he's happy to know Adam is powerful enough to need the damper unit."

She laid the case on the small table. Her eyes gleamed with excitement as she popped the latches open. As she lifted out the object, Jack saw a thin, metallic headband. He frowned. He'd seen one like it before. A friend of his wore one. She'd been a bridesmaid at his wedding. She had an incredibly snarky sense of humor, with a joke for almost any occasion.

She had a perfect beauty with dark, blue eyes and long red hair. She couldn't control her psionic ability.

He knew her as...his wife's best friend. He knew they'd fought several battles together for the past few years. He frowned harder. Why couldn't he remember the woman's name?

"Don't worry about her name, Jack. She's no longer important. Your life is with me now. We'll have to make better progress today. I'm afraid it will hurt, but with no more interference," she said, directing a hard glare at Adam, "you'll be able to feel like your old self soon enough."

Jack's gaze followed Eddie when he walked over to Adam. He yanked him to his feet and handcuffed his wrists behind his back. Vertigo activated the headband and pushed it down on his head.

Adam went still for a moment before he turned a hate filled gaze on Vertigo. "Believe me when I say I'll make sure I put a bullet in you before this is over."

She leaned close and smiled. "You're welcome to try. Your friends made the same statement. It appears everyone wants to kill me." She grabbed Jack with telekinesis and took him to the other room. "Now, it's time for you to be mine, mind, body, and soul. Eddie, I don't wish to be disturbed."

"Yes, ma'am," he said as the door slammed in his face.

****

"Do you think we'll be able to save Jack and Adam?" Kristin asked.

"We're not sure. Adam's power is out of control and Jack is being brainwashed. They may not be able to be rescued," Grayson said. "This is a very real possibility we have to face."

Kristin picked at her food and she could feel their

Annette Miller

gazes on her. "Jack and his wife have been through so much. Their lives are on a solid track and they're ready to start a family. How do I explain to her I couldn't save him? How could I go home without him?"

Her questions were met with silence. Grayson spoke again. "We have no idea what type of situation they're in. There's a chance we'll get to them before she can do any serious damage."

"But we should be prepared if they aren't," she said. "I've never failed at any situation in my life." She stared at each of them. "I don't intend to start now. As soon as the sun sets tomorrow, we'll go. I've known this showdown would come someday."

They raised their glasses in a silent toast.

Chapter Twenty-Eight

Adam tried to get comfortable on the hardback chair Eddie had shoved him onto. His arms ached and fire burned through his shoulder muscles. He was torn between wanting Trust to get there and not wanting him to ever arrive. As soon as Trust showed up, the game would be over.

Eddie Anderson stood guard in front of the closed door, and he wished he knew how Jack fared. With the power damper on his head, his power felt muted. Even attempting small acts sapped the small amount of energy he possessed. Damn headband limited any assistance he'd be able to give Jack.

He tried to roll his shoulders to relieve the pressure, but nothing helped. "Hey, Anderson, how about a little assistance here?"

"No."

Monosyllabic gorilla. "Come on. It's bad enough Vertigo tossed me around the room like a rag doll, but my arms hurt like the metaphorical bitch."

"Too bad. Vertigo will let me know what to do with you in due time. Until then, you stay put and keep your mouth shut."

So much for his grand plan, whatever it happened to be. "What do you think Benedict Trust will do with you, once he shows up? Vertigo won't have any more use for you. I know Trust won't want you around. I bet

Jack isn't the only one scheduled for termination."

"Vertigo knows my worth."

"Yeah. Zilch." Adam tried another tactic. "If you were on Jack's team at ULTRA, you guys had to have some kind of friendship."

"He was my field commander at ULTRA. I thought he respected me as much as I did him, but he didn't."

Great. Couldn't anything be easy anymore? "Come on, Eddie. A lot of time has passed since those days. You can't still be pissed about what happened."

Eddie frowned and took a step toward Adam. "No. I'm pissed how every time I'm in a good position, Grayson Styles shows up and wrecks it."

"Not the answer I expected, but okay. How did Grayson wreck what you have now?"

"Vertigo has you and McClennan, so all she does is criticize me. She knows Styles will show up with whatever loser team he's put together. I went through the same thing at ULTRA. Styles joined our team and took the squad leader position which should have been mine." He jerked his thumb toward the closed door. "My former fearless leader in there chose him over me. I hope she fries his brains. I hope Mr. Trust destroys all of you."

"Wow. You're carrying a lot of anger there. I thought you had all you wanted, you know, being Vertigo's personal stooge."

Anderson backhanded him and Adam's eye swelled almost immediately. "I did. I had a sweet position with the hidden council at ULTRA. Until Jack poked his nose in where it didn't belong. After the council broke apart, The Company hired me. They said I had skills they needed for an important job."

"I guess this is the job?"

Anderson nodded, a smug smile on his face. "If Mr. Trust can't use you, I get to get rid of any person he deems unnecessary. I know I can convince him Jack, Styles, and whoever else shows up will be unnecessary." He leaned close. "And I'll make sure it'll be slow and very, very painful."

Adam watched Anderson resume his place at the door. *And here I thought we were in serious trouble.* He couldn't stop the grin wanting to spread across his face. Even with no one to talk to, he still had plenty of jokes to keep himself amused.

He sobered when Jack's struggles sounded through the door. He'd always known Vertigo had a mean streak. It rivaled some of the most notorious bad guys on ULTRA's wanted list. Again, he wondered what happened to make her so violent. Jack's muffled screams penetrated the closed door and he decided he didn't care. She needed to be stopped, the sooner the better

****

Grayson thought about what Kristin had told him of her past. He decided it didn't matter. When he held her, she felt more real, more human than any of the women he'd been with over the years. She had a special quality about her, a unique hidden spark which lit her from within. He knew he didn't want her to go home. At least, not without him.

Tomorrow night, some of them might not go home. He glanced at her. She checked over her weapons for the fight. He'd seen her in battles. She'd never once backed down. Some of the footage Cole found showed even when outnumbered, she never gave up. Her steady determination and battle skills made him glad she would fight with them, not against them.

A woman of science, he'd told Jericho. It turned out, she lived as the embodiment of science. She may have started her life as an experiment, but she'd grown into a beautiful woman. Her eyes had a tiny tilt to the corners and gave her an exotic look. Outside, the sun had turned her hair from light brown to honey gold.

She stood much shorter than him and his team, a pocket powerhouse filled with strength and determination. He'd begun to think Jericho had hit the nail on the proverbial head. She was definitely champagne to his orange juice.

"You've stared at me for the past five minutes. Would you care to share your thoughts?"

"It's not what you think." He gave her a small smile. "Well, not at the moment. I'm worried about Jericho and Cole. I don't think I've ever seen them this skittish before. Usually, I'm the jumpy one and, believe it or not, Jericho is the voice of reason."

"I believe it. There's a steadiness in him. A friend of mine back in New York has the same air about him. It boosts your confidence when you go into a fight." She stopped. "Jack possesses the same quality. His team would follow him into hell if he asked because they know he'll get them out."

"You have it too, Kristin."

She shook her head. "I don't have those particular leader skills."

"You underestimate yourself. You forget, I've seen footage of you in some of the hardest fought battles. You never give in." He placed his fingers under her chin and tilted her head back. This close he could see her eyes were a shade or two darker than her hair. "Your team is devoted to you. And, yes, they would follow you wherever you'd lead them."

"That's quite a generous opinion of me."

"No, it isn't. It's a fact. I see it in every clip of your team. They've defended you while you've put yourself in harm's way to save a life."

"I guess you're right."

He gave her a quick kiss. "Of course, I am. The Angels have to be one of the tightest knit groups I've ever seen."

She wrapped her arms around his waist. "I guess it's because we were friends first and a team second."

"You and your team just keep doing whatever brings you together. It works." He pulled her close and held her tight. "Don't worry about Adam and Jack. We'll get them back and they'll be safe. You'll see."

"I hope you're right," she murmured.

"We'll go over the plan again tonight to make sure we've all our bases covered."

As they checked over their weapons, Kristin spoke again. "After I told you about myself, you never said what happened with Jack and his team."

His shoulders tightened, his wings twitching with agitation. He reached over his shoulder to scratch a spot right below his skull. "Let it go. I can't tell you."

"Why? I don't believe you would hurt or betray your team."

He stared hard at her. "You'd better believe it because I did. Because of my weakness, I doubted my boss and my friend. If I hadn't been susceptible to the hate spewed by other people, I would have been able to resist the manipulation more."

"Grayson," she said. "I don't think you're afraid of Jack. I think you're afraid of you. You can't forgive yourself for falling prey to the influence of others."

He turned back and continued to check his weapons. "Like I said. I don't want to talk about it."

When she didn't reply, he glanced over to see her going through her own gear. Good. Now maybe she'd take the hint and let it drop. A small knot of dread formed in his stomach, telling him she wasn't ready to let it go yet.

****

Vertigo smoothed her hair down. Jack lay on the bed and his chest heaved as though he'd finished a hard workout. In a manner of speaking, he did. The fight he'd put up had tired them both out, but she didn't doubt she'd win in the end.

"How do you feel, Jack?" she asked.

"Tired." He opened his eyes and smiled at her. "For the first time in days, my head is clear."

"I told you it would be all right. When you trust me, it's easier to see the truth, isn't it?"

He pulled himself up and nodded. "I don't understand why I wasted so much time fighting you. We're the perfect couple. I remember our whole life together."

"Wonderful. And what about the auburn haired woman who thinks she can take you from me?"

He pulled her into his lap. "We'll dispose of her together."

She could barely contain the malicious glee that filled her. "I'd hoped you'd say that."

As she walked out of the room, her confidence soared higher than it'd been in days. All of her plans were coming together. Mr. Trust would arrive soon and he'd take Adam with him when he left. His confidence in her would be restored. He'd been in a foul mood ever since an agent in upstate New York had been found dead in an "accident," and all of his notes had disappeared. Then Jack and his team broke the inner circle at ULTRA.

She stared hard at Adam as he looked up at her. This insignificant psionic would soon be out of her hair. Then, she'd have the one person she'd ever wanted. Jack McClennan. The last bit of opposition in her way were Jack's supposed rescuers. With luck, the men she'd hired would deal with them when they showed up.

After all this time, things were going her way.

Chapter Twenty-Nine

Kristin sat on the porch steps. It all came down to today. They would rescue their friends or they'd fail and everyone would die. There was a happy thought. She rested her chin in her hands. The Angels' team had faced some pretty serious villains in their time, but no one compared to Vertigo. If the team hadn't gotten some lucky breaks, the Angels wouldn't have been able to beat her on the several occasions they'd fought her.

Okay. Enough with the depression. She opened a search on her phone to look for more information on Benedict Trust. He supported some of the same organizations she did. His picture appeared on a charity website. She enlarged it and stared hard at it, but still couldn't call him to mind. Even though they'd been introduced several times, he didn't look familiar. She discovered he also sat on the board of directors at HelixCorp.

"What's wrong?" Grayson asked as he sat beside her. "You look worried."

She shook her head. "I'm not. Well, not any more than I have been. I researched Benedict Trust."

"What did you find?"

"Not much." She scrolled back to the top of the page. "He's made the list of the hundred richest people in the country every year for the past ten years. He's on the board of a lot of charity organizations. He has ties to

HelixCorp and about a dozen other scientific research facilities. I've been to a lot of the same fundraiser parties, but for some reason, I can't recall his face."

He angled her phone to get the glare off the screen. "Could he have his own powers to make people not recall him?"

"I don't know, but anything's possible." She turned to him. "I've met him at several events. I should have some memory of what he looks like. It's strange."

"Yeah, a little. Let's go in and kick around a few more ideas. Then food and rest. If we want to rescue our people tonight, we need to be on our A game."

Kristin stood and dusted off the seat of her pants. Grayson let her go in first, placing a hand on the small of her back. Would she feel his warmth again after tonight? Right now, she wished for even a little clairvoyance. Jericho and Cole were hunched over the table as they studied the map.

A heavy silence hung over the room and no one wanted to give voice to the doubts and fears which plagued them. She watched their faces. All the cockiness and bravado they'd had when she first met them vanished. If she couldn't snap them out of this funk, they were certain to be defeated.

"Are we prepared for tonight? Are there any other plans we should make?" she asked them.

"I don't know," Grayson said. "We've talked to our contacts. They've told us all they know. Sammy's injured. Tom's afraid for himself and his family."

"I had to use more force than I wanted to on the guy I talked to and now he's recovering under the protection of our boss," Jericho said.

Cole stood and walked over to his computer. "I'll

double check my sources, but I'm pretty sure there's been no new leads."

"I know you're all worried," she said. "But you can't let Vertigo affect you like this. If you can't pull yourselves together, you're of no use to me. I'll try to take down her by myself if I must." She smiled at them. "You're all the best at this kind of work, but you need to get your collective acts together."

Grayson wrapped his arms around her from behind. "Very inspirational, doc."

A sharp snap brought them all on high alert. Kristin grabbed her stun rod from the coffee table. "Is this why you never put your weapons away?"

Grayson lifted one shoulder. "Yeah, or it might be because we're lazy."

Jericho hefted his gun. "I think this is just what we all need to blow off a little steam. Let's take these asshats down. Remember…"

"You need one alive to interrogate," Kristin finished. "I believe I'm familiar with the drill now."

"Yeah, Jericho," Cole chimed in from the kitchen. "Get off the lady's back."

Jericho grinned at them. "I wouldn't touch that one with a ten foot cattle prod."

Grayson eased the curtain to the side. "Looks like about maybe ten guys. Some circled around to the back."

"I got it," Kristin said. She ran for the kitchen, glad the guys had taken time to fix the broken window on the door.

They'd completed the repairs a few days earlier. Such a short time had passed and yet, it had felt like an eternity. Troops stalked closer to the house. Grayson may not like it, but she needed to get out there if she wanted to do any damage. Eyeing the woods, she gripped her stun rod tighter. Soon, they'd be in range. Time to give them a little surprise and meet them head on. Were the attackers Company troops or just thugs for hire?

Gunshots echoed from the front of the house. Kristin took her cue from the sound, threw open the back door, and charged out. Footsteps pounded behind her, but she kept her attention on the approaching agents. She blocked a punch from the man in front of her and swung the stun rod in a tight circle. She connected with the side of his head and dropped him like a limp rag doll.

"Doc, watch yourself," Grayson called.

She dropped down to her hands and knees. A shot whizzed over her head and she wished she'd worn her armor under her clothes. She glanced over her shoulder and saw a man roll to his feet to charge her. Jumping up, she met him halfway and threw her arm up to block his punches. A sharp jab to his face broke his nose before she flipped him over her shoulder. He rolled to his feet and charged toward the front of the house.

Grayson blocked punch after punch from the agent he faced while he waited for the chance to make his move. He dodged out of the way of the next blow. When the agent left himself wide open, Grayson pounced on the mistake. He crashed his fist into the man's face before he spun him around. He wrapped his arm around the assailant's neck and squeezed until the man went limp in his arms.

He let the body drop to the ground and raised his arms. A slight breeze stirred some fallen leaves before a sharp gust of wind knocked the agents to the ground. When Kristin checked them, they were still alive, just out cold. She looked at Grayson, who shrugged. It appeared he could do more than just pull miracles out of his ass. They headed toward the front of the house to help the others.

Out front, Jericho and Cole engaged in close combat with the invaders. Jericho's shots landed in the exact spot where they'd do the most damage. Cole moved with a speed Kristin never suspected. It was subtle and dangerous, reminding her of a cat before it pounced. He jabbed his finger into his opponent's eye four times before the man even knew what happened.

Cole dodged out of the way as his opponent swung wide while rubbing his eye. He hit him in the chest, then flipped him around and twisted his head with a sickening pop. He dropped the body on the ground before he turned to see if someone else needed help.

Jericho glared at the man in front of him, while he kept the man behind him in his peripheral sight. "What, do you want an invitation? Take your shot while you can because if you don't kill me now, you won't get another chance."

Hearing the subtle whine as the energy weapon primed itself, Jericho dropped at the last possible second and the man shot his partner. He pivoted, charged attacker, and kicked the man's knee out, before he broke his arm. The man cried out as Jericho grabbed him around the neck.

"Sorry. You blew it." The man clawed at his arm and Jericho tightened his hold, ignoring the scratches the agent left. "It's no fun knowing no one will look for you, is it?"

Kristin's hair began to whip around her face. She glanced at Grayson and he nodded. She covered her face as dirt and dust swirled around them. Debris and the force of the wind made the attackers stumble back and rub at their eyes as she and Cole charged in.

She grabbed the man closest to her and gave him a brief tap with the stun rod, just enough to immobilize him. Cole simply used a more direct approach and punched the other man in the face hard enough to rattle him, but not knock him out.

Jericho walked over and squatted between them. "I don't need both of you. One of you should have the information I'm looking for." He glanced at one, then the other. "Who's more valuable?"

"I am," the one on his left said. "I led them here, he's just a flunky. I can tell you what you want to know."

Jericho looked at the other man. "Is he telling me the truth?"

The man looked at his partner and nodded. "It's true. I'm a low level agent. I do what I'm told."

"Fine," Jericho said and broke the neck of the first man who had spoken. "Oldest trick in the book, my friend. Didn't Vertigo tell you who you were up against today?"

The sole survivor spat on the ground. "A bunch of worthless heroes. She said you'd go down easy. We didn't expect this."

Grayson laid a hand over his heart. "Worthless? I don't know about you guys, but I'm hurt."

"There, there." Kristin reached up to pat his shoulder. "Jericho, would you please introduce us?"

"Gladly." He jerked his head toward the group.

"We've got the leader of a hero team, a guy who could fry you with every piece of electronic crap on your body, a winged sniper, and me. Do you know who I am?"

The man on the ground scowled. "A second-rate mercenary who can't get any other work?"

"Now that hurts." He looked over his shoulder at his team. "Too disrespectful on too many levels." He pulled the man close. This time, his smirk held less charm and more menace. "You don't need to be mean just because you lost. I, my unlucky friend, am Jericho Black."

The man paled, but kept the attitude. "I guess we know how this will end, don't we?"

"Not necessarily. I can hurt you in ways that'll make you want to die, but it's up to you. What's Vertigo's final play? Where are our people?"

The man clamped his lips together and stayed silent.

"I got all the time in the world to get what I want from you." He stood and headed to the house. "Watch him. I'll be right back."

Kristin worried what Jericho might bring out with him. She'd watched him break a man's neck. She couldn't watch him shed blood, despite the fact it would be the quickest way to get the agent to talk. He came out with a thick roll of duct tape and she released the breath until that moment, she didn't realize she held.

He nodded to Cole and Grayson, who hauled the man to his feet. Jericho pulled his arms behind his back and secured his wrists with the duct tape. "Cole, can I borrow your car for a few minutes?"

"Again?" Cole rolled his eyes but tossed him the

keys. "The last time you did this, I needed a front end alignment and new shocks *and* new struts."

Jericho popped the trunk. "Quit whining. I helped you pay for it, didn't I?"

He dumped the man inside and Cole slammed the lid down. "You should've paid for all of it. Why don't you get a sedan like mine and ruin your own damn car?"

"Because it's more fun to use yours." Jericho climbed in the driver's seat. "This won't take long."

Kristin watched him speed off. She'd been up and down the rough driveway a lot in the past few days. She almost pitied the man in the trunk. Almost. Jericho drifted off the road several times, weaving back and forth. He slammed on the brakes and did a three sixty turn over the ruts, rocks, and roots protruding from the ground.

He opened the trunk and dumped the man on the ground. "Now let's try this again. What's going on and where're our people?"

"Vertigo's still at the location where you found her the other night," he said in a shaky voice. "I don't know what her final play will be. All I know is what she told me to do." He gestured to the troops which still hadn't moved. "We were supposed to soften you up before you come for her tonight."

"I didn't think you'd know much. Couldn't hurt to hope, though." He turned to the team. "We need to call the boss for another cleanup. We don't need any distractions while we plan."

"There's a few more agents in the back," Kristin said.

Jericho jerked his head toward the back and Cole

followed close on his heels. As they disappeared around the house, Kristin turned to Grayson.

"You said you didn't have any powers."

"Yeah." As he pulled off his shirt, he stretched his wings out and jerked his thumb at them. "These came with control over all breezes and wind. My power is magic based."

"Magic," she murmured. "My team has more ties to the magical realm than I ever thought possible. I expected to meet a scientist, like myself, but I've met a man who is all magic."

He stepped closer to her and laid his hand on her cheek. "Do you believe magic and science could exist together?"

She smiled. "They have for generations. I don't see why we should be an exception. Besides, someone once said magic is science we don't understand yet."

Even though relief flooded his face, she knew something still troubled him. It had to be what happened between him and Jack all those years ago. She needed to be patient and he'd tell her the whole story, sooner or later. She hoped it would be sooner.

Chapter Thirty

Adam threw up for the fourth time in fifteen minutes. Vertigo had just given him a third dose of her damn formula and it wreaked havoc from his mind to his stomach. Small price to pay, considering with every injection his control got better. He'd opened a back door into Jack's mind and, so far, Vertigo hadn't found it. If she had, she would've been gloating about it.

With his improved control and some subtle practice, he might even be able to help stop Vertigo. His team's thoughts were clearer the more he practiced with his stronger abilities. Out of all of them, he could hear Cole's the loudest. Well, Cole did have more power than people knew. Now if he could keep it hidden and get free before Benedict Trust showed up, life would be perfect.

Vertigo came in and stood over him. "I see you've recovered a bit."

"Go screw yourself," Adam mumbled.

Vertigo yanked him up telekinetically and forced her way into his mind. She smiled and dropped him to the floor. "Well, your powers have opened up. Now if you hadn't been stubborn at HelixCorp, you and I would have made a great team."

"Now you know why I shut down my powers," Adam wheezed. "I didn't want you playing footsies with my gray matter."

Vertigo stooped and caressed his cheek. "Oh, Adam. Don't you know I will always win? When Mr. Trust arrives, he'll make sure you regret ever having crossed us. You're in for a long, painful journey of experimentation. Your defiance will come at a very high price."

Adam smiled. "So be it."

The fury in her eyes told him his jabs had hit home. After the third injection, the psychic damper was worse than useless. The damper did nothing to inhibit his psychic strength or control any longer. He heard her tell Anderson she had to go out for more supplies and to watch the prisoners. When the door slammed, Adam breathed a sigh of relief and decided to try to contact Cole.

"Cole, can you hear me?" he sent to his friend's mind.

"Adam? What the hell? Since when can you do mind to mind communication?"

"Since the psycho bitch shot me up with her formula. I've gotten better with the new power levels. I didn't wipe out any psionics this time and I can tell I didn't affect you either. How close are you guys to a rescue?"

"Close, but not as close as we'd like to be. We got hit by her troops. No damage, but it reinforced the plan we came up with the other day." Cole hesitated. *"Her guy said she knows about the attack."*

"Yeah and she doesn't care." Adam broke off to wipe at the sweat on his face. *"I've hidden my control so far. I'm going to try to help when you get here. This is harder than I thought. Got to go."*

He dozed off and on until he heard the door open.

Vertigo came in with a small bag bearing the logo of a local drug store. *Now what?*

"I'm going to add some other ingredients to the formula." Looking at him over her shoulder, she smiled. "I want to try and create a dependence in you so you'll stop thinking you can escape."

"Wow. That's kind of twisted. What made you like this?"

She laughed, actually laughed, at his question. "I made me like this. People around me were always saying, 'don't be so soft, Anita. You're just not good enough, Anita.' As soon as I developed my powers, I showed all of them how strong and how good I could be. I even joined some pitiful villain team and let them think they could tell me what to do."

"I guess you showed them they couldn't?"

"What do you think? At the right time, I tore them apart. They never knew what hit them. One of the girls you and Cole rescued from HelixCorp was their team leader. She never even realized my identity." Her smile got bigger as she glanced at him. "I hid in plain sight, just like you and your pitiful team."

"You're a real freak, you know that?"

"Oh, Adam. Do you realize how little your comments mean to me?" She put away the last of what she'd bought and turned to him. "I wanted to let you know, I've heard from Mr. Trust. He's been able to clear his schedule and should be here early tomorrow. Then, I'll turn you and your pathetic rescuers over to him. When I do, he'll put me back in charge at HelixCorp, where I belong."

As she walked to the other room, Adam allowed himself a small smile. *You keep on with those delusions, Vertigo. When my team gets here, you'll have a bigger surprise than you expect.*

****

Two very tall women stepped out of a long, black car and loaded the prisoners inside. Jericho and Cole had gone back inside to refine the plan for the upcoming fight. Grayson still stood there bare chested, his wings extended to their full length, his gun held in a tight grip in his left hand. He looked like a gun toting angel, and Kristin fought to suppress a smile.

He turned to her. "What?"

"I didn't say anything."

The way he walked over was similar to a predator stalking its prey. "You've had some kind of odd thought. I can see it in your face. You look like you want to laugh at me. Care to share?"

"I thought you looked like an angel who carries a gun. Angels and guns are diametrically opposed visual images. It made me smile."

"Almost as funny as a tiny woman who smacks people upside the head with an electrical stick?" he said.

She thought for a moment, then nodded. "Yes, I suppose so." She knew the time had arrived to ask him about his past. "Grayson, are you human?"

Her question stopped him, and he hesitated before answering. "No."

"Can you tell me about yourself? You know about me. I'm made from science. I want to know about you."

He took a deep breath. "I lived in the wooded hills in western Pennsylvania. There isn't a lot of people there. My father was human and grew up around there. He had some magical ability. He could do little things and had a few ties to the fairy realm. My mother was a harpy. With harpies, there's no halves. You're either harpy or human. There is no in between."

"You're speaking of them in the past tense. What happened?"

"They were killed by my mother's tribe. Male harpies are so rare, when one is born, they're revered and treated special." He glanced at her. "Unless the male is born with powers. Like me. Then, they scream heresy and treason. They become unreasonable."

She frowned. "I don't understand. Wouldn't they want a strong male to help protect them?"

He gave a short, humorless laugh. "You'd think so, but it isn't the case. When a male with powers is born, it summons the North Wind Brethren. They can sense the presence of male magic from the tribes. Females don't carry the same power signature. The brethren are male harpies with powers.

"The harpy tribes have feuded with the brethren for eons. The harpies believe the brethren want to train the males with power to destroy them. After all, the North Wind Brethren have kept the females in check for a long time. Not all the Greek myths are actually myths."

Kristin rubbed her chin. "You said your parents were killed by the tribe. How did you escape?"

"My parents hid my powers as long as they could. When the tribe found out, they tore my mother apart. My father and I ran. We headed down a hill to the valley. We had to get to the turnpike and we'd be safe." He stared at the sky. "My father didn't tell me he'd been injured. I saw the blood when he said we needed to split up."

He stayed silent for a long time. Kristin worried

she'd asked him to reveal too painful of a memory. "Grayson…"

"I'm all right. He drew them away and I took off. We weren't more than a hundred yards from the road. I flagged down a car and it turned out to be a state trooper. My father had given me the phone number of a friend of his in New York. The officer called him, and he came to pick me up."

She walked over and laid her hand on his arm. "Did he take good care of you?"

"Yeah," Grayson said. "He and his family aren't in New York any longer. He used to be part of a hero team which still lives underneath the city. They call themselves The Underground. They all have powers or looks which don't fit in well with regular heroes. So they hide themselves away. I hated being underground most of the time but it blocked both harpies and brethren. They couldn't find me."

"I can hear in your voice you weren't crazy about being there. What happened?"

He glanced at her before his gaze returned to the sky. "I missed this." He held his arms straight out. "I missed being in the air. I missed the freedom of flight." He snapped his fingers and a tiny whirlwind danced on his palm. "I missed the connection with this side of myself. I'd promised my dad I'd stay away from the magical realm, but it's always there and it's hard to resist its call."

"So, how did you end up in ULTRA? Not only as an agent, but on Jack's team. From what Frank tells me, you had to be the best to even be considered."

"He's right. I always had the top spot in class and on the firing range." He walked a short distance away and turned. "Because of my heritage, I have sharper than normal human eyesight and I learned how to pull my wings into my back muscles. I remembered the cop who helped me so I became a state trooper. I got all kinds of awards and recognition and ULTRA took notice. I passed their tests and got accepted. When they saw how well I could shoot, they trained me as a sniper."

His reluctant words tore at her heart and made her want to take his hurt away. Seeing the pain etched into his face and the grief in his eyes, the urge to hold him was overwhelming. If she could, she'd pull the bad memories out of him so he wouldn't hurt anymore.

"I guess Jack found out how good you were and invited you to join his team."

"You got it. I loved Jack's team. They accepted me without question." He frowned. "But we all know how the story ended, don't we."

"I don't." She took his hand. "Please, tell me what happened. The team wouldn't have let you live if they were convinced of your guilt."

"It's hard to talk about." He nodded toward the house. "Jericho knows because Shade picked me up right after it all went down. Depression and too much alcohol loosened everything inside. The whole sordid story just poured out."

She turned his face to hers, and gazed in his eyes. "Let it come out again. Let me understand how to help you."

"Are you sure you want to hear this?"

"It's not morbid curiosity. It's a genuine need to know. If there are no secrets, Vertigo can't hurt us. There's no way she could have a chance to confuse us, because deep down, we'd know the real truth."

"All right." He folded his wings against his back and sat on the porch. "Right after Jack found the files implicating some of the higher ups, lies had started to spread. I got caught up in them. The rumors claimed Jack had something big in the works. He planned to go rogue and start his own illegal operation. At least, that's what I'd heard.

"The corrupt agents planted doubt and mistrust among Jack's team, especially the newer members. At first, I didn't believe it. I knew my boss and I knew my team, but I couldn't ignore the rumors any longer. I had a teammate, Eddie Anderson, who would corner me at every opportunity and tell me all about Jack's supposed illegal activities."

Kristin took his hand and ran her thumb over his knuckles. The anguish in his voice tore at her heart. "Go on."

"I started having doubts around then. Jack, his first wife, Frank, and Amy were always huddled together. It appeared they were all in on some sort of plan together." He paused and took a deep breath, then let it out. "One day, Jack called the team together and told us what he'd found. He'd wanted to keep it quiet until all the facts were substantiated."

Grayson tightened his grip on her hand. "He showed us what he had and we all agreed we needed to stop the corrupt parties. So for the next two years, we gathered evidence and kept it all 'in house.' After Jack's arrest, Anderson and another agent came to me. They told me Jack's evidence was fake and they had the real information. I asked what they wanted me to do. All I had to do was switch the envelopes. Then there would be no doubt of Jack's guilt."

He stopped again and Kristin waited for him to pull himself together. She didn't have to wait long. The muscles in his neck tightened as he swallowed hard. She laid her head on his shoulder and squeezed his hand.

"I did what they wanted and you know the rest. The evidence mentioned Jack as the ring leader, leading to his conviction. After the beating in prison and his close call with death, they filled him with those junk cybernetic systems. All because of me. So many of our teammates lost their lives over the years. Because of me."

"But the Gravediggers team didn't take revenge on you. Why? What changed their minds?"

"Turns out, Vertigo had built a compulsion in my mind to believe the lies they told me. She had control of me the whole time."

Kristin jumped to her feet and stared at him. "Then you didn't betray Jack. Vertigo betrayed you, Jack, and the entire team because she's a vengeful, self-righteous, vindictive…"

Grayson raised an eyebrow. "Bitch?"

"Exactly." She slammed her fist into her open palm while she paced. "She's got a lot to answer for when we get to her."

Grayson's mouth curved up in a small smile. "Thank you."

"For what?" she asked.

He stood and placed a light kiss on her lips. "For believing me. For not wanting to shoot me when you found out I betrayed your friend."

"As I said, you didn't betray him. Vertigo did."

She stroked his cheek. "How did you break the compulsion?"

"Jericho took me to Shade. Our boss employs a lot of psionics. They forced Vertigo out of my head."

Her arms twined around his neck. "Good. You should now have one woman in your mind. Me."

He pulled her close. "Deal."

Chapter Thirty-One

"Jack, can you hear me?" Adam said telepathically.

"I hear you. What do you want?"

"I'm trying help you fight Vertigo's influence, but I need a little cooperation on your part." He stared at Jack. *"Can you fight her?"*

"I can, but I don't want to. She's shown me the truth. You need to mind your own business. The sooner you're gone, the better."

Adam laid his head back and closed his eyes. Vertigo completed her hold on Jack and there wasn't a damn thing he could do about it now. *We are so screwed. And she didn't even kiss us first.*

Vertigo walked in and glanced at the two men. Adam watched her eyes narrow as she stared at him and he felt she knew what he'd been up to. When she turned away, he breathed a sigh of relief. If his luck held, Jack wouldn't tell her about their silent conversation.

He needed his team. Right frigging now.

****

The atmosphere in Cole's house radiated with tension. All four of them sat in their own spot and checked their weapons. Kristin worried about Cole. He'd held his own in the skirmish they'd fought earlier, but she could tell he still wasn't a hundred percent. Suggesting he sit out the mission wasn't an option. He deserved this chance to end Vertigo and save his friend. He'd be there, no matter if it was a good idea or not.

She wished the Angels were there to help back up Grayson's team. It hadn't taken her very long to become close to these men, especially Grayson. They had a chance at a strong relationship. She bit her lower lip, wondering if they would be able to explore what she believed more and more to be their soul bonding. She had become familiar with Jericho's easy charm and Cole's paranoia and stubborn pride.

But Grayson. The hardships he'd overcome in his youth and then the manipulation by Vertigo while on Jack's team at ULTRA. His spirit, his heart, and his strength may have been bent, but it had never been broken. His fierce determination drew her. More than any physical aspect, his inner strength made love for him fill her until she thought she'd burst.

She stopped. Love? Did she love the man? As she checked her stun rods, she made the admission to herself. Yes, she loved him. He accepted her in spite of her revelations. He'd even said she was the most human person he'd ever met. How could she not love him? But did he feel the same? After they defeated Vertigo and they had their friends back, she'd ask him. If they were truly soulmates, he'd feel the same.

"I think we're about as ready as we can be," Grayson said.

Kristin nodded. Tightness in her throat stopped her words and her mouth had gone dry. She had so much to say to him, to all of them, it all log jammed up inside her.

Grayson walked over to her. "You okay?"

"Yes. I don't know why I'm so nervous. I've faced

worse criminals and steeper odds and I've never doubted we'd come out on top. This time, I feel like I want to run and hide."

"Vertigo's trying to influence us," Cole said. "She wants to take us out of the fight before we even get there. Grayson knows you from the footage. We've all seen it, too. You're the closest we've ever seen to fearless."

"Don't worry, doc," Jericho chimed in. "We're with you. With all the power we have between us, there's no way we'll fail."

Seeing them there, guns in hand, she shook off the uncertainty. "I believe you, but I'm afraid some of you may be hurt or worse." She held up her cell phone. "How about, just as a precaution, we call in an army of our own?"

The three men looked at each other. "An army," Jericho murmured. "I like it."

She hit the speed dial. "Hi, Frank. It's time. I'll text you the address. See you soon."

Grayson stared at her. "And you called Frank because…?"

"I've hidden a small detail from all of you," she said. "I asked Frank to send some agents down here when we got the psychic dampers. They've been on standby. Once we get to the location where Jack and Adam are being held, I'll call in the cavalry. Then, they'll engage Vertigo's troops so we can concentrate on the rescue."

Cole looked at Grayson and grinned. "I swear, if you don't marry her, I will."

"Sorry. You got to find your own girl." He turned to Kristin. "I think she's a keeper."

Grayson's arms went around her and she knew she didn't need to ask him about how he felt. There were no more answers she needed. What was between them was more powerful then she would have ever believed. Even if they still hadn't said the words, she knew he loved her. First chance she got, she would let him know.

Saying "I love you" spoke volumes but those three little words didn't seem to be enough. She couldn't pinpoint when it happened, but Grayson had become her whole world. If he wanted to stay here with his team, she wouldn't complain, no matter how much it would hurt. If he wanted to come back with her, she'd be ecstatic. Whatever he wanted, she'd support his decision.

"I need to put on one more piece of equipment," she said. "I'll be out in a moment."

She hurried into the bedroom she and Grayson shared. Would they make it back so they could continue to know each other? Yes. She no longer had any doubt left.

"I thought you were all set. What do you need to get?" Grayson said from behind her.

She flipped open her suitcase and took out her micro-flex armor. It flowed over her arm, shimmering like a burnished gold waterfall. The material had a satiny shine when the light hit it. She held up her mid-calf gray boots.

"I can't go without a little more protection. I left the helmet home. However, I never go anywhere without my armor."

He walked over and cupped her face. "Smart, and don't worry. We got your back."

"I know." She gazed up at him. "We will beat her."

He kissed her long and hard, and she tasted the desperation in his mouth. As he ended the kiss, he smoothed her hair back. "I wish you wouldn't go. I don't want you hurt. You aren't the only one who worries."

"You think I don't want to make you and the others stay here and let the ULTRA agents take care of this whole ugly situation? I'll be fine. You make sure you take care of yourself." She stepped back and immediately missed the warmth of his arms. "I have to get ready."

He nodded, reluctant to let her go. While Kristin stripped down, she could feel his eyes on her. How odd, the Angels tough as nails leader would feel so feminine, so desirable. She could almost hear her friends teasing her.

She pulled up the odd material and felt Grayson's hands as he hooked the back for her. It would be nice if he would always be there to help her dress. This would be very easy to get used to. She'd left her larger, silver boots at home and brought the smaller, muted gray stealth boots. These were lighter and easier to pack.

Grayson ran his hand over the material. "What's this made of? I don't think I've ever felt this kind of fabric before."

"It's a new material developed by the Challengers hero team. See how it looks like the squares don't join together?"

"Yeah?"

"It's enhanced micro-flex technology. It's different from any other armor. Each panel can absorb a lot of damage before it fails. The fact the panels aren't fused is what gives it maximum flexibility. I'm not sure what the material is, but it's lightweight and easy to move in."

"You make it look good," he said.

"Thanks." Her cheeks warmed under his scrutiny. "Should we get back to the others?"

He opened the door for her and they walked back to the living room. Jericho and Cole stopped in their tracks and stared at her. Again, her cheeks heated. If the Angels found out she'd blushed, not once but twice, she'd never live it down.

Jericho nodded. "The look suits you. It says, 'I'm more than a doctor. I'm an ass kicker.' I like it."

Kristin glanced at Grayson. He frowned a little and moved closer to her. She feared Vertigo still had a presence in his mind, giving her easy access to control him and Jericho. Even she and Cole were bound to be affected. This wouldn't be an easy fight. Too much could wrong too fast.

Cole clapped a hand on Jericho's shoulder. "You need to put your eyes back in your head. Grayson looks like he wants to cut you into tiny pieces and then burn them."

Kristin elbowed Grayson lightly in his ribs. "Please don't give Jericho the death glare. You know it's not him, but the fact he's been influenced by a psycho telepath."

"Sorry." His tone didn't sound the least bit apologetic.

Jericho feigned shock and placed a hand over his heart. "Insincerity from Grayson Styles? I never would have believed it."

"You're pushing it, Jericho."

Kristin stood in the middle of them and held her hands up. "All of you, stop. Save the aggression for Vertigo and her troops. If you fight here, all you've done is waste energy."

Cole grinned. "See what I have to deal with?"

Kristin choked back a laugh. "You're as bad as they are, so you're not off the hook."

"Maybe we should go," Grayson said. "The sooner we deal with this situation, the better. Since she already expects us to be there, we may as well go right to her front door. A surprise attack is pretty much pointless now."

The others agreed and they walked out to their cars. Cole would ride with Jericho in the SUV and Grayson would take Kristin in his car. Once they freed Jack and Adam, they might need the extra space. No one voiced the consequences if they failed.

As she watched Jericho pull out, she gazed at Grayson. The tell-tale signs of his stress showed. The muscles in his neck tightened and he reached over his shoulder to scratch at his back. He followed Jericho onto the main road and they headed for the construction out beyond the little historic village of Batsto.

Kristin laid her hand across his shoulders and scratched his back as he drove. She was certain this had to be the first job they were all so nervous about. Once the fight started, she prayed they'd all settle into what they did best.

Chapter Thirty-Two

Adam forced his eyes open as voices drifted to him from the other room. Vertigo's and Anderson's voices were familiar, but the man who spoke had a deeper tone and a slight accent. Blood turned to ice in his veins, freezing his muscles as he recognized the third voice. Benedict Trust had arrived early. He and Jack were officially out of time.

Vertigo told him Trust wouldn't arrive until the next day. Adam had hoped his team would rescue them before he showed up. They weren't escaping now. Not without a whole lot of help. His team would never make it to them in time. Footsteps approached and he pushed himself upright.

The door opened and there stood Benedict Trust. Adam could see the cold glint in his eyes as he stared at him. The man still had great taste in suits. The Armani molded to his tall, muscular, frame like a second skin. His light brown hair had some gray at the temples now and was cut in the newest, trendy style.

"Torture any puppies lately?" Adam said.

Trust clasped his hands in front of him and shook his head. "Adam, will you never learn? Your insults are pointless to me and they demean you."

He shrugged. "Yeah, but I like them. Why are you here? I thought you couldn't be bothered to show up until tomorrow."

"Vertigo informed me we could have company tonight. It appears your team will try to save you from our evil clutches."

Adam couldn't stop the laugh erupting from him. "Evil clutches? You sound like a sad parody of a Saturday morning cartoon. You had no originality before and it looks like you're stuck in the same rut."

Trust stomped over to him and yanked him to his feet. "You won't have jokes for too much longer, Williams. Soon, you'll have no choice but to obey me. And I have plans for you. Big plans. The first item on my agenda will be to kill off Cole Jamison. He hurt me, and I will use you to hurt him."

"Good luck," he snorted. "You still have no idea about how mind control works. You can't force me to act against my nature, no matter what you use."

Trust dropped him to the floor and tugged on his jacket sleeves. "We'll see. Vertigo, you've said McClennan is under your full control, correct?"

"Yes, Mr. Trust. I have made him mine."

He straightened his tie and turned to glare at Adam. "Then we have another weapon in our arsenal. He'll come in handy for the fight tonight."

"You shouldn't be here when they come," she said. "We can't afford for you to get hurt."

He laid a hand on her cheek and smiled. "I'll be out of harm's way, but I want to see how this plays out." He let his hand slide down until his fingers curled around her neck. "Don't fail like you did before. I'm tired of excuses on why you can't complete a simple assignment."

"With the troops The Company sent, we'll be able to stop whatever his team has planned."

"Don't disappoint me."

Trust walked away and moments later, the front door slammed. Adam glared at her back as she stood in the doorway. "You're in way over your head, Vertigo. You should just cut your losses and run. Trust won't forgive you forever."

She spun around and her power enveloped him as she slammed him against the wall. "Shut up. As long as I provide results, Mr. Trust won't harm me. He knows how valuable my research is."

"You're a tool to be used, like me. Your worth isn't any better than mine. How's it feel?"

Vertigo glared at him and he knew he'd gone too far. She might kill him now and suffer whatever consequences Trust would heap on her. He glared right back at her.

"When your team comes tonight, they'll fail. They have no idea what I have in store for them. Soon, all of you will learn I'm the true power here and no one else. I'll get what I want, I'll get to keep Jack forever, and no one will ever hurt me again."

She stormed out of the room and the door banged shut behind her. Adam flinched at the sound and worried what she meant. He couldn't read her mind to discover her plans but it sounded bad. He needed to warn his team before they stepped into a worse scenario than they believed.

"Cole? Can you hear me?"

He waited for a moment before he tried again. Then again. Then one more time.

Vertigo's voice slammed into his mind. *"I know the damper hasn't stopped your abilities. I know every move you make before you make it. And the back door you created in Jack's mind? I've shut it."*

When she withdrew, Adam closed his eyes. Her telepathic contact felt like a sledgehammer in his brain. All his work, all the practice he'd done had gotten him squat. She'd known about it the whole time. Probably wanted to see how much he could do. He shook his head. Not in the lab, but still a lab rat.

"Crap."

****

The two vehicles rolled to a silent stop as the sun made its final descent behind the horizon. Jericho and Cole got out and waited for Kristin and Grayson to join them. They set the psionic blockers behind their ears and stared at each other.

"I called ULTRA from the car," Kristin said. "The vans should arrive any time now. How do we want to do this?"

"Let's assume she knows we're here and doesn't care," Grayson said. "I'll get a topside look and radio you the positions of her guards. When ULTRA arrives, have them spread out through the trees to pick people off. The less we have to deal with at the house, the better."

"My job is to free the prisoners. I'll circle around to the back and try to find a way inside," Cole said. "Kristin, you and Jericho keep the fight focused on the front of the house. If her attention's on you, it'll be easier for me to sneak in."

Grayson paled a little at the plan, but he nodded. "She'll have the ULTRA agents as backup and I can even the odds by firing from up high."

"It's a sound plan," she said. "Let's hope there's no surprises."

"It's Vertigo. There's always surprises," Cole said.

She looked at Jericho. "You've been uncharacteristically quiet. What's wrong?"

As he leaned against the SUV, he folded his arms and stared at the ground. "What if she gets control of me again? It's…unnerving."

"I know," Kristin said. "It's a chance you're going to have to take. We need you. You have an uncanny ability to hit the dead center of any object you aim at. I've seen you do it multiple times. Grayson said you're an expert in hand to hand combat. Don't worry. We'll keep so her busy she won't have time to attack you. Don't forget we have the psionic blockers. They'll help."

Five black vans pulled up and seven agents climbed out of each one and Kristin recognized some of Jack's team. Frank walked over to her and shook her hand. He nodded to the others.

"Are we ready?" Frank asked her.

Jericho pushed off of his car and gripped his gun. "Let's do this."

****

"Jack," Vertigo said. "People have come to take you away from me. We won't let this happen, will we?"

He shook his head. "No. I'll deal with them for you."

She ran a finger down his cheek. "I know you will. Don't hesitate. Kill anyone in your way."

"I'll take care of them. Then we can be together forever."

She looked over her shoulder at him. "There's a woman with them. Every word out of her mouth is a lie. Do you understand?"

"I understand."

She drew him to his feet. "Are you prepared to do what needs to be done?"

"I am." He pulled her close. "Let's go say hello to our guests."

****

Adam stayed still and strained to listen for any type of battle sound. The whole area had an uneasy stillness. The familiar sensation preceded every fight he and his team had been in. He frowned. Hopefully Cole and the others were prepared for Vertigo's unwelcome wagon. The fact she had Jack mind controlled did not bode well.

Adam used his newly acquired telekinesis to throw the psychic damper headband on the floor. He could work around it, but why take the chance she'd trigger a hidden booby-trap to make his head explode. He used his telekinesis to toss the ropes binding him to the floor. He'd wanted to escape a long time ago. All he had to do was leave Jack behind, but he couldn't bring himself to do it. None of his team ever abandoned anyone and he didn't plan to start now.

Eddie Anderson pushed into the room, a gun aimed at Adam's chest. "You ain't going anywhere. Sit down."

"Really." He pulled the gun from Anderson's hand and crumpled it into a strange, metallic ball. "In case you hadn't noticed, I'm a hell of a lot more powerful now. I've also gotten better control. You're done."

Adam threw him into the far wall and watched him slide down into a large heap. He'd better get going. Anderson groaned, and he didn't want to be around if and when he came to. He opened the door and checked both directions. He didn't see anyone, so he stepped into the hallway, only to be dragged back into the room by Anderson.

"We ain't done by a longshot."

He caught Adam in the jaw and slammed him down to the floor. *Way to go, idiot. Let's make the mountain man mad. I should have made sure he was down for the count. Jericho isn't going to let me hear the end of this.*

He threw up a force shield to stop any other blows. He pushed outward and flung Anderson into the hallway. As the two men traded punches, Adam worried about the battle outside.

Chapter Thirty-Three

The entire perimeter around the house glowed bright as huge spotlights lit the yard from almost every angle. Kristin's team and the ULTRA troops were blinded momentarily when they were first turned on, but recovered enough to take the fight to Vertigo's small army. As agents poured out from around the house, Kristin's team scattered to cover as much area as they could.

"I think Vertigo called in more troops," Kristin said over her mic. "Where did they all from?"

"Thugs Are Us," Jericho answered.

She pictured his smirk and smiled before she turned her focus to the task at hand. "Grayson, can you see where they're hiding?"

"Looks like some in the basement and some from the back tree line," he answered. She heard gunshots over his mic. "Rats don't swarm like this. Where's the end to them?"

"Frank, is your team okay? Do you need assistance?" she said.

"We've taken a few hits, but so far, so good. We've rounded up a lot of prisoners. Some of them gave up when they saw us."

"That's odd," she said. "Keep your eyes open. We don't know what Vertigo may have planned."

The man she fought aimed a shot at her head and

she dodged left. When she did, another man took her out with a leg sweep. She rolled to her feet and swung her stun rod with more force than she usually used. He dropped, but whether it was from the power of her swing or the sparking energy, she couldn't tell. Another agent tried a surprise attack and she jabbed back. He made a strange *oof* sound as his breath whooshed out. She spun around and swung her leg in a high arc and caught him in the jaw, dropping him.

"If we can't catch a break, they'll overwhelm us." She spared a quick glance up at Grayson. He shot with pinpoint accuracy and stopped a lot of men before they even cleared the doors. He summoned a wind occasionally, focusing it in a tight cone toward the enemy.

Kristin saw a man aim his weapon at her and dodged behind a tree. A loud whine began before a wide, bright blast went off. A small explosion detonated a few yards to her left and where there had once been bushes and vegetation, a crater now smoked.

"What the hell just blew up?" Jericho shouted.

"Remember when you guys talked about prototype weapons? Remember the disintegration one? Well, as they say, it's in the wrong hands," she said. "This has gotten a whole lot more complicated."

Jericho laughed. "You mean it wasn't before? Doc, you have a great way of stating the obvious."

"Thanks."

She jumped out from behind the tree and threw the stun rod. It didn't hit dead center, like Grayson's shots or Jericho's aim, but she caught the agent in the chest and he dropped like a stone. A skirmish nearby caught her attention. She scooped her stun rod up and ran to lend assistance.

****

The unguarded back door beckoned to Cole and he ran in a crouch to the small porch. Despite Kristin's assurances, he didn't want his power put on hold. He yanked the psionic blocker out of his ear and stuffed it in his jeans pocket. He'd take the chance his shields would be enough.

All he had to do was sneak in and free Adam and Jack. Easy. He stepped up to the back door. It shouldn't be this easy. He heard the fight out front, but there should've been guards or some kind resistance back here. Vertigo might be arrogant, he couldn't call her stupid. If there was a door with no one around, she had a reason for it.

"Thank you for the compliment, Cole."

Her voice cut through the sounds of the fight, freezing him in his tracks. He turned, knowing what he'd see, but still didn't want it to be true. Vertigo stood behind him with a very large, very angry, and very mind controlled Jack McClennan. Cole frowned at the futuristic style gun aimed at his chest while Vertigo held Jack around the waist.

Cole gripped his cell phone a little tighter, and telepathically tapped into its battery to let the electronic power fill him. He accessed the internet and kept the power surge at bay inside him.

"What did you do to his mind?"

She laughed. "I made him see how much we belong together. He only listens to me now, right Jack?"

"Yes."

He took a step closer and stopped when Jack raised

the gun a little higher. "Is this how you want him?" Cole asked. "As a puppet?"

"If it's the only way I can have him, then yes, I'll take him as a puppet." She glared at him. "I won't let you or anyone else ruin what has taken me too long to get. Jack, darling, shoot him now."

As Jack squeezed the trigger, Cole unleashed the power from his cell phone, erecting a bright blue shield made from computer code. The shot rang off to the side, damaging the doorframe, but not him. He pulled the power back into himself and shot a bolt of electricity, hitting Jack square in the chest. He smiled as Jack stumbled back a few steps. When Jack straightened up, the hard glint in his eyes gave Cole every clue as to what was coming next.

Cole reached back and opened the door right as Jack speared him in his midsection. Jack's fist crashed into the side of his face and if he didn't have broken bones, he should. He blocked the next couple of punches, even landed one or two of his own. From the power and strength of Jack's blows, there was a very slim chance he would win this fight.

Movement to his right grabbed his attention and Adam stood there. With a slight wave of his hand, Jack flew back through the door and it slammed shut. Adam came over and pulled Cole to his feet.

"Congratulations," Cole said. "You've been rescued. You're welcome."

"Took you long enough. I expected you couple of days ago."

Cole shrugged. "You know how traffic is on the parkway. We sat in one a hell of a backup. You okay?"

"For the most part. You?"

"About the same." Cole rubbed his jaw and winced when he touched the part where Jack's fist had collided. "Remember when you said I'd get beat up enough on this job? You were right. Let's get out of here."

They walked together to the front of the house and glanced out the windows as they went. Vertigo's troops outnumbered their team by at least three to one. They looked at each other and grinned. As soon as they went out there, the tide would turn. Adam had increased power, and Cole could tap into all of their devices and fry the attackers.

"We ready to do this?" he asked Adam.

"Oh yeah."

Before they could move, Cole was grabbed from behind and thrown to the floor. Eddie Anderson kicked him in the stomach, shutting down any type of retaliation. Cole grabbed his midsection as his breath wheezed out between his teeth. *If I keep getting hit here, somebody's going to break my ribs.*

Adam telekinetically yanked Eddie's legs out from under him and he hit the floor with a hard thud. While Eddie tried to clear his vision, Cole forced himself to move and dropped on his chest. Adam held him to the floor while Cole took out his gun.

"You remember when you kicked the crap out of me not long ago?" Cole said. "Vertigo told you she didn't want to hold me in one place while you shot me. So, when I get up, you get up. I'd rather shoot you face to face any way."

He stood and Adam dropped his hold. Eddie climbed to his feet. "You won't shoot me. It's against whatever ridiculous code you two live under. I'm going to help Vertigo and you two can't stop me."

Cole glanced at Adam. "He doesn't believe us."

"No, he doesn't."

Adam pushed Eddie against the wall. "You've done too much to both of us to let you walk out of here. Grayson has said on numerous occasions he's wanted someone to put you in the ground. Looks like we got volunteered."

Eddie's eyes widened as Cole lifted the gun. "Sorry, man. You're guilty."

The shot rang out and Adam and Cole turned to reunite with their team.

****

Grayson kept the ground forces under control. Between shots, he used occasional blasts of wind, to give his side time to gain ground against the assembled troops. Kristin fell into her role as team leader, the agents listening without hesitation even though she had no real authority. He gave everyone credit. The ULTRA troops were professional, taking her orders and acting on them as though they were given by their commander.

She and Jericho had both taken several bad hits. Blood ran down the left side of her face from a cut on her forehead and she favored her right leg. Dirt and blood covered the front of Jericho's shirt from when he decided to take the fight up close and personal. He and Kristin fought side by side, then back to back. Grayson had to admit, they worked well as a team.

He couldn't stop the swift pang of jealousy stabbing through him. He wanted to be on the ground at her back. Jericho fought to keep her safe while she did the same. An odd buzz filled his mind. He increased the frequency on the damper unit and the strange sound faded into the background. Thank God the little device worked. He pushed Vertigo's telepathy aside and battled to keep both of them safe.

Grayson allowed himself a small smile as he watched Kristin fight. For refusing to take a life, the woman had a natural mean streak. She could disable a person without doing them too much bodily harm. Would she be lenient when it came to Vertigo? The telepath had yet to make an appearance at this little shindig.

"Has anyone spotted Vertigo yet?" he asked. "I haven't seen her from up here, but she has to be nearby. They wouldn't fight this hard if she'd left already."

"Negative," Jericho said. "We need to find her and soon. If this keeps up, we'll be too tired to fight her when she shows."

"It's probably her plan," Kristin said. "It explains why she has all these extra troops here. She'll want to wear us down so we'll be easier to pick off."

"Watch it," Grayson called out. "We've got a fresh batch coming out from the trees."

He summoned a stronger wind, using it to push the fresh troops back several steps while his team took those precious seconds to recover. On his left, another contingent headed toward Frank and his team. He redirected the winds and pinned down Vertigo's men while the ULTRA team charged over to surround them.

As he flew higher for better accuracy, his vision blurred. He squeezed his eyes shut and blinked furiously to refocus on the battle. He sent a small cyclone to engulf the enemy agents while his team pushed forward to take as many prisoners as they could in the confusion.

Annette Miller

His vision blurred worse and the world tipped on its side. His power cut off and he hit the ground hard enough to jar his teeth. Pain lanced through his left shoulder when he pushed himself up. Kristin did warn him. Vertigo's namesake power hit him worse than he would've believed. In addition to everything looking like it had been submerged in a swimming pool, now his ears rang from the hard impact when he hit the ground.

"Grayson, can you hear me? What happened?" Kristin said.

He groaned as he sat up and grabbed his ribs. A broken rib or two would be the icing on this rather unappealing cake. "I had the field almost clear. The winds stopped and I couldn't tell up from down. To shut me down so fast, she's a lot more powerful than any of us thought."

A cold laugh echoed in their minds. "Thank you. I didn't think anyone appreciated me."

They all turned to the porch and the ULTRA agents raised their guns while Grayson got to his feet. He readied his rifle as he and Jericho stood on either side of Kristin while Vertigo gave them a sly smile. How could she look smug and so hateful at the same time?

She clapped her hands. "Bravo. I have to applaud all the effort you put into this grand battle. I knew my men would be defeated. Every smart villain knows not to count on hired minions."

"Where are Jack and Adam?" Kristin shouted. "Give us back our people and this can end now. If you don't, I can't guarantee your safety."

"I don't need your assurances," Vertigo spat. "Those two are mine. Adam will be sent to The

288

Company and Jack, well, we've planned to start a new life together."

She used her telekinesis to open the door. Jack walked out and put his arm around her waist. "You need to leave." He glared at Kristin. "I won't let you hurt her."

"No," Kristin whispered. "We failed."

Chapter Thirty-Four

Grayson didn't hesitate. In one smooth motion, he aimed and fired. The shot ricocheted off the telekinetic shield Kristin had come to expect. With a small flip of Vertigo's fingers, they were pushed back while their enemy stood and laughed.

Jack looked at her. "Don't play with them any longer. Let's end them now and then we can go anywhere you want."

"Jack, darling," she purred. "You have a lot to learn about revenge. These people want to hurt us, to separate us. Are we going to let them?"

"No." He raised his gun and his eyes narrowed. "Who wants to be first?"

"Jack, stop," Frank yelled. "She's in your mind. You've got to fight her."

Kristin watched as Jack squeezed the trigger and Frank stopped, then collapsed to the ground. She ran over to him and her feet kicked up little clouds of dust when she slid to a stop. Blood covered his left upper chest and Frank groaned.

"He just hit your shoulder," she said. "His gun has to be another prototype. It shouldn't have gone through your armor like this."

"You've got to get him to listen to you." Frank grabbed her arm. "Make him remember who he is."

Kristin waved over some agents and they pulled

Frank to the cover of the trees. Kristin raised her gaze to Vertigo. The telepath stood on the porch, gloating over her soon to be won victory. If Jack didn't hesitate to shoot his best friend of many years, what hope did she have? She would make Jack listen to her because she refused to leave without him.

She rose to her feet while she held her hands out from her body and stepped cautiously toward the porch. "Jack, I know you're in there," she said in a low voice. "You have to fight her. You know who you are. She's in control of what you're doing and what you're thinking."

"No, she isn't. She's shown me who I am."

"Is that so?" She walked a little closer. "She showed you how you fought for your innocence? She showed you how you learned to trust and love again? She showed you you're one of ULTRA's best agents?"

Jack squeezed his eyes shut and rubbed the back of his neck. "Stop. You're confusing me. I'm Anita's husband. She proved to me we're married."

"You aren't married to her. You married my friend Misty. She's my height with auburn hair and brown eyes. She helped you clear your name. Remember her. Remember all of us!"

Vertigo scowled. "Enough of your lies."

Nausea slammed into Kristin as Vertigo unleashed her namesake power. Most of her team had fallen over or had begun to vomit. Kristin had been through the psychic assault before, but not like this. Vertigo had put all of her strength, her hate, and her revenge into it. Kristin closed her eyes and prayed for the sensation to end.

"You see, little angel," Vertigo said. "You can't

stop me. Not now. Not ever. I will always win."

Vertigo held all the cards, as much as Kristin didn't want to admit it. They had no hope against her. Not with the power she wielded and a brainwashed Jack at her side.

****

Adam looked at Cole. "This is bad."

"Buddy, this sucks on a universal scale." Cole stared at the fallen heroes. "If they can't fight her power effects, they don't have a chance. Jack will walk out there and shoot them all."

As they stared at the scene on the front lawn, Adam smiled. "I got an idea. You want to hear it?"

"Sure. Lay it on me."

Cole had to admit, Adam had a solid plan. If they could implement it before Vertigo found out what they wanted to do and fried their brains, it might work. Adam would need absolute control over his increased abilities, but he'd already demonstrated he could reign in the power.

"Are you sure you can take her? You're still pretty new at this whole telepathy game." Cole glanced at him and Adam nodded once. "You need a weapon?"

Adam tapped his temple. "Nope. Thanks to her drug, I've got all the firepower I need." He gestured to the front door. "Shall we?"

"Be rude not to show up when we were invited to attend."

They walked to where Vertigo stood on the porch. Cole shot her from behind while Adam telekinetically restrained Jack. Vertigo stumbled forward, but no mark showed on her. Cole squeezed off more shots, each one bounced off the shield she erected.

Her eyes narrowed as she stared at him. "Honestly, Cole. You get more predictable all the time. I knew you two were in there. I knew you wanted to ambush me. I should kill you both now and be done with it."

He grinned and built electricity in his hand. "And here I thought you didn't miss me."

She shifted her gaze to Adam. "Let Jack go."

Cole watched as Adam did as she told him. "What's going on, man?"

Adam's eyes glazed over and he threw Cole from the porch. "You won't hurt Vertigo. She's promised to take care of us."

"Terrific," he muttered.

Cole pushed himself to his feet, before dropping back down to one knee as the vertigo affecting everyone slammed into him, too. Adam's plan better work because he needed him to kick it in right about now. Jack had moved again to Vertigo's side and stared at everyone like they were beneath the two of them.

Cole crawled over to Kristin and grabbed her hand. "Any time now, you'll have the opening you need. Talk to Jack. Make him listen. Adam will try to help you, but most of it has to come from you. He's known you the longest out of everyone he can see."

She glanced over her shoulder. Grayson crouched on the ground with his head bent down. His wings dragged in the dust behind him. "No. I tried. Turns out he's known Grayson as long as he's known Frank. They were teammates in ULTRA. If anyone needs to talk to Jack, it has to be Grayson."

"Grayson," Cole called out. "Grayson, listen to me."

When Grayson lifted his head, he stared at Cole.

"What do you want? Can't you see all of my guts want to come out right now?"

"Fight it. You have to talk to Jack. Make him remember who he is. I thought Kristin had known him the longest, but she told me after Frank, it's you."

Grayson glanced to where Jack stood with Vertigo. "I can't. I betrayed him. He hates me."

Kristin gazed at him. "If you don't, we're all dead."

"How do you expect me to get to him? She's got us right where she wants us."

Cole nodded toward the porch. "We have a plan. You'll know the time when it happens."

As they watched, Vertigo flew off the porch. With her power interrupted, Kristin and her team climbed unsteadily to their feet. Vertigo got up, her eyes blazing with rage and hate as she marched back to where Jack stood. Adam stepped out from behind him and telekinetically threw her again.

"Surprise, psycho," Adam said. "You thought you had control of me? Talk about over confidence."

While Adam kept her occupied, Grayson ran for the porch.

****

The time had come. The boss told him he needed to confront his past and it looked like the perfect opportunity just dropped into his lap. He hoped Jack would listen to him and not follow Vertigo's orders to shoot him. If so, the end result would be radically different from the one everyone hoped for. He glanced back to where he'd last seen Frank and took a deep breath. He had to do it now.

"Jack," he called. "Listen to me."

Jack stepped down off the porch, his gun aimed at Grayson's chest while he strode toward him. "I remember you. You betrayed the team. You lied to me."

Grayson slung his rifle over his shoulder. "We had some good times back in ULTRA. Remember the first time you saw my wings? After I certified as a sniper, you gave me the codename Nemesis. You said I dispensed justice like the Greek god. I thought the name sounded a little pretentious, but I went along with it."

Jack hesitated and the weapon lowered a little. He frowned and looked like he wanted to pull the memory out. The anger returned to his face and he raised the gun higher. "You're a liar. Vertigo is my world now. She said all you people would lie to me."

"And she told you the truth? Listen to yourself. When have you ever blindly followed anyone?"

In one smooth motion, Jack raised the gun and fired. Grayson flinched but held his ground. He looked at his right arm where the bullet had grazed him. "You see? You won't kill a friend." When he walked closer, Jack backed up a few steps. Grayson showed him his left shoulder, pointing to the Gravediggers tattoo. "Remember when the team got this? We wanted you to know you had our loyalty."

His steps faltered and his shoulders sagged. "I'm so confused."

Jack focused on a sight over his shoulder and Grayson turned. Adam battled Vertigo to keep her occupied while he tried to get through to Jack. When they'd stop and stare at each other, he suspected they fought on the psychic plane. Grayson turned back just as Jack squeezed the trigger. He felt a familiar burn on his skin and knew Jack grazed him again.

"Damn," Grayson muttered as Jack ran by him.

Blood dripped down his arm as he swiped at the wound and the one his side before he wiped his hand on his pants. Could their plan get any more derailed? They needed a lot more help to get her out of his head than they realized.

His earpiece crackled. "Are you all right?" Kristin said. "What happened?"

"Jack shot me, once in the arm and once in the side, but I'm okay. He just grazed me. It hurts, but it won't kill me. He's headed for Adam and Vertigo."

"Copy."

Grayson ran over and tried to ignore the pain in his side. He met up with Kristin and Jericho. "Where's Cole?"

Jericho shook his head. "He came out of the house with Adam, but I lost track of him. Could you get through to Jack at all?"

"Some." He glanced at his friends. "She's got her hooks in deep. We need to try again."

Jericho reloaded his gun. He smirked again, this time a twinkle in his eyes accompanied it. "I bet if we put a bullet in her, it would break her hold."

"There's one way to find out."

Grayson took to the sky as Kristin and Jericho ran along his shadow. Cole joined them and Kristin nodded. If they were to have any chance to stop her, it had to be now. As they drew closer, Jericho fired. Kristin sent out a static electricity burst from her stun rod. Grayson took aim and let loose a barrage shots at Vertigo. All of their efforts were deflected.

"When are you all going to learn, I can't be

stopped." She pulled Jack to stand by her side. "You're all pathetic."

Adam pounced on the distraction to throw her high in the air and slam her into the ground. Jack pulled her to her feet and held her close. She pointed to Kristin and Jack fired at her. He hit her in the center of her chest and she fell backwards. Again, she gave thanks for the experimental armor she wore. It stopped the serious damage, but she knew from the force, her whole upper chest would be sore and bruised the next day.

"You've got a lot to learn about how to fight a cohesive unit," Adam said. He used telekinesis to rip her out of Jack's arms. He yanked the gun from Jack's hand and yelled, "Grayson, grab him. Get him out of here."

Grayson flew over, grabbed Jack's wrist, and lifted him into the air. He summoned a wind to push him higher. He'd forgotten how heavy Jack's cybernetic systems were. "Come on, boss. We need to get you out of here."

Jack struggled in his grip. When he slipped, Grayson held on tighter. "No. I can't leave her."

He secured his grip on his former field commander. "Yes, you can. For one thing you don't have a choice."

****

On the ground, Kristin, Jericho, Adam, and Cole surrounded Vertigo. Her chest heaved and her legs shook with exhaustion. "Now is the time for you to surrender, Vertigo," Kristin said. "Your energy is depleted. Most of your troops are captured. Give yourself up."

"Never. You'll have to kill me first."

Cole leaned close and whispered. "You guessed

my plan and ruined the whole surprise."

Before anyone could stop him, he held his phone and pulled power from the internet. A blinding blue-white beam of light hit Vertigo square in the chest. She threw her head back and screamed as the light consumed her. Thin traces of light zigzagged through her body before coalescing in her chest. A bubble of force built and expanded out from her until it exploded, knocking them all off their feet.

As the light dimmed, they glanced over at where she had stood. Her body lay smoking on the ground and scorch marks marred her once flawless skin. Her hair had been burned almost completely from her head. Jericho walked over and nudged the body with his foot. When she didn't move and no sound came from her, he glanced at his friends.

"I think we got her," he said. He stared hard at Kristin. "No offense, but I don't want you anymore. All the crazy emotions she implanted in me are gone."

"None taken. It's a good sign. It means the extreme force we were forced to use worked and her influence is out of your head."

Cole and Adam fist bumped. "Here's hoping you're right."

They turned as Grayson set Jack on the ground and landed next to him. He rubbed his eyes and looked up at the gathered team. "Is she dead?" he asked.

Jericho pointed to the body. "What do you think?"

Jack turned to Kristin. "I could hear you when you spoke to me. I tried so hard to fight her, but she had taken my will. She'd taken over my mind." He looked at Adam. "The back door you created. She never destroyed it, did she?"

Adam shook his head. "Nope. She found the one I expected her to find, but not the secondary. It's how you kept a tiny part of yourself. I couldn't let you run off and do weird, perverted acts with her. That would've been so wrong, man. So wrong."

"We need to get you home," Kristin said. "The psionic doctors at ULTRA need to check you out."

He nodded. He stopped and jerked upright before jogging toward the trees. "Bloody hell. I shot Frank."

They hurried to the ambulance to check on the wounded men. Frank sat on a gurney and complained loud enough for them to hear him from where they emerged. Jack pushed through the agents. "I'm sorry, Frank. Are you all right?"

"I'm fine, or I will be as soon as they quit poking me. You weren't you." He grimaced as the paramedic taped a large gauze pad to the wound. "I knew you were in there because this isn't even close to fatal. If she had totally compromised you, you would've taken the head shot."

"True. Even as I got more and more lost in my mind, a small part of me knew this couldn't be right. The other man she held prisoner, Adam, helped me."

"Great." Frank looked over at Kristin. "I need to take some agents and start cleanup procedures. We need to shuttle the prisoners and the bodies back to ULTRA."

"I'll take care of it," Kristin said. "Get some rest."

Next to her, she felt Grayson stiffen. "Glad to see you're safe, boss," he said.

Jack held his hand out. "You know, Grayson, I held a lot of anger at you for many years. After I escaped from the hospital, Frank and Amy found me and helped me get back on my feet. They told me you were under telepathic influence. You didn't betray me. I listened to the evidence they had and when they told me how guilty you felt, well, the anger faded away to regret. Can you forgive me?"

Grayson hesitated, then took Jack's hand in a firm grip. "There's nothing to forgive. You knew what the evidence said at the time. If I hadn't been weak, Vertigo's mind control wouldn't have been so effective."

"You're welcome back any time you want to return."

"Thanks, boss."

Kristin walked away, Grayson behind her as their team walked back to the fight zone. ULTRA agents rounded up the survivors and placed the deceased in body bags. Smoking holes dotted the once flat yard. She shook her head, never doubting they'd win, but happy to see the confirmation of their victory in front of her.

After she cleared the area, Kristin stopped the lead agent. "You've gotten all the bodies?"

"Yes, ma'am."

She focused on the burn spot where Vertigo's body had so recently lain. "Where did you put the woman's body from the middle of the yard? Special precautions need to be taken with it."

"We didn't find the body of a woman, ma'am. The only bodies we found were the troops."

Kristin turned to Grayson as the agent walked away. "I should've known she'd have energy for one last illusion."

Chapter Thirty-Five

Kristin sat on the couch in Jericho's living room, glad she and Grayson would have some time alone. Grayson moved around in the kitchen, fixing dinner for them. She thought about the battle they'd just been through. She wished they could've taken Vertigo, but her instincts told her it would be a lot easier said than done.

Grayson dropped down in the chair across from her. "Mission's completed. Jericho, Cole, and Adam had to go see the boss and will be back tomorrow. What do we do now?"

"I don't know. Your team is here. Mine's up north."

He gave her a small smile. "Don't suppose you'd consider a move to south Jersey?"

"I thought I could, but I can't. All my work is there and my team depends on me." She paused. "I have to head home tomorrow. I need to see the head of ULTRA and file my report. Since it involved one of his field commanders, he'll need to know the details. He also needs to be warned Vertigo is still on the loose. I want to get checked out by their psionic doctors, just to make sure she's out of my head for good."

"I understand. We'll be getting checked out by our own people, too."

He walked to the kitchen, dishing up dinner on two

mismatched plates. He set them on the coffee table and stared at her.

"I guess this is our last dinner together."

Kristin picked up her plate and sat back. "I guess it is." They ate in silence for a few minutes before she spoke again. "You could come back with me. I mean, I've had Angel Haven renovated for my friend and her wizard husband. Another one of my friends is married to a human/gargoyle hybrid. Don't forget the cyborg we just rescued. A harpy would fit with the rest of them."

"Sounds great." He shook his head. "But like you, my team is here. They need me. I know you understand."

She placed her empty plate on the table and toyed with the end of her shirt. "For the first time in my life, I don't want to understand. I don't want to see the practical side of this. I want to scream and rail at you. I want to drag you back with me."

He chuckled. "That's quite an admission, doc. You think I don't want to lock you in the bedroom and force you to stay here? My team is better with you." He hesitated. "I'm better with you. You know my background. I lost the two people I cared most about in the world. I hurt a good friend. I don't want to lose you like I lost them."

She walked over to stand in front of him and drew him to his feet. "We'll worry about tomorrow when the sun rises. Right now, we have tonight. Let's not waste it."

"And if Jericho comes back early?"

"We'll put a do not disturb sign on the door."

He swept her up in his arms and carried her to the room they shared. "I like the way you think, doc."

****

Kristin slammed the trunk of her car a little harder than she'd meant to. Grayson, Jericho, Cole and Adam stood on the lawn as they waited to say goodbye. Tears burned in her eyes and her throat had closed tight. In the short time she'd been here, she'd grown close to the four of them. It became harder to leave the longer she stood there.

"Well, I've got everything. I'll call you when I get home. It's only a couple of hours drive so I should be back by lunch time."

Adam shook her hand. "I'm sorry we didn't get to work together longer. Take care of yourself, doc."

"I'm going to miss you," Cole said. He hesitated, then pulled her into a tight hug. "Thanks for saving my life."

She squeezed him. "You are more than welcome. You're a good guy, Cole."

Jericho walked over to her and stared. "Are you sure you won't stay? It's pretty here in the fall."

"I can't. I'm needed back home."

He planted a light kiss on her cheek. "I get it. Sometimes we get up to your area. I'll give you a holler next time we're in the neighborhood."

"I look forward to it."

Grayson shifted from foot to foot, his expression unreadable. He closed the distance between them and grabbed her in a fierce hug. "You won't forget me, right?"

She laid her hand on his cheek. "How could I? Grayson, you made me understand the emotional side of myself. You'll always be a part of me."

He buried his face in her hair and held her like he'd

never let her go. "I wish you didn't have to go."

"I know," she whispered.

He kissed her lightly and stepped back. "Be careful on the road."

"I will." Then she got in her car and drove away.

****

The four of them watched Kristin drive slowly down the rutted driveway before she turned right and disappeared. The dust settled around their feet and no one moved. Without warning, Jericho smacked the back of Grayson's head.

"What the hell is wrong with you?" Grayson shouted.

"You're an ass. I've told you that before and I'll tell you again." Jericho stomped up to the porch. "I can't believe you stood here and let her go. What are you thinking? You don't have to answer. I'll tell you. You aren't. You should've told her you love her. Maybe then she would've stayed or you could've left with her. Either way, you two need to be together."

Grayson looked at Cole and Adam, who shrugged. "We're on Jericho's side on this one," Cole said. "You should've gone with her."

Grayson stared in the direction Kristin had driven off in. He turned to reply to his friends and but they'd all gone inside. He glanced back down the driveway and took a step. Almost against his will, he turned back to the house. His boss wanted him here.

He stripped off his shirt and flew to the top of the house. He stared at the sun and wished he knew what to do. No one went against the boss's orders and yet, his friends and his heart told him to do the very thing he'd never done. He faced west and closed his eyes as a soft breeze caressed his face, reminding him of his mother's gentle touch. A falcon flew overhead, its lonely cry mirroring his own turbulent emotions.

Soulmates weren't all they were cracked up to be. The memory of her was a spike to his heart. He'd never known such emptiness in his soul before. He and Kristin were bonded and they belonged together. If Jericho hadn't smacked him, he would've banged his head against the wall himself. He really needed more sense about his own emotional state and worry less about what others wanted him to do. He needed to get her back in his life at all costs.

Twilight fell and shrouded him in its soft, lavender light. He replayed the first time they made love. He'd seen a DNA strand in golden light appear as his harpy soul flew around it. They were soulmates. They weren't meant to be apart. He'd tell the boss he wanted to be in New York and would refuse to take no for an answer. He leapt off the roof and glided down to barge through the front door.

"You're right. All of you." He turned to Jericho. "Champagne and orange juice, man."

The three of them glanced up. "Mark this day in red on the calendar. Grayson admitted we were right," Adam said.

Grayson grinned. "You guys want to help me with a plan?"

"If it involves getting her back, count me in. What have you got in mind?" Jericho said.

He pulled out his cell phone and dialed. "Here's what I want to do." He held up his hand and spoke to the person on the other end. His friends nodded as they understood what he had in mind.

****

Kristin avoided the Angels ever since she arrived home. It had been two days since she left Grayson and his team. She'd be in the middle of her latest research project, when memories of him would pop in and jumble her thoughts. She'd lost more than a few pens from throwing them across the room. She missed Jericho's charming smirk, Cole's paranoia, and Adam's joking nature, but Grayson had showed her what true strength of spirit could be.

She missed every little aspect of him, from his beautiful wings to his rare smiles. His embraces had warmed her heart and soothed her spirit. His touch made her feel like a woman, a human woman, not like the experiment she knew herself to be. But responsibilities called her home and she left him.

He'd told her about soulmates and she'd seen the evidence of that truth with her own friends. Why was it so hard for her to believe it could happen to her? Well, it did and she'd made a real mess of it. As she'd driven home, the ache in her chest had worsened until she was in tears as she pulled up to Angel Haven. He had to be back in her life. He just had to.

More tears burned her eyes as she thought about the hard choice she'd been force to make. Her traitorous cell phone hadn't rung since she'd gotten back. Of course, she could've called him. Phones did make, as well as receive, calls.

Why hadn't she told him how she felt? She should've told him she loved him. Most of her research was conducted online. It wouldn't have been any trouble at all for her to stay in south Jersey. Her father would've understood. After all, he'd tried to get her to date and meet someone for several years. The guys had begged her to stay. She held her head in her hands. For the first time in her life, she'd had the chance to follow her heart instead of her head, and she'd made the wrong choice.

Laughter drifted in from the hallway. From the sound, all of her friends had come in at the same time. Someone would peek around the doorframe, then disappear as quickly as they appeared. Then more giggles and laughter would resume. She didn't find any humor in her present state of mind. When they'd been hurt, she'd always been there for them. Laughter had no place in her life right now. She stomped over to the door and slammed it shut.

Sitting down with a hard thump, she stared at her computer and drummed her fingers on the desk. Her mind did not want to work right now. However, it did want to dwell on Grayson Styles a little longer. With every passing moment, the temptation to run out to her car and leave consumed her. Bach's fifth concerto blasted from her phone and she shot to her feet.

"Hello? Oh, hi Frank," she said, not bothering to hide her disappointment. "Yes, I know St. Michael's church. We had a wedding there not too long ago." She paused. "A problem? I can be there in about twenty minutes. See you soon."

When she stepped out of her office, she couldn't hear any noise. First, the laughter from her friends and now, total silence. Her teammates seemed to be on board with her emotions to drive her crazy.

"Hello?" She waited for an answer. "I'm going to St. Michael's. Frank just called me. There's a problem he needs help with." Silence. "I'll be back soon. I have my cell if anyone needs me."

She grabbed her car keys and hurried out to the driveway. She headed for the church and tried very hard to not exceed the speed limit. The priest at the church had ties to the magical world, being a powerful wizard in his own right. If a magical problem had arose, Kristin didn't know how she could help.

There were a dozen cars in the parking lot and some looked suspiciously like her friends'. Did Frank call the whole Angels team in? At one in the afternoon on a Thursday, there shouldn't have been any services planned. Someone must have tried to rob the church. She hurried to the side door and pulled it open. She paused by the door to let her eyes to adjust to the low light.

As she headed for the altar up the side hallway, she heard low voices and slowed her steps. She peered around a column and Grayson and his team stood there, talking to Frank and Jack. The rest of the Angels were there, too.

"What's going on?" Kristin demanded.

Frank walked over to her and took her hand. "We thought we'd invite you to your wedding. After all, this is a trend for the Angels these days. You know, go on a dangerous mission and then tie the knot. Today, it's your turn."

She stared at Grayson. "But I thought you decided to stay down south. How are you able to be here?"

"The boss transferred me to the New York office. I'll also work as a go between for Shade and ULTRA." He walked over and kissed her hard. "I hope you say yes, since we have everyone here and all."

"But we've known each other less than two weeks.

Are you sure about this?"

He laughed at her surprised tone. "You have so many ties to the magical realm, you should know when true love and soulmates are involved, there's no such thing as too little time. We were destined to be together. Remember our first time together? Our souls bonded that night."

"How did you put this together so fast? We've only been apart for two days."

Grayson shrugged while his friends just grinned. "First, I called Frank. He called Jack, who told his wife, who called her friend and her wizard husband, who is friends with the good father here. It all just sort of fell into place."

"I see. So, you planned a whole wedding in two days?"

"More or less."

She wrapped her arms around his neck and kissed him. "I should have said this before I left. I love you, Grayson Styles."

"I love you, too, Kristin Mentor." He kissed her one more time. "I guess this is a yes to my awkward proposal?"

"Yes."

Her friends surrounded her and pushed her down the same small hallway she'd come in at. In the bathroom, they stripped off her street clothes and yanked a wedding dress with simple, classic lines over her head. Kristin couldn't stop the protests from coming out as her feet were stuffed into white shoes with low heels. They anchored a short veil to her hair with what felt like a thousand bobby pins. Before she had time to catch her breath, they dragged her back to the church.

Kristin looked at them. "Well, this explains the laughter before you all left the house."

The priest cleared his throat. "Shall we get started? I need to meet up with my team to take care of some nasty creatures who want to open another portal."

Grayson took his place with Jack, Jericho, Cole, and Adam next to him. With Kristin's father out of the country on business, Frank walked her down the aisle. The ceremony began and she didn't hear any of it. The man next to her commanded her full attention as they made the appropriate responses. He slipped a ring on her finger and gave her a matching one for himself.

After the ceremony ended and their friends congratulated them, the priest led the way to the rectory where he laid out a small reception. Kristin sighed when Grayson's arm went around her waist as they walked over.

Grayson smiled at her. "I have a friend in south Jersey. His name is Tom. He'd like very much to meet you."

"Oh? How does he know me?"

"He's a clairvoyant. He told me I would marry you and to make sure to bring you by."

She smiled, not surprised at his answer. "Then I guess I should meet this man who knew about all this before we did.

As they all entered the rectory, they picked up a champagne flute with orange juice in it. Soon, talk and laughter filled the small home. Kristin eyed the non-orange juice bubbles and turned to Grayson.

"Mimosas?"

"My idea," Jericho said behind her.

"And what prompted this particular idea, if I may

ask?"

He pointed at Grayson. "Him. When we first met you, he didn't know if you two would suit. I believe his exact words were 'oil and water.' After all, he's magic and you're science. I gave him a better comparison."

She nodded, a smile curving her lips. "This is what you were talking about when you said champagne and orange juice." She glanced up at Grayson. "I like his comparison better than yours."

He pulled her tight to his side. "I don't mind, as long as you like me better."

"Of course. Jericho has his own charm, but you are all mine." She shrugged at Jericho. "Sorry."

"It's all good." He gave her a quick kiss on the cheek. "Welcome to the family."

She watched as he walked over to rejoin Cole and Adam. As she gazed at Grayson, she decided she couldn't have asked for better friends or better family than her teammates and the men who had been her new team. The woman made from science had joined with a man made from magic. Oil and water. Champagne and orange juice. Comparisons didn't matter. The love joining their worlds together did.

She smiled at Grayson. And he was the most important thing in her life.

Epilogue

Vertigo trembled beneath Benedict Trust's glare. She'd followed his plan to the letter and yet she failed. Again. Her boss would only tolerate so many negative results. One more failure and he'd cut his losses and be through with her.

"You're a disappointment to me, Vertigo. I'm not sure why I should let you live."

She stood on the rich carpet in his office, her head bowed as she tried to get the nervous tremors under control. "You shouldn't. Those worthless heroes defeated me and they shouldn't have. Give me whatever punishment you deem appropriate. I deserve it."

He leaned against his desk and folded his arms. "The best thing to come out of this mess is the disposal of Eddie Anderson. I'm comfortable blaming him for your failure."

"I'm sorry, Mr. Trust. I don't deserve your faith in me."

"Don't worry." She glanced up, startled to see him smile. "I still need you, but be warned. I'll only tolerate so much failure. If you can complete the next assignment I have in mind for you, I'll forgive your past mistakes."

"I understand, sir. What do you need me to do?"

He walked around his desk and pulled out a folder.

"As you know, I've picked up some lesser known supers for experimentation. At this time, most of them are in a holding facility before they're transferred to HelixCorp."

When he said experimentation, excitement lit her eyes. "What can I do to help?"

He handed the folder to her and sat. "A member of the Angels team is from a negative, sometimes called an anti-matter, dimension. The belt she wears stabilizes her here. It may have a link to the wormhole to take us to her world. I need to analyze her belt. Bring it and her to me."

"Yes, sir. Should I take her to the holding facility first?"

"No. I want her brought straight here. I would like to talk to her, find out what she knows about the science which brought her here."

"And then?"

His smile left no doubt to the hero's fate. "Then, she'll be another component to give me unlimited power."

Vertigo flipped through the folder and a plan began to form in her mind. "You'll have her soon, sir. My network has told me of a recent power surge not too far from here. There may be a connection."

He drummed his fingers on the desk. "I assume you need more resources?"

"Yes." She snapped the folder shut and smiled. "As soon as I have a solid plan in place, I'll send a list of necessary items. It shouldn't be as much as the previous assignment."

"Fine. Stay in contact with me. And Vertigo." He stared at her. "I expect better results this time."

"You'll have them, sir."

She tucked the folder under her arm and marched out of the office. This time, it would all go her way.

Dear Reader,

Thank you for spending time in my world. As you know, these days, reviews are very important. I would love it if you leave feedback on amazon, goodreads, and any other review site you frequent.

Please visit my website at:

www.annettemillerauthor.com

I've posted some character backgrounds and music that inspired me. While there, please leave a comment. I love hearing from readers. You guys are the ones that keep me writing.

If there's any character you particularly liked and want to see in their own book, feel free to let me know.

Thanks!

Annette Miller

A word about the author…

I graduated from Mercy High in Baltimore, MD in 1981 and got married to an Air Force man in 1982. We have two amazing boys who have grown into amazing young men. We spent sixteen years in southern New Jersey, four of them at McGuire AFB and the rest in Hammonton. We currently live in Memphis, TN, where science fiction, wrestling, and hockey take up what time the cat doesn't.

www.annettemillerauthor.com